CHANTS TO

PERSEPHONE

Jennifer Macaire

Published by Accent Press Ltd 2018
Octavo House
West Bute Street
Cardiff
CF10 5LJ

www.accentpress.co.uk

ISBN 9781786154613
eISBN 9781786154606

"The soul, at the moment of death, feels the same impression as those who are initiated into the Great Mysteries ... first it is like being lost on a long, winding walk through eerie darkness. Then, just before the end, the terror, the cold sweat, and the horror are at their greatest. At once a marvellous light appears to the eyes: we pass into a green meadow where singing is heard ..."

Themistius – Religious Chants to Persephone

Initiate: 'I come from a virtuous people, O pure Queen of Hades ... for I believe I belong to your kind, but destiny struck me down ... I broke free from the circle of pain and sorrow and I leapt lightly toward my chosen crown; I took refuge in the arms of the Lady, Queen of Hades.'

The goddess replies: 'O Fortunate One! O Blessed One! You have become a god, from the man you once were.'

And the initiate concludes with this mysterious reply: 'Kid, I fell into the milk.'

Words which form the rites of initiation to the Cult of Orpheus

Chapter One

Alexander looked across the waves toward the new city. The arms of the bay curved out from either side of the wide port. White marble buildings lined the shore. Behind them stood brightly painted stone houses. The sea was very blue, the buildings sparkled in the light, and he narrowed his eyes to slits as he stared.

'It's still not very far along,' he said.

'It looks wonderful.' I took his arm and smiled. The sun was blinding. I wished I had a pair of sunglasses. Well, maybe I could invent them. The new city of Alexandria looked much better than I'd expected. I'd been there once before. Three thousand years in the future Alexandria, second largest city in Egypt, would be a steaming, sprawling, noisy, smelly city.

Right now, it was probably just smelly. I wrinkled my nose. We were arriving in the port and men were rushing up the wharves toward us. Someone had a basket of fish in his arms.

When we reached the dock, Nearchus leapt lightly ashore and tied the boat. I was impatient to disembark and walk on dry land. We'd been at sea for weeks.

In June 323 BC, we had sailed from the mouth of the Euphrates, down the Persian Gulf, into the Indian Ocean, and through the Red Sea. We'd taken a camel caravan across the desert to Gaza. Afterwards, we'd taken another ship to Alexandria. It had taken three months. I was tired of travelling, tired of boats and camels. I wanted to stay in a real house with a real bath and sleep in a real bed.

Alexander, my husband, felt the same. He didn't much care for boats. Every time he boarded one, he was seasick. Unlike Nearchus. The tall blond admiral was more at home on a boat than on land. At this moment, he was reefing the sails as we got everything packed. We were planning to spend at least a month here. Then we would head to Memphis, where Alexander would meet Ptolemy Lagos and discuss what was to be done with the kingdom.

Not that Alexander had a lot to say in the matter. Officially, he was dead. Alexander the Great, King of Heaven and Earth, had contracted malaria and died after seven days of high fever and delirium.

Only he hadn't died. I'd saved him.

I, Ashley of the Sacred Sandals, born three thousand years in the future, ex-time-travelling journalist, and kidnapped by Alexander eleven years ago in Arbeles, had cheated the Fates. I was reputed to be Demeter's daughter, Persephone. At least, that's what people had thought. Now they believed I'd returned to Hades, God of the Dead. A fitting end, I thought.

Yet here I was, on a beautiful morning, standing on a stone pier in Alexandria. By my side was my husband and in my arms a baby girl. Cleopatra was a tiny infant with dark grey eyes, a sweet smile, and a loud voice. When she was hungry, *everyone* knew.

My eldest child, Paul, was ten. He was helping Nearchus square the boat away. He was a tall boy, slender and blond as a young Viking. I thought he must look very much like my ancestors. We shared the same broad cheekbones and slanted blue eyes. The sun had bleached his hair almost white. He was big for his age and had his father's proud nose and mobile mouth.

My other son, Chiron, was six years old. He was darker than Paul, with brown curly hair and bright hazel eyes. His face was triangular, with a mischievous expression. He looked very much like his father Plexis, better known as Hephaestion. Plexis was busy down below getting our baggage ready, not that we had very much. He was completely at ease on a boat, although he preferred horses. He had been Alexander's cavalry general.

Nearchus had been Alexander's admiral. And Usse, the thin-faced, dark man coming up on deck was Alexander's doctor. He was Egyptian and stood very still and breathed deeply. I wondered what he felt like being back in the country where he'd been born, grown up, and sold as a slave. He was a slave no longer.

He caught me looking at him and smiled. When he smiled his teeth looked very white in his dark face. His hair was starting to turn silver at the temples. He was a handsome man. I thought perhaps he would marry Chirpa and settle here. Chirpa was Greek, from Athens. She had been a slave in Babylon. Now she was free, and as she came on deck the wind whipped her copper hair around her face and turned her cheeks pink.

'This is beautiful!' she exclaimed.

Alexander heard her and smiled. 'I planned the whole city myself,' he said proudly. 'I can't wait to go see it.'

I couldn't wait either, but first we had to get settled in our new house. Plexis had found it, and assured us it was comfortable.

'With a bath?' I asked, suspiciously.

'Of course.' Plexis grinned. 'You'll love it. It's one of the new villas beyond the city walls. There's even a kitchen.'

'*Even* a kitchen?' I raised my eyebrows. 'I certainly hope there's a kitchen – and a *decent* bathroom as well.' But in the general rush and excitement of arrival, my comments went unnoticed.

I wondered what the house would be like. I'd just spent ten years in a tent. The last house I'd lived in had two kitchens, fifteen bedrooms, ten bathrooms, a service elevator, and a ballroom. I didn't think the houses here even had doors that closed. I imagined something along the lines of a mud-daub building, with all of us crowding into a smoky living room and sharing a cramped bedroom. Well, at least it wouldn't rock under our feet.

At the waterfront, a horse and cart waited to take our baggage. Alexander put me in the cart and settled Cleopatra in my arms. Paul and Chiron clambered in the back, and Chirpa found a seat next to the driver. The driver touched his whip to the horse's back, and we set off through the city.

We must have seemed a strange group. I was tall for a woman of that time, and with my white-blonde hair, stood out like a dove in a flock of crows. Chirpa was a redhead, and her penny-bright hair reached her hips.

Walking beside us were the men: Alexander, who caught the eye and held it because of his magnetism; Plexis, who was tall, dark and handsome; and Nearchus, who was even taller with a shining helmet of red-gold hair. Brazza and Millis were eunuchs. Brazza was an older man but graceful and walked lightly as a dancer. His head had always been shaved smooth and he had no beard. It was impossible to give him an age – only the wise look in his eyes made me think he was older than any of us even guessed. Millis was young. He was Darius's son by a slave woman. He was the tallest of all the men, standing nearly one metre ninety. His long and straight hair was golden brown, and he had golden eyes. Brazza and Millis were mutes. A particularly horrible practice of the time was the cutting out of slaves' tongues. Both men had been castrated and Brazza was deaf as well. Neither of them wanted pity from anyone. It would have been a terrible insult. Axiom, Alexander's valet, was a Jew. A serious man, he had voyaged with Alexander for thirteen years now. He was also a philosopher and loved to discuss new ideas and theology. He had been Alexander's slave until we set him free, as we had Usse and Brazza. Now, according to law, they were our godchildren. Most of all, they were our friends.

We looked around the city in admiration, commenting on everything we saw. Plexis pointed out particular features for us. He had been in Alexandria when the plans had been laid. He showed us the great library, the courthouse, the baths, and the gymnasium. Nearchus admired the deep bay with ample moorings for trading boats. Chirpa exclaimed over the market place, and Usse was thrilled to see a large hospital. I watched Alexander. As we drove through the new city his smile grew wider and wider. He turned to me, his cheeks flushed, and he laughed.

'It's just as I'd imagined it!' he cried. 'Look, over there. That's where the sewage goes.'

'I'm speechless,' I teased.

He looked at me sharply, but nothing could ruin his good mood. 'And see the road? See how there are crossings, so when it rains you don't get your feet wet? The water all runs down to the harbour. There's no garbage in the streets, did you notice?' His voice was excited, like a child's.

I nodded. 'I did notice. This was your first city and I think it's marvellous.' Following the harbour's curve was a waterfront main avenue, lined with tall date palms and classical-style buildings of golden stone.

He turned toward me again and I saw he was crying. He was always crying or laughing. Like nearly everyone of his time, he wore his emotions close to the surface. And his emotions were stronger than most. He reached up and grasped my hand, squeezing it tightly.

'Ashley,' he whispered. 'I can't believe I'm seeing my city again. By rights I should be a dead soul, fluttering like a dry leaf in the kingdom of Hades.'

'I'm so glad you're not,' I told him gently.

'Sometimes I have nightmares that I'm trapped in that darkness, and I wake up in a cold sweat all over. But today, with the sun shining so brightly, and the city new and sparkling all around us, I feel as if I've just been born. Like Aphrodite from the waves.'

Plexis cocked an eyebrow at his friend. 'Aphrodite?'

Alexander grinned. 'Don't say it. I know I sound ridiculous, but I'm in such a good mood I feel like singing …'

'No!' we shouted at him.

'No, don't sing,' said Plexis, shaking his head. 'We're very glad you're so happy, and we're happy too, believe me, but don't sing, all right?'

Alexander looked at us, his head tilted to one side. 'Fine, I won't sing, but I would like some music. So you sing.'

We sang. The wagon rolled smoothly over the streets as our voices rose to the heavens. We sang the 'sacred' song I'd taught everyone on the boat as we sailed through the wine-dark sea. *'Sailing, sailing, over the bounding main, oh, many a stormy wind shall blow 'ere Jack comes home again …'*

Alexander held my hand as he walked alongside the wagon. The sunlight turned his hair to gold. He turned his eyes to me, one blue, one brown, and smiled. And when he smiled like that, I thought fondly, I would gladly follow him to Hades and back.

Chapter Two

Our villa was a pleasant surprise. It was built on the site of a spring. There was a well in the house and a fountain in the courtyard.

I was impressed. Not only by the proportions, but by the decorations as well. In the dining room, the entire floor was covered with tiny blue tiles, like an ocean, and brightly coloured fish of every kind seemed to swim and splash about. Frescoes depicting scenes from the Greek myths covered the walls, and even the ceilings were painted. The doors were double, opening at the top and bottom. The windows were large with latticed shutters, making it bright and airy yet cool when the sun was high.

The furniture was made of painted or gilded wood. Cushions of every colour lined the sofas. The bedrooms were furnished with large beds and dressers. It was as luxurious as a palace.

We stared, our mouths hanging open.

Plexis smirked. 'Nice, isn't it?'

'It's incredible,' I admitted, sinking down on a sofa and looking around. 'This house is beautiful.'

'Well, it should be,' Plexis said, 'It's mine.'

'Yours?' We gaped at him, and even Nearchus, always serious, looked surprised.

'I had it built before leaving for Persepolis. I've been renting it out since then. Now there's money in the bank for us here, and we won't have to worry about a roof over our heads.'

The thought that we were practically penniless had crossed our minds. Only Plexis had seemed unconcerned, and now we knew why. He grinned.

'And you haven't seen the best part. Come.' He led us out of the garden and down a shady path. There was a wooden door in a tall stone wall. He opened it with a flourish. We gasped. A swimming pool.

Alexander laughed shakily. 'Well, perhaps I am dead after all, and this is the paradise Ashley spoke of.'

Chiron and Paul streaked by us and jumped into the cool water. The boys were soon splashing each other, while I sat in the shade and nursed Cleopatra. The boys played in the pool all afternoon, only leaving the water to eat the fruit and cheese Axiom brought us.

I sat on a cushion and held Cleopatra. I never grew tired of watching my children. Paul floated on his back and wiggled his toes in the pool. Chiron sat next to me, his curls full of sparkling drops of water. Both boys looked healthy. Paul had suffered from nightmares on the first half of our journey but was settling down now. Chiron was used to travelling, he had been born in the army.

I was so happy to have both boys close. I would sometimes burst into tears thinking of all the years I'd been separated from Paul. He was ten years old now, and I hardly knew him. He smiled at me; perhaps he sensed I was thinking of him. He rested his arms on the side of the pool, his chin in his hands.

'Will we stay here long?' he asked. His Greek was clear, with a faint Persian accent. He also spoke Sogdian and Bactrian, and I was teaching him Latin and English.

'I don't know,' I said. 'A month, maybe two. We have to go to Memphis and meet one of your father's generals.'

'I know, Ptolemy Lagos.' Paul cocked his head to the side, his father's gesture. 'And then where will we go?'

'I don't know.' I yawned. 'Does it matter?'

He shook his head. 'Not as long as I'm with you. Please, Mother, don't ever leave me again.'

My eyes filled with tears, and I touched his cheek. 'I will never leave you again, I promise.'

His face relaxed, and he slid back into the water. In an instant, he'd become a little boy again, shouting at his brother to watch him do a somersault in the pool.

I watched them until the shadows grew long. Then we dried off and went back up the path to the house. Axiom and Brazza had prepared dinner, and we ate together in the dining room. The garden's flowers spread their perfume.

When the air turned navy blue, and the stars started to show on the night sky, we lit the lamps and I put my children to bed. Paul and Chiron shared a room with Brazza. Axiom slept in the small room next to the bureau, Usse and Chirpa took the two rooms facing his.

Alexander and I shared a room in the back part of the house with Cleopatra and Millis. Cleopatra had a new cradle, and Millis always slept at the foot of my bed – nothing would make him move. If I ordered him away, he'd look at me and his eyes would fill with tears. I had finally become used to having him sleeping on a pallet nearby.

Alexander didn't mind. Actually, after spending ten years living in a tent with five other people, I didn't mind too much either.

Hardly anyone slept that first night in our new house. Cleopatra, unused to her new surroundings, kept waking up and crying. When I got up to nurse and change her, I fell and sprained my wrist. Alexander leapt up to help me, forgot where Millis had put his pallet, and tripped over him.

Axiom was afraid he'd forgotten to dampen the fire correctly and got up in the middle of the night. Usse thought Axiom was a robber and tackled him in the dining room. Chirpa screamed because she thought Usse had been wounded. Nearchus ran out of his room, terrified that the house was being ransacked, and tripped over a toy nearly breaking his knee. He howled, waking the neighbours, who started yelling.

Paul and Chiron, frightened by the din, woke Brazza, who was deaf and hadn't heard anything. He went out to investigate and managed to calm everyone down, including the neighbours, by bringing them a jug of wine with a note from Usse, apologising for the ruckus.

Plexis slept through everything.

Next day we staggered into the garden where Axiom and Chirpa were serving breakfast. Nearchus limped. Axiom had a black eye. Usse had a lump on his head. Chirpa had dark circles under her eyes, and the boys yawned widely. Alexander and Millis had bruises where they'd collided during the night, and I cradled my swollen wrist and yawned with exhaustion. Cleopatra had finally dropped off to sleep just as dawn was breaking.

'Good morning everyone,' I said wryly.

'Good morning.' Usse winced as he sat down. Chirpa made a clicking sound with her tongue and handed us cups of fresh orange juice.

'What a terrible night. I can't believe that we slept crowded on a tiny ship or squeezed into a tent, yet we can't seem to sleep in a spacious house,' I said.

Alexander shrugged. 'It's like getting used to civilian life after the army. It will take a while.'

Plexis stared at us, an expression of puzzlement on his handsome face. 'What happened? You spend one night in a decent house, and you all look like you've been in a battle.'

When the sun was not so high and the city was cooler, Chirpa, Plexis, and I went shopping. I wanted to get clothes for everyone, Plexis had to stop at the bank, and Chirpa needed to go to the marketplace.

We went to the bank first, so we could get money. Plexis counted out his silver, giving some to me and Chirpa, and putting the rest in his belt. Chirpa put her money in her mouth.

At the market, the biggest news was about Alexander's death. It was all anyone could talk about.

'Great Iskander is dead!' a newscaster called out loudly. We dropped a few coins in his pouch and stood back. The newscaster took a sip of beer and wiped his lips. 'What do you want to hear first?' he asked. 'The prices or the latest news?'

'The prices,' said Plexis, always money-minded.

'Very well. Silver and gold have gone up since the Great King Iskander's death. Grain and cotton are stable. Bread is selling at a quarter of an obol, olive oil is five obols a jar, a goat will fetch two drachmas, and a suckling pig is three drachmas. Let's see, there's a sale on parrots by the temple, the hair ribbon stand is by the fountain, and a caravan from Tyre just arrived with fish.'

'Fish?' Plexis wrinkled his nose. 'Why would they bring fish? We're right on the water, and Tyre is two weeks' march from here!'

The man peered closely his parchment and gave a laugh. 'You're the first to catch that one. I'm sorry, it says cedar planks.'

'How can you confuse fish and cedar planks?' Plexis asked with a frown.

'Well, it's an honest mistake. Look at this writing! It's all over the place. How can you expect me to read that?'

'It is illegible,' conceded Plexis. 'Who wrote it?'

'I did. But it was after the party last night at the new consul's house. I was invited so I could write about it in the Society column.'

'The Society column? Will you read that too?' I asked.

'I'm afraid that all I wrote is "Party, consul's house, and don't forget your … something."'

The man frowned at the parchment and turned it over. 'Can you read that word?' he asked Plexis.

'No.'

'Me neither. I must have had too much to drink. I don't remember anything about the party. It must have been fantastic. Now for the news: the Great Conqueror Iskander is dead. The news from Babylon has been confirmed. His body was being taken to Greece, but rumour has it that Ptolemy Lagos hijacked the funeral cortège and is bringing his body to Egypt.'

I gasped and Plexis muttered. Chirpa looked at us with round eyes.

'Go on,' said Plexis.

The man nodded. 'In Greece, the lawyer Demosthenes has offered a vote of thanks to whoever poisoned Iskander, and Demades, a Greek orator, said, "Iskander, dead? Impossible, the whole world would stink of his corpse.".'

'The bastards,' I swore.

'Do they believe he was poisoned?' Plexis asked.

The man shrugged. 'Some do. Sisygambis is dead. She starved herself. Olympias, the queen mother, has fled to Macedonia. Before leaving she had Iollas, Iskander's cupbearer, killed.'

I gripped Plexis's arm tightly. 'He was just a child! He was Antipatros's son!'

Plexis turned a pale face toward me. 'Hush,' he said, 'let's hear the rest.'

'Stateira is dead, she was poisoned by Roxanne. It wasn't proven, of course, but everyone knows it,' the newscaster added in a confidential tone.

'Oh, no,' I whispered.

'The goddess, Alexander's wife Persephone, went back to Hades, taking her children with her. The poor harvest and cold spell are proof of this. The priests are sacrificing heavily, but to no avail. A famine is predicted for Babylon this winter. And for the latest news, Roxanne gave birth to a son she named Alexander.'

'That's enough,' I said hoarsely. I turned away. 'I can't hear any more. It's dreadful.'

Plexis put his arm around my shoulders. His voice was soft. 'You knew what would happen,' he said.

Chirpa put her hand on my arm. 'Don't think about it now,' she said kindly. 'I saw some pretty cloth over by the fountain. Let's go see what we can get for the boys.' Her eyes were dark with pity.

I nodded, and we turned away. What broke my heart the most was the general air of indifference everyone had for Alexander's death. Perhaps, because his death was so recent, the full extent of his accomplishments couldn't be appreciated. But the Greeks' snide jokes chilled me.

Shopping took my mind off the news. I bought cloth for everyone. Then we went to the sandal-maker and gave him the villa's address; he would come to fit shoes for us later that evening. Chirpa ordered a goat and jar of olive oil from a merchant. Plexis bought some wine and fresh fruit. When we finished shopping, we walked back to the villa on the hillside.

My thoughts drifted back to the newscaster's stories. I had known beforehand everything that would happen. Well, almost everything. I didn't know, for example, what we would do now. Alexander wanted to meet Ptolemy, and there were discussions about trading with Carthage or Rome. Right now though, I was glad to settle down in a real house and take care of my children. I wanted them to have a tutor, so Alexander said he'd find one. He'd had Aristotle as his teacher. I wondered if the old man would take Paul for a few years. He had an academy in Athens, but I didn't know if Alexander would go back to Greece.

After hearing the news, I was even more sceptical. The Greeks had always resented Alexander. They thought he and his father were barbarians and were mortified when they found themselves conquered by the Macedonians.

Back at the villa, I found Alexander in the pool with Paul and Chiron. Brazza was sitting on the lounge chair with Cleopatra.

Alexander grinned when he saw me. 'What happened?' he asked.

I sighed. He'd better hear it from me. I told him the news. He was shocked about Iollas and Sis, saddened by the news of Stateira, and furious that his mother and Roxanne had fled.

'So who's ruling Babylon now?' he fumed. 'Honestly, I die for two months and everything goes, what's that expression you say? Down the train?'

'Down the drain,' I said, kicking my feet disconsolately in the pool.

'The drain. Thanks. I knew about Ptolemy, by the way. I told him to hijack my funeral cortège.'

'You told him to?' I stared.

'Well, yes. How do you think we're going to live? I have no money; the only things I owned belonged to the state except my golden cup, my tent, and a rather nice glass lamp. I asked Ptolemy to bring the cortège to Egypt. That way I can get the gold it contains.'

I looked askance at my husband. 'That's sordid,' I said.

He shook his head. 'I inherited seven silver cups from my father along with eight thousand soldiers and no way to pay them. Plexis and I were not speaking back then, but he invested his family's entire fortune in my army, enabling me to buy thirty thousand more men. With that, I defeated Darius and his one hundred and fifty thousand soldiers. That was just the beginning. Now that I'm dead, I have nothing again, except what Plexis wants to give me. But I can't accept it. Ptolemy is just bringing me what's mine. Think of it as pay.'

'I'll try.' I smiled weakly. 'There's more.'

'Oh, you mean, what Demosthenes and Demades are saying about me?' He chuckled.

'I think that's terrible!' I cried.

'So do I, but, Ashley, you can't expect them to mourn. They weren't with us on our great adventure. No one else can really understand.'

Great adventure? I sighed and looked up at the sky. The sun was setting. Evening shadows crept over the garden. 'We'll talk about this later. Now I think I'd like to see about dinner.'

I rose and made to leave but Alexander got to his feet, picked me up, and tossed me into the pool.

'Why did you do that?' I cried, sputtering.

'Just to see if I could.'

'The same reason you conquered Persia or went to India?' I asked, wading to the steps and taking my tunic off. It was soaking wet. I threw it at Alexander, who dodged.

His smile was blinding. 'Why else do anything?'

Chapter Three

After a month had gone by, Alexander, Plexis, and I sailed to Memphis. I was uneasy. We were going to meet Ptolemy Lagos, the most mystic and ambitious of all Alexander's generals. He'd been born in Macedonia, in Pella, but his grandfather had been Egyptian. He'd been sent to study in Egypt and worshipped the Egyptian gods. Like most Egyptians, he believed that Alexander was the son of Amon.

At the royal palace in Memphis, he met us wearing the crown of the Egyptian rulers and bearing the serpent sceptre, symbol of his powers. He was not yet officially king. Only the priests could anoint him by declaring him the son of Amon, their god. He'd taken over the government though, and was effectively ruling in Alexander's stead.

I was nervous. I'd never trusted Ptolemy, but Alexander did, and I'd supposed he knew his generals. Ptolemy stood when we entered the throne room. He waited until we were nearly in front of him, then he removed the crown and laid the sceptre on the empty throne. He bowed very low, touching his forehead to the floor.

'No, my friend, do not prostrate yourself. I am your king no longer.' Alexander stepped forward and pulled him to his feet.

'You will always be my king.' He swallowed hard and touched Alexander on the arm. 'It really is you. My heart is singing with joy and my eyes overflow with happiness.' It was true. Tears rolled down his cheeks.

Alexander was crying too. He embraced his general and then held him at arm's length. 'I am so glad to see you. I was worried that you'd have trouble leaving Babylon.'

'No, my men remained faithful to me. You were right to divide the army in the last days.'

'And Seleucos, is he having any trouble?'

'No. I didn't have to fight him to get your funeral cortège. He escorted me as far as Tyre.'

'Very good. I'm happy to hear that. So what will you do with it now?'

Ptolemy looked confused. 'I'm giving it to you,' he said.

Alexander nodded. 'Very well. I will take what's mine. I only want to be buried in Alexandria. Nothing fancy, just a little tomb.'

Ptolemy flipped his wrist and smiled. 'I hear you, Iskander.' He shook his head. 'I can't get used to seeing you again. When you died, it was as if the heart of the kingdom stopped beating. The man who took your place, who was he? I'd never seen him before nor had anyone else. He bore only a fleeting resemblance to you.'

'He was a man from another world,' said Alexander, shrugging. 'My wife killed him.

Ptolemy blenched, but he smiled bravely. 'He looked enough like you to fool most people.'

I was shaking now. I had tried to forget about the man who had travelled three thousand years through time to interview Alexander on his deathbed. I hadn't touched him, but because of me, he was dead. I had ordered Usse and Millis to put Alexander into the cold beam of the time traveller, and the beam, regulated for only a certain mass, had rejected the other man, throwing his frozen body against a wall and killing him. I swallowed hard. The memory was making me feel ill.

'Is everything going as planned?' Alexander's question to Ptolemy startled me. I raised my head and stared.

Ptolemy shrugged. 'There is one thing that we didn't count on,' he said.

'What's that?'

'Lysimachus. He's allied himself with Roxanne and has declared war on Cassander.'

Alexander's brows drew together in a fierce scowl. 'If true, it is a surprise. And the child?'

'Roxanne says he's yours. She's claimed half of Macedonia and Greece for him.'

'What about my mother?'

'A prisoner of Cassander. He will keep her alive as long as she behaves.'

Alexander was silent for a while, digesting this. 'I suppose I shouldn't be concerned, but it still hurts.' His voice was bleak.

Ptolemy and I looked at each other. His bald head gleamed like polished wood. His dark eyes were hooded. I noticed a small twitch in his jaw. If I was wary of him, he was twice as wary of me.

'I will not stay long in Memphis,' said Alexander. 'There is one more place I would go, and then I will head south. If you have any messages for me, you know where to find me.'

'I want you to stay in the palace,' said Ptolemy.

'I thank you, my friend, but I will not risk being seen by those of your soldiers who knew me well. It would only confuse things for them, and you are now king of all Egypt. I wish you well in all your undertakings.' Alexander stood very straight, his hands on Ptolemy's shoulders.

'I would never have taken Egypt except for your advice.'

Alexander smiled wryly. 'Ah, well, I think perhaps you would have thought about it sooner or later, but I'm glad you acted promptly. You took the seal and you have the sceptre.'

'I do, and I have your funeral cortège. I put aside what you wanted. I hope it pleases you. I added more.'

'Thank you.' Alexander sighed. 'Now I will go to Siwa to consult the oracle of Amon.'

'I will give orders to accompany you.'

'No, I will go alone this time. I need no guards. I am simply Alexander, not Iskander, king of Greece, Egypt and Persia. That person has truly died.'

Ptolemy was sombre as he escorted us to the door. 'Are you sure you won't stay?' He sounded almost plaintive.

'I will not put your authority in jeopardy, and that's what would happen if someone saw me here. So I will bid you farewell once more, my friend, and repeat what I said. May your reign be prosperous and your descendants many.'

'I wanted to ask you one last thing,' said Ptolemy, with a sideways look in my direction.

'If it is mine to give you, I will give it to you,' Alexander said with a smile.

'I heard you had a new daughter. I would marry her to my son.' He spoke in a rush, and I felt my cheeks grow hot.

Alexander stepped back a pace. 'She is but three months old,' he said, 'I don't know what to say.'

'Say yes,' begged Ptolemy.

Alexander cleared his throat. I was busy staunching a sudden rush of blood from my nose. I suffered from nosebleeds when something upset me, and this was *very* upsetting. Alexander had promised to give Ptolemy what he'd asked for – and he'd asked for our daughter. In those days, words were law. Especially from one king to another.

'I gave my word,' said Alexander. 'But you must agree to wait until her eighteenth birthday.'

'I agree.' Ptolemy smiled broadly. He bowed once more to us and showed us to the door. The sight of my nosebleed, for him, was auspicious. He was emboldened to bid me farewell.

We walked out. The hallway seemed to stretch on for ever, and I thought we'd never get to the street and fresh air.

Once outside, I stood on the palace steps and glared at Alexander.

'I'm sorry,' he said, 'I'm sorry, I didn't know he would ask for that. I'm sorry, I'm …'

'Shut up!' I cried. 'Just shut up! I know you're sorry. That doesn't help. So now what? Do we leave Cleopatra here?'

Surprise showed on his face. 'No! No, of course not.' He frowned and looked at his feet. He flushed. 'We just have to make sure she's back here for her eighteenth birthday.'

'And what if she falls in love with someone else?' I hissed. 'Are you going to be the one to tell her she has to marry a man she's never seen?'

'I didn't think of that,' he admitted.

'Well, I did. What if Ptolemy's son is a brute? Or if he's cruel, or, or … oh Alex, how could you?'

He looked around frantically, but Plexis was nowhere to be seen. He'd dropped us off at the palace and said he was going shopping. Now we had to wait for him on the steps. Two of the guards watched us curiously. 'Woman problems,' Alexander said to them with a shrug.

I kicked his ankle, the one he'd broken. He yelped. 'Will you stop it!' he said. 'You're making a spectacle of yourself.'

'I don't care. You just gave our daughter away in marriage to someone we've never seen …' I broke off with a gasp. 'And what if he's much older than she is?'

'A difference in age? You're worried about a difference in age? They can't be more different than you and I, and we get along fine. Most of the time,' he added, dodging another kick. 'Three thousand years is quite a difference, don't you think? By the way, who's older? You, or I?'

'You are, you beast.' I sank down on the steps and cupped my chin in my hands.

Alexander looked down at me, then smiled broadly. 'I know what we can do, we can marry her to him when she's twelve, then we won't have to worry about her falling in love with anyone else, Hey! Stop kicking me, *ouch*!'

Luckily, Plexis drove up then and we climbed into the cart. He touched the horse lightly with the reins and off we trotted. Plexis looked at me, then at Alexander, but didn't say anything about our thunderous expressions. Instead, he told us all about the marketplace and the news he'd heard, which was similar to what Ptolemy had said. Then he pointed out some graffiti on the walls as we drove by the city gates.

'Do they have graffiti in your time?' Alexander asked me, most likely hoping to change the subject from Cleopatra's engagement.

I gave him a look that told him the subject wasn't forgotten or forgiven. 'In the future? Lots. Mankind has always loved drawing on walls.'

Plexis was whistling, his hands light on the reins. At the mention of the future, he cocked his head. 'You never did tell me *when* you came from,' he said.

'You were ill for so long,' I explained. 'I didn't want it to be a shock.'

'And now? Can you tell me now?'

'I come from three thousand years in the future,' I said.

'How? Did the gods send you?'

'No, we have a machine that does it. It's very complicated to explain.'

24

'Try me.' He grinned over his shoulder.

'You won't understand.'

'Well, you told me about flying machines and chariots that rolled without horses.'

'That's right,' I said. 'And you weren't even impressed.'

On the long voyage through the Red Sea, I'd told stories about the future. They had listened with interest, but they had been hearing stories since their childhood about men who flew – the gods flew all the time. And the god of the forge had two robots that spoke and helped him walk. The gods made magical things happen in most tales, and, as I'd discovered, magic and technology seem very similar. My stories had entertained them, but nothing more. This was a wee bit aggravating to someone who came from three thousand years in the future. If I thought I'd impress anyone, I was mistaken.

Plexis continued, 'But you didn't tell me about the machine that pushed you back in time. Why can't you go back to your own time? Why are you still here? I don't understand that. Does everyone travel in time? It must be very odd. What if you meet yourself as an old woman or a child? Can one go forward as well?'

'That is against the law,' I said. 'No one can go into the future. We can only go to the past. The machine works with lightning and the earth's magnetic field, and only one person can go at a time.'

'I see.' Plexis said lightly. 'So, three thousand years from now, the people still speak of Iskander here? What do they say? That he was a great hero, like Achilles?'

'Oh, much better than Achilles,' I said seriously.

'Really?' he cocked an eyebrow. 'And do they say he was a skinny horny bastard?'

'No, they say that about you,' said Alexander, chuckling.

'They don't!' He looked amused. 'They don't say anything about me, I hope.'

'They refer to you as Alexander's alter ego,' I said.

'Alter ego?' He was shocked. 'How awful. I suppose they also said I died falling off a horse, and I never fell off a horse. Well, maybe once or twice, but nothing serious. It was a polo accident. Do they say that?'

'No, they don't. Nobody in my time knows how you or Alexander died.'

Plexis brightened. 'I don't care. Just think, I'm known three thousand years from now, and all because I hung around this fellow.' He dug an elbow into Alexander's side. 'What a laugh. I suppose all your generals are famous too, and your trip to India was hailed as a big success.'

'It was,' said Alexander modestly. 'They say I united East with West.'

'Nice work. And they realized you were chasing a baby?'

'No, they say nothing about that. They think I did it on purpose.'

'Amazing,' repeated Plexis. 'I shall have to get used to being next to such a famous person.'

'Do,' Alexander said. 'And while you're at it, could you please never mention it again, or ask any more questions of Ashley? I hate hearing her answers.'

We both stared at him. Plexis's face grew serious when he saw Alexander's expression. 'All right,' he said. 'I'll ask no more. I'm sorry. I wasn't thinking. To me it seems so ridiculously far away.'

'To you, ten years is an eternity,' said Alexander with a spark of humour.

'That's true. I never thought I'd live to see my twentieth birthday, and here I am, nearly thirty.'

'You are thirty-one,' said Alexander.

'See, time has no meaning for me,' Plexis waved airily.

'It has for me,' said Alexander. 'Sometimes it feels as if the very air around me is made of stone and I must struggle to stand up.'

'That's your melancholy,' said Plexis. 'Ever since you were a young boy you've been prone to moodiness. It used to drive Aristotle crazy.'

'Perhaps.' Alexander's voice was bleak. 'But you've never suffered from it, so I'll thank you not to mock me.'

'I'm sorry.' Plexis could sound contrite when he wanted, and soon he had Alexander smiling again as he told him a story he'd heard in the marketplace about two Egyptians, a Persian, and an over-sexed camel.

We stayed in Memphis for a week; enough time to sort out the treasure that Ptolemy had brought back to Alexander. It was immense: gold statues; bolts of cloth; chalices; enamels; and coins of gold and silver. Alexander put most back. He had never wanted to be rich.

After beating Darius for the first time, Alexander had entered the royal tent and seen its gold chairs, precious carpets, and silk curtains. 'So, this is what it's like to be king,' he'd said ironically.

He sent what he needed to his bank account in Alexandria or to Plexis's house. He also put aside a large amount for Usse as a gift for his wedding. Usse and Chirpa were married in a simple ceremony in the courthouse in Alexandria.

Alexander, as her godfather, gave Chirpa away. The ceremony went like this:

ALEXANDER. I give you this woman so you may have legitimate children. Do you take her?

[*All questions are posed to the man., The woman stands next to him and tries to look as demure as possible*.]

USSE. I take this woman.

ALEXANDER. And I offer you a dowry of three hundred gold talents.

USSE. That's too much!

ALEXANDER [*frowning*]. Just say yes!

USSE [*stammering*]. I accept, with thanks.

Afterwards we held a banquet and invited our neighbours. We decorated the house with laurel and olive branches, and Paul had the honour of carrying a basket of bread around to all the guests while saying the ritual words, 'I fled from the dark and found the light.' – a saying that no one could explain to me, but that everyone said was 'traditional'. I had to be content with that.

Chirpa, as befitting her new status as a newly married woman, was showered with gifts: a spinning wheel; a new cloak; some fine wool; a package of precious dye; three baby pigs; an olive tree in a large pot; some new dishes; a rug; and a beautiful bedspread.

Paul and Chiron were entranced with the baby pigs and played with them all afternoon, until someone left the door open and the piglets ran squealing down the street.

And that was it. Chirpa and Usse were married. Plexis asked them to stay in his house in Alexandria. Usse got a job working in the new hospital. Chirpa started to manage the household. Then Alexander and I readied ourselves for a trip to see another oracle.

Alexander wanted to see the temple of Amon in the Siwa oasis. He had been there once before, just before he'd set out on his journey across Asia. Now he wanted to consult it again.

Chapter Four

We rode camels across the desert and slept in tents. Axiom and Brazza came with us, and Cleopatra too. The nights were chilly, but the sand beneath us held the warmth of the sun. The only sound we heard at night was the rustle of the wind moving the millions of grains of sand.

Alexander and I lay beneath the starry sky and spoke in whispers.

'Do you truly believe in the oracle?' I was interested.

'The last time I went, the oracle said something very strange. I want to go back and ask again.'

'What was so strange?'

He seemed to hesitate a long time before he replied. 'The oracle forbade me to tell anyone. But I will tell you this, it said I would be buried in Alexandria.'

'Ten cities carry your name now, and in three thousand years there will be ten times that many.'

'Really?' he looked pleased, then his face grew serious. 'The oracle told me I would ask to be buried in Egypt. That's all I can tell you for now.' He paused, then said, 'No, I'll tell you one more thing. The oracle told me I would die at the age of thirty-two.'

I was startled. 'What?' I cried.

He looked at me. His immense eyes were half sad, half amused. 'So you see, I always knew.'

I shook my head to clear it, and tears flew off my cheeks. I blinked quickly. 'You always knew?' I asked, my voice shrill in my tight throat.

'I didn't want to believe it at first. I was young and rash. I thought I could overcome anything. I felt invincible. Then the oracle told me I would die aged thirty-two. And that I would be buried in Alexandria.' He sounded apologetic.

I pulled my covers tighter around my shoulders. Despite the heat radiating off the sand, I felt suddenly chilled to the bone. 'You never told me that.'

'How could I tell anyone?' His voice was gentle. 'When we found Paul in the sacred valley, I nearly spoke to you then. You couldn't understand why I wanted to leave him behind, but I didn't know if he would ever be safe with me. The oracle didn't say *how* I would die, and if I'd died at the hands of an enemy, you and the children would have been sold into slavery.'

'You're thirty-three now,' I said.

'I want to ask the oracle where I should go next.'

'Don't you want to go to Africa and see the elephants?' I tried to make my voice light but it wavered.

'I do. However, I would ask the oracle to guide me. I feel like a ship without a rudder now, or like the empty wind blowing over a desert. I feel as if I were an empty cup or a hollow gourd. I have no more substance, and it is a feeling I fear. Some mornings I wake up and wonder where I am. I have to touch my face to make sure I haven't changed. It's very strange. I feel ...' His voice tapered off and he frowned slightly, searching for the right words. 'I feel as if I *had* died, and that my soul has left my body. I want to ask the oracle where my soul has gone. I want it back.'

I stared at him, frightened. 'Is it like your melancholy?' I asked. 'Did Usse leave you some medicine?'

He shook his head. 'No, it's nothing like that. It's the strangest feeling I've ever had. I feel incredibly light, as if the wind could lift me up and carry me away.'

I smiled shakily. 'Perhaps it is simply the weight of the world leaving your shoulders,' I said. I wiped away the tears that seemed determined to blur my vision; I wanted to see his face.

'Perhaps.' A smile tugged at the corners of his mouth. 'I would like it to be so. All my responsibilities, all my worries, all the stress of having a million people in my care suddenly gone. Maybe it was simply too much for one man to carry by himself. Only you would be the one to tell me that. Everyone else wants to follow, don't they?'

I looked at him. My heart beat hard. 'If you could see how much I loved you, you would feel as if a hundred million people were nothing at all,' I whispered. 'My love is as big as the desert, as deep as the endless sea, and as vast as the sky above us.'

He leaned over and he kissed me. His hand caressed my cheek. 'Don't look at me like that, for surely the gods will become jealous and cause me harm.'

'I would fill up that emptiness inside you.'

'I think that you're the only person who could,' he answered. The breeze tugged at his hair. His face was pale in the moonlight. His eyes were brilliant.

He felt the weight of my gaze and smiled at me again. His teeth were very white and even. At least the battles had spared them. A scar made one eyebrow higher than the other. Other scars decorated his body. 'Do you like what you see so much?'

'I do.' I grinned back at him.

'Well, I like what I see too.' His regard was frankly admiring.

I blushed. 'You don't have to say that.'

'It's true though. When I look at you I feel cool, even in the hottest desert. Your eyes quench my thirst. They are as ice-blue as a mountain stream. Your skin is like the white marble the sculptors love so well. I feel the breezes of spring when I see you. I feel refreshed and new again. It's a magic you have. I would stay by your side for ever.'

Cleopatra's little hammock swayed in the breeze. I lay back in my husband's arms. He raised his arm and pointed to a bright star near the horizon.

'That's my star, Regulus, in the constellation of Leo.' He spoke softly. His words were so low they barely detached themselves from the whispering wind. He leaned on one elbow and looked down at me. 'Your eyes are silver in the starlight,' he said, bending to kiss me. I felt his lips tremble against mine. His body seemed to grow hotter. I reached up and pulled him on top of me. He was urgent, his muscles tense. I stroked his back then took his hips in my hands and pulled him into me. My breath caught in my throat. There was an instant where neither of us moved, where we didn't even breathe. Then he moaned softly and put his forehead against mine. I arched up to meet him but he held himself still. I moved slowly, sheathing him inside me, pulling nearly out then pushing in again. I wrapped my legs around his waist to gain more leverage and moved smoothly against him. The image of the waves came to me, the slow slide of the water onto the beach back and forth, in and out. His arms shook with the effort of not moving. His eyes were closed in concentration.

I moved until I felt a throbbing start in the pit of my stomach. My legs slid off his back and I abandoned myself to my own pleasure, feeling it growing like flame inside me. My body shook. I tipped my head back and groaned aloud. Alexander gave a cry and thrust into me. Holding me tightly against him, he drove himself to my very womb. Over and over he pounded into me, his breath coming in deep groans. My own breath was torn out of my throat in sharp gasps. When his release came, he cried out. I held him to me. We shuddered together; our bodies joined in that mysterious gift of pleasure we could share. Afterwards, he stroked my belly and arms until the trembling stopped, then we both slept.

Chapter Five

The Siwa oasis was a magical place three thousand years ago. Perhaps the desert has claimed it for its own again, I don't know. I had never been to this part of the world three thousand years in the future. In my time, deadly little land mines lay buried under much of the Egyptian soil, which made it one of the most dangerous places on earth. I didn't tell Alexander that though, he hated hearing about the impersonal massacres of our wars. The stories of the atom bomb and the biological weapons had literally made him ill. So now I kept my musings to myself, and I was glad, fiercely glad, to be back in Alexander's time, when the world was pristine.

We entered the timelessness of the oasis at noon. Entering the blue shade was like diving into cool water. Over our heads rustled the stiff fronds of thousands of palm trees, and little streams had been diverted to form a huge irrigation system within the oasis. Tall trees shaded the gardens. Olive, lemon, pomegranate, and fig trees spread their sweet perfume in the air. We rode along white sandy paths next to fast-flowing irrigation streams. We rode all day then camped in a large clearing that night. The oasis was so vast it would take us another day to reach the centre, where the temple for the oracle of Amon was built.

I could see it in the distance sometimes, through the trees. It was built on a high, peach-coloured rock.

That evening, I was happy to be able to take a bath. A spacious bathhouse stood next to a stream. I was less happy about the huge scorpions that came out at night. We made sure that Cleopatra was secure in her little hammock. I hardly slept, but they didn't bother us. Usse said the farmers worshipped them, and I suppose they helped keep the insect population down. And from the size of them, the lizard and mouse population as well, although Alexander said I exaggerated.

Small houses were set in the groves of trees. As we rode by, people would sometimes wave, and children would trot behind our camels. The men who cared for the immense oasis bowed low as we rode by. 'Do they know who you are?' I asked Alexander, as another farmer put his wooden hoe down and knelt in the sand.

'I don't know, maybe.' He sounded unconcerned.

I was disappointed when we finally arrived. I'd expected a great stone temple – perhaps with beautiful carvings or statues. Instead, two mud-brick buildings stood high on an outcropping of rock. A small staircase had been hewn into the cliff. The first house was the Temple of the Question, and the second house was the Temple of the Answer.

Thirty priests stood in a line to greet us as we rode down the dusty path, and they prostrated themselves. 'Welcome, Alexander, Son of Zeus, to the oracle of Amon,' said the head priest, when he'd raised himself from the ground and brushed off his robes.

'Ptolemy must have sent a messenger ahead,' I declared.

Alexander nudged his camel with his whip, and the elegant beast knelt down. Alexander hopped off lightly. 'How did you know I was coming?' Then he added, 'Hadn't you heard I was dead?'

'The oracle said you would arrive,' the priest said. 'And we did hear the rumours, yes. Apparently they are false.'

Alexander flushed, something his skin did easily. However, it wasn't to be confused with a blush of shyness. He flushed with pride or pleasure. Any emotion could change the colour of his skin. Now his eyes glittered with something I didn't recognize. He turned away from the head priest and helped me descend from my camel. I hated when it pitched forward and backward as it knelt down. Even Cleopatra squealed loudly.

'I've got you,' I said to her reassuringly. Then I was in Alexander's strong arms with my feet on the sand. 'And I've got you,' he said.

'Where do we go from here?' I asked.

'I don't think you will be admitted.'

'Baloney,' I said hotly.

'I have no idea what you just said, but if it's anything like 'holy shit', I think you should be ashamed of yourself. You're in a sacred sanctuary here.'

I looked at him sternly. 'Baloney is not a bad word. It's a kind of meat and also a bunch of nonsense. It means I don't believe that I can't consult the oracle. Tell them I'm a goddess's daughter.'

Alexander made a choking noise.

'What's the matter with you?'

'It just doesn't seem right. You drag your identity out and only use it when you need it.'

'I'm tired of being a second-class citizen. Women have just as much right as men to …'

'Fine, fine. I'll tell them. Let's not get into another argument about what men and women can and cannot do.'

He spoke to the head priest, and the man, after dubiously consulting his colleagues, shrugged. 'You will be allowed into the adyton, which is a restricted area. It is a great honour, but you have to take off your clothes,' Alexander translated for me.

'Oh, really?' My voice turned icy. 'Or is that a rule made up just for me because I'm a woman?'

'No,' Alexander spoke hastily. 'Everyone takes off their clothes. And we bathe in the sacred spring before going to the Temple of the Question.'

I was mollified. 'All right. I believe you.'

'I thought you never wanted to see another oracle?' Alexander asked me.

'This is an Egyptian one. I know nothing about their gods. It's going to be very educational.'

Alexander continued to look doubtful, but we handed Cleopatra to Brazza and walked up the stone stairs together.

Once at the top, I turned to see the view. The oasis stretched its green arms around us, keeping the desert at bay. The edges were lost to view – it was a two-day ride in any direction to reach the desert sands. Mountains surrounded the oasis like a gold setting holding an emerald. It was breathtaking.

The priests motioned us toward the doorway. I took Alexander's hand in mine, then we disappeared into the gloomy darkness of the temple. The hallway ended in a stone courtyard. There, a spring bubbled out of the ground and flowed into a large square basin. The pool had been cut out of solid black stone. There were no benches, flowerpots, or anything decorative. It was stark. On one wall, wooden pegs were driven into the mud daub. Alexander took off his short linen tunic and hung it on a peg, then jumped in the pool. The water was waist deep.

'Come on in,' he called to me, 'the water's fine.'

I took off my tunic, hesitating a second before shrugging off my home-made underwear. Then I stepped into the pool and gasped. The water was like ice.

Alexander grinned widely, then sat down, ducking completely underwater. He came up again, shaking water off his hair, letting his breath out with a *'whoosh!'*

I shivered but did the same, closing my eyes as I sank beneath the dark water. When I got out, I felt refreshed.

We padded barefoot down another hallway before coming to an antechamber. This one was lit by a lamp, and benches lined one wall.

'Wait here,' Alexander told me. 'I'll go first.'

'Fine.'

He disappeared through a doorway. I looked around. There was nothing to see or hear, so I sat on the bench and leaned back against the wall. I was in the middle of a bored yawn when I turned and met the faintly disapproving stare of the head priest.

He motioned me through an open door. I found myself in small chamber. There was a torch flickering on one wall, but no windows. I wondered what I should do. Did I speak first? Did I wait for the oracle to speak? As I stood there, undecided, smoke from the torch billowed outwards and a choking cloud surrounded me.

I stepped backward, waving my arms. That's when the voice spoke.

'Hello again, Ice Queen.'

I froze. It was the same deep voice I'd heard twice before, in two different places. For a minute, I panicked. I tried to find the door, but the smoke was thick.

'Aren't you going to ask me a question?' The voice was softer now. I hesitated. It sounded almost human.

I coughed. 'What are you doing here?'

'That's your question?' Amusement coloured the words.

'All right.' I sighed. I might as well get used to it – I was being followed by Apollo, even here in the deep desert. I thought for a minute, then asked, 'Will my daughter Cleopatra marry Ptolemy's son?'

'That's a good question. The Ptolemys' reign shall begin with a Cleopatra and end with one; how's that for an answer?' The voice was sly, deep, and mysterious. The perfect oracle voice.

'Cleopatra is a common name. You didn't answer anything.'

'Oracles rarely do. That way, we're never wrong.'

'You told me I'd return to my own time, but I didn't. I saved Alexander and I didn't go back.'

'I said you would go back to your own time?'

'Yes, you did.'

'No, I said you would have the *choice* to return.'

40

I thought of the terrible yearning I'd felt when I'd seen the blue magnetic field, that urge to throw myself into it and go back to my own time. 'I didn't go back.'

'I can see that,' the voice said dryly. 'And now you are here with the king.'

'He says he has lost his soul; is that true?'

Silence. I craned my head, trying to see past the haze and the flickering torchlight. Smoke swirled lazily in the air.

'Are you still here?' I asked.

'I'm here. I think I'll answer you.'

'Where is Alexander's soul?'

'He hasn't lost it. It has been stolen. To find it you must go to the land of the Eaters of the Dead.'

I shivered. 'Where do they live?'

'In the land where the sun never rises or never sets. Your ancestors are waiting for you, O Queen of Frost and Ice.'

I stared into the smoke. 'Will I speak with you again?' I asked.

'Perchance. I like speaking to you. Do you remember everything I told you when we first met?'

'I think so.'

'Be sure you forget nothing, child. Or else the search for Alexander's soul will be in vain. Beware of two things: the sickle moon and the Thief of Souls. He is very powerful. I can say no more than this.'

I wondered what a 'thief of souls' was, but when I asked, I was met by silence. I sighed. 'All right, don't bother. I suppose I'll find out. I would like to know one more thing though.'

'Ask. Perhaps I will answer.'

'I always wondered why you decided to help the Trojans? In *The Iliad* it says you were on their side.'

'I liked Hector,' said the voice, a smile in it now. 'And I thought Achilles was an ass for sulking so much.'

'Well, you certainly showed him,' I said.

'I did, didn't I?' He chuckled softly.

'So why did you forsake them in the end? They loved you, they believed in you and in your power to help them. So why did you let them down?' I asked.

There was a long silence. I thought perhaps he wouldn't answer me, but at last he sighed. 'I suppose that we gods always forsake you mortals in the end,' he said sadly. 'We love you, but we love ourselves more. Do you know what your namesake is called?'

'My namesake?' I was startled. 'No, I don't.'

'Persephone the Terrible. All men fear her, the cold bride of Hades. You must learn her chants – the Chants to Persephone – Child of the Future.'

'I'm not a child,' I said, 'I'm nearly thirty.'

'And I'm nearly thirty centuries. To me you're just a whisper, a faint breeze that stirs my hair, the trilling of a bird at dawn, a leaf that moves on the tree.' The voice was fading away, growing steadily fainter. 'Learn the chants. Tell Iskander to give his shield to his son.'

The smoke swirled and disappeared, leaving a smell like dry leaves in its wake. The torch flared and a warm glow filled the room. A thumping noise sounded above my head, and a man spoke.

'Ask your questions, my daughter.'

I frowned. 'Your voice has changed,' I said. 'Are you still there, Apollo?'

He said, 'Er...I am but the messenger. I will hear your question now and pass it on to the oracle. Only three questions, mind you.'

I thought for a moment. What other questions could I ask? 'Will Alexander and I have any troubles in Africa?' I asked.

There was a pause. 'Is that all?'

'Yes.' I frowned. I should have prepared a list.

'Very well, I will transmit your message. You may leave now.' A door opened and I saw a glimmer of sunlight. I followed the hallway to the courtyard, and I saw Alexander standing in the sacred pool again. I was feeling warm so I jumped back into the water. It was just as cold as before, taking my breath away. I rinsed the smoke out of my hair and felt much better. Afterwards we dressed, and a servant led us to another antechamber.

'What questions did you ask?' Alexander turned to me, his eyebrows raised.

'Well, it was more of a conversation. I chatted with him for a while. I asked him if Cleopatra would marry Ptolemy's son.'

Alexander looked flabbergasted. 'You talked to the oracle?'

'You'll never believe this, but I spoke to Apollo again. He seems to be following us around. He said that we had to go to the land where the sun never sets and never rises to find your soul. Isn't that strange? Then a different voice came from the ceiling and asked for another question, so I asked ...'

'Wait a minute, two voices? But, there's only one messenger.' He shook his head.

'It wasn't a messenger, it was Apollo. I asked him why he sided with the Trojans, and he said it was because he liked Hector and he thought Achilles was an ass.' I said smugly. 'Oh, and he said something about a soul thief, my learning Persephone's chants, and that you should give your shield to your son.'

Alexander was leaning toward me, an expression of disbelief on his face. He opened his mouth to speak, but nothing came out.

A knock sounded on the door and a very old man entered. Alexander sprang to his feet and bowed.

The old man greeted Alexander as Son of Amon, King of Egypt. Then he bowed to me and called me Daughter of Demeter, and he held out two scraps of papyrus with some hieroglyphics on them. 'Here are your answers, O Mighty Ones.'

'Thank you.' I said, taking my papyrus and looking at it. I turned it upside down and sideways, but I had no training in reading hieroglyphics. 'Can you translate these?' I asked the priest.

'Certainly.' The priest first took Alexander's papyrus. '"Will I go to the land of the wild elephants?" Answer, "You will go, but not until you've found what you are seeking." Question, "Where will I find my soul?" Answer, "In the land of the never setting sun." Question, "Will I live to be an old pan?" Answer, "You are not a pan, how can you grow old as one?".'

'I didn't say "pan", I said "man",' said Alexander.

44

'The messenger is hard of hearing,' said the old priest. 'Two out of three questions isn't bad.'

I gave him my papyrus and he cleared his throat. 'Question, "Will Iskander and I have ant troubles in Africa?" Answer, "Definitely. There are many ants in Africa and some are quite dangerous. Beware of ants in Africa.".'

'I didn't ask about ant troubles, I said, *any* troubles!'

'Well, now you know that you'll have troubles with ants. I would consider your question answered.' The old priest shrugged.

I took the papyrus back. 'Thank you.'

'It was my pleasure.' The priest bowed, and we bowed back, all of us bobbing until he finally backed out the door. Alexander tossed his papyrus into the brazier's flame. I did the same. Supposedly, you couldn't take your answer out of the temple.

'Ant problems.' I shook my head. 'If I had known he was deaf I would have spoken louder.'

Alexander put his arm around my shoulders. 'What do we do now?'

'We find your soul.'

'Do you have an idea where it could be?'

I spoke hesitantly. I had no clear idea what Northern Europe was like in 300 BC. 'The land where the sun never sets or never rises is near the Arctic Circle.' I tried to imagine the journey in my head. 'Our best bet would be to take a boat to Marseille, and then go up the Rhône River as far as we can. Then across land to Paris and, if Nearchus wants, we'll take a boat again at Calais and go up the coast.'

'Nearchus will be glad about the boat part.'

'The voyage will be long. We'll be gone for months. I believe the best thing would be to leave the children with Usse and Chirpa in Alexandria,' I said.

'I agree,' said Alexander. 'We have to be careful. I've heard stories about the Eaters of the Dead.'

I was so startled I jumped. 'Eaters of the Dead? You've heard of them?'

'Yes, why? Ashley! You're so pale!'

I took a deep breath. I'd had a fright. 'That's where Apollo said your soul was.'

Now it was Alexander's turn to lose a few shades of colour. 'Are you sure?'

'I'm not deaf yet.' I clung to his arm.

'The Eaters of the Dead.' Alexander shivered. 'I don't like the sound of that. Especially since I'm supposed to be dead myself.'

Chapter Six

We decided we would take a boat to Marseille and then plan the rest of our trip. Even in the year 323 BC, Marseille was known as a busy port, and we were sure of getting information about the north of France, or Gaul, as they called it then. We could join up with merchants, and that would be even safer.

We left one windy December day with Nearchus, Axiom, and Millis. Axiom wouldn't let Alexander go anywhere without him, Millis wouldn't leave me, and Nearchus was thrilled to be going on a sea voyage to the great unknown. I was miserable to be leaving my children. Cleopatra was only five months old, but she had been weaned, and Brazza, Chirpa and Usse would take care of her. Cleopatra was too little to understand, but I knew that she would be a toddler when I next saw her. I was devastated, although part of me was reassured as I watched her tuck her head under Brazza's chin and fall asleep in his arms. She would be well loved.

Paul had been upset when I'd told him he had to stay behind, because I'd promised never to leave him again. I tried to tell him that he would be happy in the house, and that Plexis would buy him a pony of his own, but he still begged to accompany us.

Plexis stayed behind as well. He had business to attend to and would make sure everyone was well cared for.

I didn't know whom I was going to miss more; Cleopatra my sweet daughter, my precious boys, or Plexis.

As the boat sailed away, Alexander and I stood on the deck and waved. Plexis stood on the dock, seeing us off, with Chiron by his side.

Paul was nowhere to be seen. He had been begging to come with us so much that Alexander had lost his temper and yelled at him. Paul had never been yelled at in his life, I think, and it had crushed him. I tried to comfort him, but his pride had been hurt, and he wouldn't speak to me. I cried as the boat left the dock, but Alexander told me not to worry.

'Paul will be fine, he's a big boy now.'

'I hope you're right; I feel dreadful leaving him like this.'

'We'll be back in less than a year. You can bring him loads of presents and he'll get your letters, never fear.'

I nodded, my hair whipping around my face. I waved until I couldn't see Plexis and Chiron any more then went to sit down on the deck and leaned against the mast. The boat creaked and the wind whistled in the sails. The water made a wonderful whooshing sound as it flowed by, and Alexander leaned over the rail and was sick.

'I miss everyone so much,' I said. It was our fourth day at sea and we'd entered the deep currents now. Dolphins leapt at the bow.

'I do too. It seems so strange not to have Brazza and Plexis around. I keep expecting them to show up.'

I looked around the boat. 'Me too, but most of all I miss my children. It's awful. Every time I think of Cleopatra I want to cry. I hope that Chiron is behaving and not making too much mischief for everyone. And I wish I could see Paul. I wanted to speak to him before we left. He wouldn't even talk to me. I'm so worried about him.' I sniffed loudly.

'Don't worry, Mother, I'm right here!'

I spun around, gaping. Paul popped his head out of a hatch. His blond hair was tousled and his eyes were as bright as his father's when he'd accomplished a particularly difficult feat.

'Wha ... wha ... what are you doing here?' I managed to gasp.

'Paul!' Alexander lifted his son out of the hatch. 'What *are* you doing here? Answer me, boy!'

Paul grinned. His face was pink with excitement. 'I stowed away. I've had enough of being left behind like mouldy millet seed in a storeroom. I'm coming with you. Besides, you need me,' he said proudly.

'What do you mean by that?' Alexander was stern.

'I speak Keltoi,' he said, saying the Greek word for Celt.

'What?' We both asked in unison. 'Where and when did you learn that?' asked Alexander.

'They spoke Keltoi in the valley of Nysa. Didn't you realize that?'

'No,' I said. 'I always heard them speaking Greek.'

49

'They spoke Greek to you because you wouldn't understand anything else, but they were a Celtic tribe. When you left that's all they spoke. So now I speak Celt. And when you go to the north, in Gaul, everyone speaks Celt.'

'They speak Gallic,' I said.

'And Celt, mostly Celt.' Paul's face was serious. His eyes were dark blue, his cheekbones high, and he had a proud nose. It was hard to believe he was only ten. He looked much older. He had a stubborn set to his mouth and a determined chin. I knew where those came from. I stole a glance at Alexander.

'Do you really speak Celt?' he asked.

'Of course,' and he said something that sounded like a clay pot breaking.

'What was that?' I asked him.

'I said, I'm coming with you.'

'I suppose you are.' Alexander looked half vexed, half proud. 'But I'll have to send a message to Plexis, he must be out of his mind with worry.'

'Oh no, I left a message, and Chiron knew what I was up to.'

'Chiron?' I sighed. 'He is such a little troublemaker. And it never occurred to him to tell on you?'

'Oh no! He would never do that! He nearly wanted to go with me but preferred to stay with Papa and the horses. I think he likes horses as much as Papa does, and I told him he had to stay and guard Cleopatra.'

'Well that's a relief.' I rubbed a cold hand over my face. 'You have been hiding out on the boat for four days now, are you hungry?'

Paul looked guilty. 'I was hiding in the storeroom. I'm afraid I ate most of the figs and the flat bread.'

Alexander frowned at him. 'When we get to Massalia I will find a Celt, and if you can speak to him, you can come with us. But if you've been telling stories, I will put you on a boat with Axiom, and he'll take you straight back to Alexandria. Fair enough?'

Paul smiled sweetly. 'Very fair, Father.' He came over and put his arms around me, kissing my cheek. The he kissed Alexander. 'I won't be any trouble at all, you'll see.'

I winced. 'Don't say that, please. Every time I hear that, there's trouble.'

Nearchus came up on deck and strolled over. He saw Paul and said, 'Oh, greetings, Paul.' Then he did a perfect double take, tripped over the railing, and fell head first into the water.

'Man overboard!' I screamed, leaping to my feet and waving my arms.

Alexander was more practical. He threw a rope into the water and Nearchus caught hold of it. Since we were sailing along at a fast clip, it took a few minutes to lower the sails and come about. The sailors hauled Nearchus onto the boat just in time; a large shark had started to circle around him. Nearchus was chalky white when he landed back on deck. He sat in a large puddle of saltwater, gaping first at Paul, then at the shark fin cutting through the water.

'What are you doing here?' he gasped when he had gotten his breath back.

'He stowed away,' said Alexander wryly. 'Don't worry. We've got Persephone the Terrible, and the Harbinger of Destruction. What could possibly go wrong?'

'The Harbinger of Destruction? Is that what they call me?' Paul looked pleased.

'Oh great,' said Nearchus. 'We'd better batten down the hatches and put the storm sheets up. Paul's with us.' He looked at Paul and a smile tugged at his mouth. 'The gods must think I was getting soft, or bored.'

Chapter Seven

The trip from Alexandria to Marseille took us little more than four weeks, and only one storm battered us, only one sailor broke his leg, and our boat didn't catch on fire when the clay cooking stove exploded. Nearchus said that Paul, as Harbinger of Destruction, might be losing his touch.

Marseille, or Massalia, as the people called it then, had been founded in the year 600 BC by Graeco-Phoenicians as a trading post. The Greeks were the first to build a port there. When we arrived, the large and prosperous city was already three hundred years old.

Long wharves reached out into the bay, and a small rowboat escorted us to our slip. Customs officials welcomed us.

'I can't believe it,' I complained to Alexander after we'd stood in line for an hour. 'The Gauls and their officials! They aren't happy unless they're doing paperwork of some sort. They haven't changed in thirty centuries!'

We had filled out what seemed like hundreds of parchments, papyrus, or wax tablets by the time evening came and were finally cleared to enter the city. There were documents for everything: for us; for the sailors; for the boat; and for the cargo. The customs building was large and we got lost twice trying to find an exit. Finally, we found ourselves on a busy street full of merchants pulling wooden carts and carrying sacks of grain.

Massalia seemed a nice city. The buildings were made of stone and the streets clean. We followed the main street toward the marketplace and then searched for an hotel. Alexander wanted to get us settled, then needed to go the courier office to send a message to Plexis telling him we'd arrived and Paul was safe.

We stayed in Massalia just long enough for Alexander to sell his cargo of dates, and make sure Paul really knew how to speak Celtic.

Then we headed for the Rhône to catch a boat upriver. We stopped in a town called Glanum, which nowadays is called Saint-Rémy-de-Provence. It was our introduction to Gaul, although the town was a mixture of Gallic and Greek architecture. It was built around a sacred spring as were many towns at that time. The spring had two temples near it, one for Glanis, a local divinity, and one to Athena, the Greek goddess of wisdom. We found a guide, Camimilulix, who told us everything as we walked through the town.

He was a Gaul, which meant he rarely answered a question directly.

'What's that building near the stream?' Paul asked, pointing to a line of women standing in front of a long shed.

'Perhaps the river goddess will help you guess,' Camimilulix replied.

'How do I ask her?' Paul was all for it, leaning over the little stone bridge.

'How does one ask anything?' Camimilulix usually answered a question with a question.

'Well, they ask, that's all.' Paul rubbed his nose, then leaned further out over the bridge. 'I only wanted to know what that building was,' he yelled at the stream in Greek.

A fisherman, sitting on a mossy bank, shouted back at Paul, 'It's a washing house, my boy, the local women wash their clothes there.'

Camimilulix looked smug as Paul gaped.

'I didn't realize the river goddess was a Greek fisherman,' I said ironically.

Camimilulix shrugged. 'The goddess has many forms and speaks in many tongues.'

'I'll say!' Paul stared at the fisherman until we were well down the road. Even then, he kept turning around.

'What are you doing?' I asked him.

He grinned sheepishly. 'I want to see the river goddess change forms.'

'Paul!' I looked at him sternly. 'There is no such thing as a river goddess.'

He looked abashed but cast one last glance over his shoulder. 'Mother!' he cried, pointing.

I turned. Where the fisherman had been sitting, there was a sleek brown otter holding a fat perch in its whiskered mouth. With what looked suspiciously like a wink, the creature slid into the water and disappeared without a ripple.

'Did you see that?' asked Paul.

'I saw an otter,' I sighed, taking his hand and walking after the others.

'But do you think it could have been the river goddess?'

'Don't you think you saw an otter?' I said.

'You're beginning to sound like Camimilulix,' he complained.

I smiled at my son. 'Well, if it *was* the river goddess, I'll say this much for her, she's got a superb moustache.'

We were in the heart of Provence. Three thousand years later tourists would flock here in droves and jam the streets, but right now it was pleasantly provincial, and there were no hover camper-vans lining the dusty roads or tourists on rider-drones soaring about with their 3-D cameras whirring.

Nothing whirred here, but we did see traffic jams. Horse-drawn chariots would often get stuck behind plodding en ox-drawn carts, and there would be hearty shouting and swearing from the charioteers until the ox drivers decided to let them pass.

The Gauls invented the first iron-bound wheels. Alexander was always marvelling over the chariots, very much like a man from my time would exclaim about new hover cars.

'I've got to get one of these!' cried Alexander, running his hands over a gorgeous *biga* with two large iron-bound wheels. 'Imagine how fast it would go. I bet Plexis would love this.' He decided to send two of the chariots back to

Egypt, so he spent an entire day at the customs house filling out export forms.

Chapter Eight

We arrived in Arles – or Arelate, as the Romans called it – and found a trading boat willing to take passengers upriver. The boat stopped overnight in different villages along the way, and I noted the differences between the Graeco-Gallic villages, the Gallo-Roman villages, and the purely Gallic villages. However different they were, one thing was the same: they all had dogs.

Paul was captivated and started to pester us to get him one. I suppose every boy wants a dog, although Alexander said he'd never had a pet.

'My mother had a parrot, not a dog, and my father was bitten by a dog as a child and never wanted one. We had no dogs in our palace, although there were hunting hounds in the kennels. I wouldn't know how to care for one,' admitted Alexander.

'But, Father, I'll take care of him. Please? The captain says he'll give me a baby dog.'

'They're called puppies,' I said, 'and they have the habit of growing quickly.'

'And the habit of peeing everywhere.' Axiom spoke with assurance. 'I had a dog once. It was not easy to train. It peed on everything I owned. I think it was marking its territory.'

Paul shrugged. 'I don't own anything but a linen skirt, a tunic, and a bow. I don't even have any arrows yet. Please, Father, I would *really* like a dog.'

'We'll see.'

Three thousand years later this would still be a parent's last resort. 'We'll see'. What a wonderful saying. It could mean anything and Paul knew this. His face darkened, and I could practically see sparks in his eyes.

'Paul,' I said in my best *'watch out'* voice. 'Your father said he'd see about it. Now is not the time to ask. We're travelling on a small boat up a deep river.'

'But the captain of the boat said …'

'I don't care what he said. You listen to your father.'

Paul stomped away. I sighed and went back to my mending; there was always something to mend. Paul was forever catching his cloak on something sharp, and Alexander wasn't much better.

I was also cross with the boat captain. After all, it was none of his business. It didn't matter to me if his bitch had given birth to a litter of hopelessly mongrel mongrels. I had never seen a dog like her before. She was huge, with matted grey fur and wary, yellow eyes. She looked like a cross between a bear and a wolf. The captain was fond of his dog, but he should know better than to get a boy's hopes up like that.

We stayed on the river for ten days, long enough to get as far as the present-day city of Chalon-sur-Saône – or Cabillonum as the ancients called it. Soon, I knew, it would become an important trading post and city, but it was just a small settlement when we were there. Our ship's captain waved farewell, a huge smile on his face, and it was not until we'd walked for nearly five hours through the countryside, that we found out why he'd looked so cheerful.

Paul trailed behind us. He carried his luggage over his shoulder. His luggage consisted of a rough sack containing an extra pair of sandals and a tunic. He was wearing his skirt, low boots and his warm, woollen cloak; it was winter and the wind was chilly. He also had his new bow slung over one shoulder. I wondered why he was puffing. He looked tired and I kept turning and calling back, asking if he were all right.

'I'm fine, Mother,' he cried. He was far behind, and I grew nervous.

'Maybe you had better go to help him carry his bag,' I said to Alexander.

'That's ridiculous! All he has in it are his sandals and an extra tunic.'

And a large puppy. The boat captain had managed to give Paul his biggest puppy.

We stopped to eat lunch. Paul set his sack down near his feet and took the bread Axiom handed him. Immediately there came a sharp howling from inside his bag. A shaggy grey head popped out, and two hungry yellow eyes surveyed us.

'Yap!' it said sharply.

Alexander jumped. 'What in Hades is that?' he cried.

'I named him Cerberus. Please let me keep him!' cried Paul.

I opened my mouth, then shut it. This was between Paul and Alexander; I was staying out of it. However, the name brooked no good. Cerberus was the three-headed monster that guarded the Underworld.

'The Harbinger of Destruction and his hound from Hades.' It was Nearchus, looking at Paul over his lunch. To me, he said, 'It should make you feel right at home, O Queen of the Underworld.' Then he started to laugh and nearly choked.

I was speechless. Nearchus, usually the most serious person in the world, never joked about anything. However, perhaps that had just been the effect of being at war. Now that he was a tourist he seemed different.

Alexander was at a loss for words. It was one of the few times I saw him caught off guard. When I'd told him I was from the future, he'd been more composed. He stared at the huge hound busily gobbling up Paul's food. Finally he said, doubtfully, '*That* is a *dog*?'

'He's *my* dog,' said Paul firmly. 'I love him and he loves me.' He seemed to be right about that. The dog paused long enough to lick Paul's face thoroughly. Then he went back to eating.

'But, but … but I know nothing about dogs.' Alexander searched for an argument.

'That's all right. The captain told me all about what to feed him and what to do when he's sick.'

'They get sick?' Alexander leaned over to get a better look.

'They get fleas and ticks, and they pee all over,' said Axiom, with a large grin.

Alexander glared at Paul. 'Didn't I tell you to wait and see?'

'Yes, but I knew that I could wait until I was old and grey. Admit it, Father, you were never going to ask the captain.'

'Well, actually, I do admit it.' Alexander scratched his head and then muttered an oath. 'I feel like I've already got fleas.'

'You probably do,' I told him. 'The boat was hopping with them.'

We finished our lunch and set off for the nearest village. Since it was winter, I hoped we'd make it before nightfall. I wanted to take a hot bath and sleep in a comfortable bed; the boat had neither of these things.

There is nothing so reassuring as the sight of lights in the distance when night is falling. The sun had set, and I was cold and weary by the time we reached the village and found an inn. To our delight, a whole wild boar roasted on a spit in an immense fireplace in the dining room. There were other travellers too. A group of merchants from Rome had a load of wine to trade. When they found out we were heading north, they invited us to journey with them.

After dinner, I was glad to take a hot bath in the bathhouse. I made Paul take one too. Like most boys his age, he hated bathing. Then he and Cerberus curled up together in a bed of warm straw. Since there was only one bedroom free, Nearchus, Axiom, and Paul slept in the large, well-built stables, while Alexander and I were privileged to sleep in a bed.

After his bath, Alexander came to our room. The bed was narrow, lumpy, and hard, but there was a cheerful fire in the fireplace to keep the chill out. Alexander gazed out of the window for a moment then closed the wooden shutters. Millis, wrapped snugly in his cloak, was already asleep on his pallet at the foot of our bed.

Alexander sighed and took me in his arms. His lips tickled my cheek as he spoke. 'Well, it's not the palace of Nebuchadnezzar, but it's clean.'

'Do you miss living in luxury?' I asked.

'I spent twelve years living in a tent, remember? This *is* luxury compared to that.'

I shook my head, remembering the opulent tent with the Persian rug, the ebony table, and the delicate glass lamp. 'We were spoiled,' I said.

He chuckled. 'I remember the first time I saw the palace in Babylon. It was the night I married Stateira. I wasn't allowed in the palace before my purifying ceremony. After the ceremony, they took me up on the roof and tied ropes around my chest. I had no idea what they were doing. Do you know what they did next? They lowered me into the bridal chamber from the roof.'

'How funny!' I was amused. 'Why?'

'As king of Persia I was supposed to be divine, remember?'

I snorted. 'How could I forget?'

He ignored my sarcasm. 'There were mirrors in the ceiling, and when the trapdoors opened in the roof, they reflected the light in such a way it seemed I was riding a golden cloud. I was lowered into the room where Stateira was waiting on the bed for me to …'

'That's enough,' I said hastily, 'you don't have to tell me any more.'

'Why? Aren't you curious about the nuptials of the god and his queen?'

'No, I am not,' I said firmly. 'I'm jealous about you and anyone else. I don't want to hear about it ever.'

'Sorry.' He kissed me gently, making a warm glow in my tummy. I arched my back, pressing close to him. I could feel his ardour against my thighs. With a deep sigh I opened my legs.

Alexander chuckled. 'Not so fast,' he whispered. His hands roamed over my body, his mouth followed. I moaned softly and closed my eyes, savouring the gentle caresses. He knew me too well. He knew all the places that made me shiver, that tickled, that delighted. I tried to wriggle away but he held onto my waist, not letting me move. When I was breathing in shuddering gasps, he rose up on his elbows and then lowered himself onto me.

I wrapped my legs around his hips, urging him on. My head was spinning. When I opened my eyes, I saw only shadows. There were faint cries coming from my throat. I tried to stop, to slow down, but my hips were moving of their own accord.

He grasped my hips and pulled me even tighter, thrusting deep with each movement. His breath was coming in short gasps, I felt the room tilt as he rammed into me. There was a brief moment when we both froze. Then the throbbing began and I let myself dissolve into my husband's body. The fire flickered and went out, but I was secure in Alexander's warm arms. My whole body felt as if it were wrapped in a golden cloud. I fell asleep with a smile on my face.

That night Alexander had one of the nightmares that made his dreams unbearable. He hadn't had one in so long, I had almost forgotten the trembling that woke me. Confused, I opened my eyes. There was a faint red glow from the fireplace, but otherwise all was darkness.

Alexander was sitting upright, his eyes open, seeing nothing but his own demons. His lips were drawn back in a grimace of fear. In the reddish light his hair was copper and his eyes black pools.

I knew that to touch him would only exacerbate his horror. Whatever it was that he saw in the dark corners of his mind, only he could overcome it. I shrank away from him, waiting until his consciousness took over enough for me to pull him out of his sleep.

It didn't take long. Sweat appeared on his brow, and he thrashed his legs in the covers. A low moan in his throat grew into a harsh cry.

Millis was instantly awake. He raised his head, and I saw his eyes glowing in the light of the embers. His face grew tense. I shook my head at him, motioning him down with my hands. Millis sank back onto his pallet. He had seen Alexander's phantasmagorias before. He knew that there was nothing to be done except wait.

I took Alexander in my arms. I had to grip him tightly. While I held him I felt his heartbeat slowly return to normal, and his body stopped shaking. Soon his head dropped onto my shoulder, and he took a deep breath. When he could open his hands, he placed them on my thighs. I could feel them trembling.

'I'm sorry,' he whispered.

'Don't be.' I stroked his back, calming him. I hesitated then asked, 'what was it this time?'

'Does it really help to talk about it?' he asked.

'I don't know. Only if you want to.'

'It was Tyre.' When he said the name his whole body shuddered.

I was silent. I hadn't known him when he'd taken the island of Tyre. The siege had lasted four months. Thousands had died. The people had put up a bloody, desperate fight before falling to Alexander's army. He had built a causeway sixty metres wide from the mainland to the island. Then he'd leapt from a siege tower onto the wall of the city, brandishing his shield and his lance.

His army swept into the town, burning buildings and slaughtering anyone that put up resistance. They spared anyone who had taken refuge in the temples. The city had fallen, and he was master of Tyre.

However, I didn't think that the memory of that battle would cause him so much distress. That was part of his warfare. He planned his attacks with care and accepted the consequences. No, most of his nightmares were about his family, or the death of his friend Cleitus, whom he'd killed in a fit of rage.

I didn't say anything though; I just tightened my arms around him and put my cheek against his.

Alexander stirred restlessly. 'I saw my brothers and sisters in the fortress. They were waving at me from the ramparts. They kept asking me if I recognized them, and I said "Yes, of course I do." Then they started shouting and told me I was lying. "How can you recognize us? Your mother killed us when we were just babes!" But I knew who they were; they looked just like me. The men and the women looked just like me.' He shivered. 'I told them to go to the temples where they would be safe. But they just laughed at me. They yelled back that the gods had long ago stopped caring what happened to them. I wanted to save them, so I told them again to go to the temples. They looked at me, and all of them had two-coloured eyes. They said, "We can tell you where your soul has gone." Then arrows fell like rain upon them.'

'Oh, Alex,' I murmured. 'It was just a dream, nothing more.'

'Dreams are messages from the gods,' he said, his voice muffled in my neck.

'No they're not. We've had this discussion before.' I took his face in my hands and smoothed his cheeks with my thumbs. They were wet with tears. 'Remember what I told you about the unconscious, the subconscious and the conscious? I told you that dreams were a sort of safety valve that lets off excess stress. Anything that your unconscious can't handle is turned into nightmares. It gives you a good scare, gets your adrenaline pumping, and you learn how to deal with what's frightening you.'

'You also told me stories of people who couldn't bear to sleep any more because their dreams were too awful, and how doctors had learned to stop their dreams. Do you think you can make me some of that medicine?' His voice was hopeful.

'I don't know. Are your dreams so horrible then?'

He shuddered. 'I feel as if they tear me apart.'

'I wish I could help you.' I kissed his mouth, nibbling on his lips. He smiled, and I gently licked his upper lip, taking it between my teeth. 'Does this help?'

He chuckled weakly. 'Mmm. Maybe.' He kissed me back and I tasted the sharpness of fear.

'I think that there must be something you need to face. Something that you've been avoiding. If you finally got it out in the open it might cease to torment you.' I chose my words carefully. Alexander was a strange combination of strength and fragility. He was opposing forces brought together.

I knew that, in his youth, he had thought of himself as a descendant of Achilles. His mother had told him that he was directly descended from Zeus. His mother also worshipped Dionysus, the most mortal, most terrible of the gods. Worshipping Dionysus meant living on the very edge of folly. His adepts would often drink themselves blind and make bloody sacrifices before abandoning themselves to huge orgies.

Unfortunately, the edge of madness is not a place to live if you're the least bit vulnerable. Alexander's mother, Olympias, had given her son his own Achilles heel. Olympias was mad. She had killed eight of Alexander's stepbrothers and sisters. It was rumoured she'd had a hand in her husband's murder, and that she'd forced his new wife with her infant son onto the funeral pyre.

I had no idea how far Alexander was implicated in his father's murder, but judging from his nightmares, I thought he was in rather deep. But he never spoke to me about it. Even in allusions. So all I could do was hold him closely when he awoke from his nightmares.

He listened to my words but wouldn't answer. Instead, he made love to me as if he wanted to chase away all his dreams with my body. Afterwards, he pretended to sleep, but I always knew when he was awake.

Chapter Nine

Dawn came, eventually. Alexander hardly ever showed the effects of a sleepless night. His face was unlined, his skin fresh. He went to the window and opened the shutters, looking with clear eyes out into the morning mist. 'I forgot where we were,' was his only comment.

We ate breakfast in the common room. Paul and Axiom were already there; Cerberus sprawled at Paul's feet like a shaggy grey rug. He lifted a twitching muzzle and watched us closely as we arrived, but he knew us, so just sighed and put his nose back on his oversized paws.

Breakfast in Gaul consisted of bacon, porridge with honey, scalded milk with chicory, eggs, and a delicious sausage made of leftover wild boar fried with spices. I stuffed myself. The food was wonderful.

Frost lined the windows that morning. It was February, the month of Dionysus. The month Alexander hated the most. It was the month he'd killed Cleitus, the month he'd destroyed Persepolis, and the month he'd nearly died in India from an arrow wound. It was the month of all his nightmares. I watched him closely. He only appeared to eat, pushing his food around his plate, not even tasting anything.

The Romans came to eat their breakfast. They were heading toward Lutetia, which I knew as Paris, and wanted to leave right away. Since we'd elected to travel with them, Alexander went to town and bought a small farm wagon pulled by two solid-looking brown ponies. We put our meagre belongings in it, and I had the dubious honour of sitting in the back with Cerberus, who was still too little to walk very far without tiring. *Too little*? I stared at the beast as he lay with his head on my leg. Already he was nearly as long as the wagon was wide. I reached over and scratched his head. He beat his tail on the wooden floorboards hard enough to raise a cloud of dust. I sneezed. With a sigh I leaned back and tried to get comfortable. The men walked ahead of the wagon. Axiom drove the horses. Paul walked just behind the wagon; his head tilted to the side, like his father's, his eyes lost in his own daydream. Sometimes he'd stumble. Then he'd grin sheepishly at me and trot to catch up.

The sun rose high in the sky, and just after noon we stopped at a stream to eat our lunch.

The Romans were a garrulous bunch. They were going north to sell a load of fine wine. The amphorae were carefully packed in straw and filled three large farm wagons. They had guards and slaves with them. The slaves wore brass torcs engraved with their master's name. They slept in the wagons with the wine and drove the horses.

I was interested, because the Romans were the new 'up and coming' people. They would soon take over the entire Mediterranean and push north to the British Isles. Well, they were certainly *pushy*. To them, everything Roman was wonderful, and anything else was quaint. A bit like the Athenians, I decided.

They started telling us about their city, making it sound just incredible.

'As if we've never heard of sewers or running water,' said Alexander to me.

I laughed. 'Ask them if they have central heating. No, I'm just kidding,' I said, tugging on his sleeve. However, it was too late.

'How do you heat your houses?' he asked, and we were obliged to listen for another hour about hypocausts and how the Romans had invented central heating. I mouthed *'I told you so'*, to Alexander, but he seemed genuinely interested.

'I'll have to get Roman architects to come to Alexandria and build the baths. Did you hear, Ashley? They have heat coming up from the floor, and they have an amazing new system where the hot water circulates all through the house.'

'Amazing,' I said, grinning.

'Don't be sarcastic,' said Alexander.

'Who, me?' I raised my eyebrows. 'By the way, Rome will soon be the big guy on the block, so we'd better be nice to them. They'll conquer all this land, and all the way north to the islands I showed you on the map.'

I'd brought my map with me and we looked at it every evening to see how far we'd gone. Maps, back then, were very rudimentary, so mine was like a television. Nearchus and Axiom would ask me questions for hours. The men and Paul would pore over it, tracing routes with their fingers, asking about the different mountain ranges and deserts.

Alexander frowned. 'I could have conquered that,' he said haughtily.

'That would have been interesting,' I said reflectively. 'I'm not sure it would have changed the Europe as I knew it. The Romans are very like the Greeks in many ways, but it would have spread Persian civilization much further. I wonder ...'

'What?'

'I was just wondering how that would have changed the story of Jesus.'

'Do you mean the man who died when he was my age? Who changed the world even more than I did? And who never led a single army, nor killed a single man? That one?'

'That's him. He was born in a country under Roman occupation, and the Romans were less tolerant than you were about religion and things. They will try and force their gods on everyone else, and the Christians will become martyrs, thrown to the lions and all that.'

'Ah yes, the entertainment.' He tilted his head to the side. 'Do the Romans invent television as well?'

'No, you're getting your history mixed up.'

'It's not history yet,' he told me.

I made a face. 'You're right. What else do you want to know?' He was so curious that once he got started on his questions, he could go on all day. 'Why don't you come with me in the wagon?' I asked him.

'All right. I want to find out more about these barbarians.' Alexander had picked up the Greek habit of referring to anyone who didn't speak Greek as a barbarian. It was a form of antique snobbery.

That afternoon, Alexander and Paul rode in the wagon with me, and we talked about the future. I was in charge of Paul's future education, and Alexander took care of his reading, writing, and history. Axiom helped him with arithmetic, and Nearchus gave lessons in navigation, geography, and astronomy.

Millis loved to listen. As a slave, he'd never had any schooling. I was astounded that one of Darius's sons could be treated so badly: enslaved, castrated, and made mute. Persians had their own terrible rules applying to their royal family. Poor Millis, his father had been one of the most powerful men in the world, but his mother had been a lowly slave. Babies of slaves were slaves, no matter what.

All afternoon, we travelled down the dirt road. The horse's hooves made a clinking sound every time their iron shoes struck a rock. The iron wheels of the cart had no shock absorbers, so we kept getting out to walk and rest our sore backs. It was chilly enough to make walking attractive.

The Romans were sociable and they would often drop back to chat. They loved to complain, and criticized everything they saw.

'Look at that,' said Marcus Quintus Caius, the head of the Roman expedition. 'We travelled twice as far as necessary because of the loop. If we had gone straight, back there, we could have shortened the route by ten leagues.'

'There was a big ravine,' said Paul.

'It would have been easy to cross,' said Marcus, waving his hand airily. 'A Roman bridge builder would make short work of that.' Then he frowned and looked up at the sky. 'Perhaps we'll get some snow.' The temperature had dropped, and we were wrapped tightly in our woollen cloaks.

'Are you from Rome itself?' I asked.

'No, I come from Po, just to the north of Roma. It's a lovely place. I can't wait to go back and be buried there.'

I wasn't sure I'd heard correctly. 'Pardon me?' I asked. 'Did you say, buried there?'

'Why, yes. The only way to have a decent house is to be in the necropolis. The houses for the dead are all made of stone or brick. They're very nice. The living have to make do with shacks.'

'How odd,' I said, making a face.

'No, not if you think about it logically.' His voice held a note of triumph in it. 'Think. How long do you live?'

'Well, that depends,' I said cautiously.

'No, no. I mean, in general – about sixty years for a man and fifty for a woman. And how long are you dead?'

'Is this a trick question?'

'You stay dead for ever!' he crowed.

'So the houses of the dead are built to last them all their, uh, deaths?' I asked.

'Exactly. See? We Etruscans are very logical.'

Alexander saw me talking to Marcus Quintus and came over. He took my arm and drew me back. 'Don't mingle with that man,' he said in English – I'd been teaching him English for four years now and he could speak it fairly well.

'I'm not "mingling",' I corrected him. 'I'm talking.'

'Don't talk to him. He's a Lydian.'

'He told me he was an Etruscan.'

'They call themselves the Rasenna.' His voice was low and mysterious.

'So?' my curiosity was piqued.

'They believe that the dead walk among them like the living. They build great cities with streets and houses, and even temples, only for the dead.' His voice was still low.

'Why are we whispering?' I asked him.

Alexander frowned. 'You can't be too careful with Lydians. They're very strange. They seem to think that they'll be better off dead.'

'Whatever it is they think, they won't be able to understand English, I promise. It won't be spoken for a few more centuries at least.'

'Marcus Quintus isn't his real name,' Alexander said.

'No? What is it, and why did he change it?'

'His real name is Marce Tarquinius Iolaus. He's related to the actual king of Etruria.'

'What's wrong with that?'

'They wrap their dead in linen.'

'Get to the point, Alex.'

'If they really like you, they kill you.'

'That's a good reason not to get friendly with him.' I looked at Alexander. 'Are you speaking the truth or are you just jealous that I'm talking to another man? You're not going to get all Persian on me now. I'm not locked up in a harem any more and I intend to stay free.'

'Nearchus is growing a beard, did you notice?' He changed the subject.

'How could I miss it? It's very thick and curly,' I said. 'Now tell me the truth, who are these Lydians, and why don't you like them?'

'Oh, they've been warring with Greece for ages. They are a very rich people, and they have been fighting over an island in the Inner Sea that is full of iron ore,' he explained. 'Aristotle told me their towns were full of music, they play flutes for every occasion, even kneading bread. However, it's true about the necropolises. They really do think the dead walk around on earth. How bizarre.'

'Really,' I teased. 'Instead of flitting like dry leaves in a conventional underground realm ruled by a guy called Hades, his terrible wife Persephone, and a three-headed dog. Quite frankly I can't understand how they can believe something like that!'

'You're being sarcastic again.'

'You know, Alex, I come from a place and time where we study religion but nobody believes in it any more. I'm sorry.' I shrugged.

'Don't be. It's not important to me, but be careful how you speak to others. For them, their religions are very powerful.'

'Did you notice that one of the Romans sculpts in clay?' I asked. Now it was my turn to change the subject. Serious talk about religion made me uneasy.

'I did. He's doing a study of Nearchus with his new beard. I think he means to use him as a model for Zeus. Zeus! When Nearchus takes himself for Poseidon?'

We looked at each other and laughed, then went to join the others. Alexander, who was jealous, held on to my arm possessively for the rest of the day.

Late that afternoon, we arrived in the next village. A high wooden wall surrounded it, and several hairy men stood guard at the gate.

I hoped they were Gauls. If they were Gallo-Romans they would insist on checking every single scrap of document we carried with us, and if they were Graeco-Gauls they would insist on rewriting the very same documents.

They *were* Gauls, so after some strange questions they let us through.

To me they asked, 'Where did your hair come from?' To which I answered, 'My ancestors.' I must have hit it right the first time, because they waved me through.

Nearchus and Paul were blond as well, so they were waved through. Millis was mute, and the Gauls didn't hold with writing, so they looked suspiciously at the wax tablet he used to communicate with and hurriedly waved him through.

'What's your dog's name?' they asked Axiom.

'He's not my dog, he's the boy's dog.'

'Very well, carry on.'

They looked at Alexander and asked him, 'How far can you run?'

'How far can I run? What kind of question is that?' Alexander frowned. 'I think I can run pretty far. My legs aren't the same since I was shot in the calf with an arrow, and my ankle was shattered once. It's still stiff. My knee was broken. Another arrow I think. No? A lance? Well, you'd probably remember better than me, Axiom. I always fainted when something like that happened.'

'You faint easily,' said Axiom blandly.

'Ah, you faint?' The Gaul looked interested. 'So, you can run far and you faint. Very well, you can enter.'

We left the Romans at the gate arguing with the Gauls about whether or not a curve in the road was akin to a winding river or a low hill, and at any rate, whether or not they should all be straightened.

Chapter Ten

We found a small comfortable inn and settled our horses in the stables. Then we took turns taking a bath in a trough in the yard. It was in plain sight of everyone. As I stripped, a man stuck his head out of the upstairs window and whistled. Alexander looked around for a spear, and I hastily covered myself and shouted at Axiom to take Alexander for a long walk.

Paul bathed, and so did Nearchus. Alexander came back from his walk, still simmering, and bathed too.

In the dining area, we sat in front of a roaring fire and ate roasted wild boar. After dinner, Cerberus sprawled at Paul's feet. Nearchus brought his helmet to the table to polish, and we watched as Nearchus put a mirror-bright shine on his bronze armour.

'This fireplace is great,' said Paul, holding his hands toward the heat. 'It's so big, Daddy could stand up in it and not hit his head on the mantle.'

'Only your father,' said Nearchus, rubbing hard. 'A regular-sized man would bang his head.'

Paul giggled, and Alexander, always touchy about his height, bristled. 'I'm not short,' he said.

'Of course you're not,' I said, giving him a kiss. 'You're average.'

'Maybe in Macedonia, but here in Gaul you're on the small side,' said Nearchus, holding his helmet up to the light and admiring it. 'But don't feel bad. You're short and you walk funny, but you're still a handsome man. The serving woman couldn't keep her eyes off you.'

'I might be short and walk funny, but Barsine taught me how to throw a javelin.' Alexander spoke blandly.

Nearchus glanced at him, a smile flitting across his face. 'Oh? Did she? When? When she threw one through my tent, or when she was threatening to cut my balls off?'

'And stuff them down your throat,' agreed Alexander, nodding sagely.

'That sounds like a good story!' cried Paul, climbing onto his father's knees. 'Tell me about it, will you?' He was getting too big to sit on laps. His legs dangled to the floor, but Alexander wrapped his arms around him and held him fondly.

'Well, Barsine was my first wife. Remember, I told you about her.'

'You said she was very large and good at sports.'

'She certainly was. Well, she was also very jealous, and she didn't want anyone else to share my bed.'

'She threw Plexis out of the tent one morning,' I said. 'She had a fearsome temper.'

'Stop interrupting.'

'Of course, you wouldn't remember that, you were unconscious. She knocked you out, and you slept for a whole day,' I added.

'She did?' He looked at Paul and tousled his bright hair. 'Well, she told Nearchus that if she ever caught him sneaking around the tent, she'd cut off his balls and stuff them down his throat. To prove it, she threw her javelin right through his tent. She did the same thing to Plexis's tent. He never mended the holes. He claimed they made a nice breeze.' He shook his head, smiling. 'I miss Barsine.'

'Did she die a long time ago?' asked Paul.

'Oh, years and years ago. I've forgotten when, exactly. I'm not very good at dates, I'm afraid. She had a son, your half-brother. His name is Heracles, and he lives with his grandparents. Artabazus is his grandfather.'

'I'd like to meet him,' said Paul.

'Perhaps someday you will,' Alexander said. He sighed and looked into the fire. The flickering light cast deep shadows on his face.

Paul settled his head under his father's chin and blinked sleepily. His mouth went soft as he relaxed in Alexander's arms. I caught Nearchus staring at Alexander. His eyes were full of longing.

I knew that Nearchus was in love with Alexander. He had been for ever, but he'd always stepped back. He'd never tried to take Plexis's place as Alexander's best friend. Now Plexis was not with us, and I wondered what Nearchus was thinking. His expression was always serious. His golden hair swallowed the firelight and threw it back in sparks. His hands tightened on his helmet. Then he put it carefully on the table.

Axiom and Millis were playing dice. The soft click of the bone dice as they rolled onto the wooden table was all we heard, except for the crackle of the fire and a loud scratching as Cerberus worried his fleas.

My eyes met Nearchus's. I had always been slightly afraid of the blond admiral, but now I knew him well enough to admire him. He'd never married, following Alexander throughout the years.

He'd watched as Alexander married Barsine, Stateira, Roxanne, Stateira again, and me. He'd watched as Alexander's children were born and died. When Alexander was wounded or ill he'd always been there. He was Alexander's childhood friend; they'd met in Aristotle's school. He had been born in Crete. He was one of the most intelligent men I'd ever met and had written a fascinating log of our voyage from the Persian Gulf to the Red Sea. It would still be read nearly three thousand years later. He was the only man who could always beat Usse at chess.

I wondered if Alexander loved him, and if I were jealous. I had seen them kissing once before, years and years ago. Before Alexander had destroyed Persepolis, and before he'd made peace with Plexis after killing his brother. Nearchus had always been close, but he'd never made the slightest move toward Alexander. Would he do so now? I frowned. Whatever happened, I had long ago learned never to interfere. Until now, it was because I was terrified I'd somehow change history. Now that we were free from the pitiless gaze of the Time-Institute, I could relax. I looked at Alexander and sighed. Habits are hard to break. I still couldn't bring myself to interfere.

I stared at the fire. There was something extremely hypnotizing about flames. I fell asleep with my head on the table.

Alexander shook me awake. He had Paul in his arms. The boy had fallen asleep as well; his face was pale with fatigue and his arms hung straight down at Alexander's sides.

Before we went upstairs to the bedrooms, Axiom had to clean up the puddle of urine that Cerberus had left in the corner. The dog looked sheepish, the innkeeper stood by with his hands on his hips, and Axiom muttered balefully all the time he was scrubbing.

Chapter Eleven

In the morning, we set off again with the Romans. The weather took a turn for the worse. I clung to Alexander and took refuge under his cloak. It was definitely warmer huddled together. Alexander was never cold. His body was always toasty, and I felt as if I were next to a heater.

I looked back and saw Paul talking to Nearchus. Paul had a cloak made of warm wool; he wore that over a linen shirt. None of us had underwear, although I had made some for myself. I wore them on occasion.

This was one of the occasions, and I was feeling crabby. Alexander hugged me; he was always sympathetic. I had to stop every hour or so and change the primitive feminine napkin I'd invented. I wished, for the thousandth time, there was something disposable I could buy in a shop. However, until then I would have to make do with cotton rags.

That evening we camped out; the next village was still two days away. The Romans had brought a couple pigs with them, and they slaughtered a small one and grilled it. One thing I had to say about them, they knew how to live.

We parked the wagons in a circle, built up a huge fire in the middle, and opened an amphora of wine. The smell of the meat as it crackled and sizzled made our mouths water. The wagons were set in a circle for protection, and I caught flashes of metal beneath the men's cloaks. We were travelling through a savage land now. The Romans posted guards near the pony lines. Even Cerberus was watchful. He kept lifting his head and sniffing the air.

We ate dinner in companionable conversation about the wine market and the new inventions everyone had seen lately. The Romans wanted to perfect their roads, so they were asking about the blacktop someone had told them about. Alexander explained to them about asphalt. The Romans used it for sealing, but hadn't used it on roads yet. Alexander had seen blacktop roads on his travels in Persia. He was still interested in the heating system the Romans had in their houses, so they drew diagrams in the dirt and talked about plumbing.

I had my own problems. I wanted to bathe, and I wanted to change. There was no place to do either. Finally I murmured to Alexander that I'd be right back. There was a bend in the road, and just beyond the pony lines was a copse of trees and a stream. I thought I'd go over there to wash and get ready for bed – 'bed' being a pallet made of a cloak and a pile of straw in the back of our wagon.

I made my way through the darkness toward the trees. Near the pony lines, the guards were sitting on large rocks gnawing on succulent pork ribs. A pile of bones lay at their feet, and a game of dice was temporarily put to the side. I told them I was just going to take a quick wash in the stream, but they barely glanced at me as I passed.

The horses stomped their hooves and snorted softly as I weaved through them. I couldn't see very well, as night had fallen. However, I knew that there was a path leading to the stream. I'd taken it earlier when I'd helped Nearchus tie up our ponies and fetch water for them.

The trees were very close together, and I had to pick my way through a thick hedge of bramble before I made it to a small clearing where a stream glittered in the dark.

Wintertime meant no nettles, thankfully, and the hedge of brambles hid me from view. There was a nip of frost in the air, and although no ice formed on the rushing stream it was cold enough to make me hurry. I rinsed out the cloths I'd used for my period and stuffed them back in my pouch. I'd hang them on a stick over the embers tonight and hope they dried by morning. My hands were icy cold now. I rubbed them together and squatted down to finish my business. I didn't want to have to come back into the woods before morning.

When I was finished, I stripped and washed myself. I felt better when I dressed, but I was upset to see that I'd run out of clean cloths. I'd used the last one. There was one good thing though; I ate fewer calories than in my own time and exercised constantly. My periods tended to be heavy for one day, light for two, then finished.

Today had been the first day, complete with cramps, crabbiness, and greasy hair. Tomorrow I'd feel better. I tied my pouch around my waist and plucked a twig from my tightly braided hair. I would have to wash it as soon as I arrived at the next town. Well, another nice thing about winter besides no nettles: no lice.

Faintly, I could hear the men's voices. They sounded loud, as if they were arguing or laughing. From a distance it was hard to tell. I shrugged and started to push through the trees when I heard a sound I knew well. It was the sharp clang of metal against metal. Then I heard screams. *Paul!* My breath caught in my throat and I leaped forward. My panic was for my son. I figured Alexander, battle-scarred warrior that he was, could take care of himself. The tree branches clawed at my throat and cloak, hindering me. I broke out of the forest.

The guards no longer sat on their rocks. They lay in a heap on top of the bones they'd been eating. A dark, steaming puddle spread beneath them. I choked back a cry. Slowly, I eased past them, pulling my dark cloak over my pale hair.

Orange firelight wavered as shadows crossed in front of it. Fighting was taking place around the fire. The wagons were partially blocking my view. As I drew closer, I could hear the harsh breathing of the men and the clanging of swords.

I saw Paul huddled underneath one of the wagons, his arms around his dog, and his face a mask of terror. Millis was guarding him, holding a large shield. I was still beyond the edge of light. I bent low, meaning to crawl under the wagon with Paul. However, the sight of five men standing in the road stopped me. They seemed to be waiting to capture anyone foolish enough to try and flee.

Inside the circle of wagons, Alexander and his men stood back to back, their weapons raised, as figures circled them warily. I could see Alexander, Axiom, and Nearchus. Alexander held his sword with a casualness that was deceptive. It was bright red, and blood ran down the blade and dripped off his hand. Nearchus wore his helmet and held a sword and a shield. Axiom held a sword and a lance. I couldn't see the Romans. On the ground lay at least ten bodies. Some were writhing, and others were still. I caught sight of Marcus Quintus's dark hair. I closed my eyes and took a deep breath.

There were still five men circling Alexander, Axiom, and Nearchus. However, they looked decidedly wary. None of them dared get within reach of Alexander's blade. They'd already picked Axiom and Millis as the weak links, but Axiom was armed with a long lance, so they had to keep their distance.

I took stock of the situation. The men inside the circle didn't worry me too much. The men outside worried me. Perhaps Alexander didn't realize they were there. I tried to think of a way to alert him and glanced once more towards my son. He was hiding under the wagon directly behind Millis. Paul was in front of me, the men on the road off to my right, and at my back was the pony line.

The horses were standing stiffly at the end of their tethers. Their eyes rolled in their heads and their nostrils flared as they snorted nervously. They weren't used to battle. One broke free. He leapt backward and spun around, galloping madly down the road. Frightened by the sounds of fighting and the overpowering smell of hot blood, he headed home.

The five men jumped out of the horse's way and looked towards me, but I had hidden behind a pony. They didn't bother to investigate. They stayed grouped together in the middle of the road. That gave me an idea. Hurriedly, I tied the next two ponies together. I set them free and watched as they streaked toward the men. They saw the ponies coming. However, they didn't see the rope dangling between them. The ponies galloped on each side of the road. As the road was narrow, the men grouped quickly in the middle to avoid being run over. The rope mowed them down. One man was caught under the chin, and I heard his neck break. The others were luckier; they were lifted off their feet and thrown backward. The noise they made caused Alexander to spin around and peer into the darkness.

Now that there was no more possibility of surprise, the men fighting Alexander tried to finish their job quickly. They thought to take advantage of Alexander's apparent distraction, but he was never distracted. As the man on his left jumped toward him, Alexander parried with his sword, and Nearchus ran him through with a mighty thrust.

The four remaining men on the road staggered to their feet. They were armed with swords, so I didn't dare approach. They separated. Three stayed where they were and one came towards me to investigate.

As I looked for a weapon, another horse pulled loose and galloped away. The men scattered, but not quickly enough. The frightened horse struck one of the men a glancing blow. The man stumbled and fell, landing near the wagon. He saw Paul and gave a triumphant yell. He reached toward the boy. Suddenly, a dark shape surged out from under the wagon. Cerberus. The puppy flung himself on the man, growling and snapping. I heard Paul's frightened cry and thought I would faint.

'No!' yelled Paul, scrambling out from under the wagons, his arms outspread. 'Don't hurt my dog!'

I choked back a cry of my own. The fighting intensified. The man heading toward me wavered then turned to see what the yelling was about. He had his back to me, so I didn't hesitate. I had a large rock in my hand. I'd read enough of *The Iliad* to know how handy those things could be. I rushed over to him and smashed the rock on the back of his head. He dropped to the ground and I bashed him again. He made a strange noise and grabbed at me, but his hand only brushed my sleeve before it fell to his side. He shuddered once and grew still. I thought I'd vomit. I clenched my teeth together. Then Paul screamed.

I wiped my hands on my tunic and sprinted toward the wagons.

Millis protected Paul. But, unlike a soldier or an aristocrat, he'd never studied sword fighting, archery, or even wrestling. His speciality was massages; a useless defence against two armed men.

He saved Paul's life. As Paul ran towards his dog, the man on the ground rolled over and stabbed Cerberus. The puppy howled in agony. Then the man stood up and Paul flung himself at him, fists flying. The attacker was so startled, he dropped his sword. Millis saw Paul leave the protection of the wagon, and he came running. Picking up the sword with one hand and pulling Paul to safety with the other, he stabbed the attacker. Not being a swordsman, his blow was poor and deflected off the man's ribs. The second blow managed to stick in the attacker's arm, putting him out of the fight. However, the second man appeared out of the darkness. I saw him leap forward and thrust his sword at Millis.

There was a moment when the darkness fooled me. I thought he'd missed Millis completely, because he seemed to touch him with his hand. Then I saw a glint of metal shining from Millis's back. Paul screamed. Millis staggered.

When I turned around, Millis was on the ground. The two men began chasing Paul and me toward the woods. My breath was coming in sharp gasps, and I was shaking so badly I could hardly run. Luckily the two men chasing us were wounded, or we would never have made it to the cover of the trees. I plunged into the brambles. I knew where the path was and that helped. The branches and thorns slowed the men. Paul and I scrambled beneath a fallen tree. I knew our hiding place would not last for long. The copse was small and the men, if they were methodical, would soon find us. However, we had no choice. We were unarmed and physically much weaker than them. I peered through the dead leaves and branches and watched as they started to search.

They were tall, dressed in dark tunics with striped leggings. They had beards, and one wore a helmet. The helmet puzzled me. It had horns, not unlike the helmets I'd seen in the museum exhibits of Viking artefacts. One man was blond, and I narrowed my eyes trying to get a better look at him. Vikings were known to have voyaged nearly everywhere. When Crete fell, mysteriously, a thousand years before this time even, the only clue from the writings said, "the marauders from the sea came and destroyed the cities". Were they speaking about the Vikings? Everyone feared them. Their savagery was legendary. The Vikings would sail as far as Paris, and conquer all of Normandy, but not for another thousand years. So, what was he doing here?

Paul huddled against me, trembling, his breath coming in little gasps.

'Hush,' I breathed. 'He's coming this way.' There was a crunch of dried leaves beneath stealthy feet, and I saw a dark form heading toward us. I shrank back, trying to will myself invisible. If we were captured, we might be spared and sold as slaves. However, I didn't think I wanted that to happen. I saw the man's eyes; they were flat and cruel. He seemed to be staring at us. My muscles tensed, preparing to fight. Instead, a sharp cry stopped him in his tracks. His companion looked up at the sky, pointed, and dashed off. The blond man hesitated, then spun around and ran off through the trees. Bare branches clawed at his cloak, and he made a huge racket as he crashed through the undergrowth. He was gone in seconds. I waited until I heard no more noise, then we eased out from under the tree.

I could hear shouting.

'Ashley!' It was Nearchus. He came running into the woods.

'We're here.'

When he saw us, he cried out in relief. 'Thank the gods!'

'How is everyone?' I asked. 'Who were they?'

'Alexander and Axiom are fine. The raiders were Gauls. But they spoke in a strange tongue.' I noticed he didn't mention Millis.

Alexander ran to us. His was limping, but he still moved with a rapid grace. He grabbed Paul and me and held us tightly. 'I was so worried about you,' he gasped.

His arms and hands were drenched in blood, and a fine spray of crimson covered his torso.

'Are you wounded?' I gasped.

'No, not a scratch. Axiom has a cut on his leg, and Nearchus lost a finger.'

Nearchus held up his hand, a bandage swaddled it.

'Has it stopped bleeding?' I asked.

'I cauterized it,' he answered. 'Don't worry, it was my little finger, and somewhat crooked after I broke it twice.'

'You won't be breaking it any more,' Alexander told him grimly. He turned to me and said, 'Millis is dead.'

I just stared at him. My face must have been a picture of misery, because he cursed softly and drew me into his arms.

'I'm sorry. I tried to help him. I saw him fall, and I saw you and Paul running, but I couldn't do anything, I was fighting. Then they just broke and ran.'

'Did he ... did he ...' I swallowed hard. 'Did he suffer?' I asked, tears blinding me.

'He died quickly. I don't think he suffered.'

Paul started to keen. He stumbled toward the fire where Axiom bent over the body of our friend.

'I'm so sorry,' Paul said brokenly, kneeling by the dead man's side. He took Millis's hand in his and pressed it to his cheek. Then he carefully put it down. He reached out and touched his eyelids, his cheeks, and his lips with his fingertips. 'Oh Millis,' he cried, and he put his face in his hands and sobbed.

We dragged the dead men into the circle of firelight. The Romans had been slaughtered. Businessmen, not fighters, they had succumbed easily. Their slaves had put up more of a fight, but they had been mercilessly cut down. The guards, who were there to defend the precious wine, had been taken by surprise while eating.

I shed tears for Marcus Quintus. In death he was still darkly handsome; I hoped he was happy, walking around his spirit world right now.

Alexander believed that the wine was the reason for the attack. Three wagon loads were worth a fortune, and there was a sack of silver coins in a chest. We carefully wrapped the dead in their cloaks and lay them in the largest wagon, their weapons next to them. Alexander took off his own cloak to wrap Millis. His hands shook as he tucked the corners under the body, and he leaned forward, pressing his lips to Millis's cold mouth. 'You saved my son,' he whispered, 'and I couldn't even thank you.' Tears ran down his cheeks and fell upon the pale face of Darius's son.

In death, Millis's perfect features were even more apparent. In the golden, flickering glow of the fire, he looked like a sleeping god; no mortal could be so beautiful. Alexander smoothed Millis's hair back and then gently pulled the cloak over his face.

It was like extinguishing a light.

Cold fury possessed us. Working quickly, we buried the silver. Then we piled wood under the wagon, and then, one by one emptied the amphorae of wine onto the bodies. When the air reeked of alcohol and the space below the wagon was crammed with branches, Alexander lit the pyre with a torch. There was a huge *'WHOOSH'* as a fireball bloomed in the night. We jumped back, our faces singed. Then Axiom started intoning a prayer. The moon had just started its ascent into the sky, and all the tree branches were cast in silver. It was the sickle moon, the moon of Artemis the huntress, the cold and unmerciful goddess.

We stood with our heads bowed until Axiom was finished praying, then we put our belongings in packs and tied them to the remaining ponies. We each rode one. Paul rode the smallest pony, with Cerberus carefully cradled on his lap. Somehow the hound had survived being stabbed, and when Axiom finished bandaging him, he seemed better. We carried shields, swords, and Alexander had given Paul a quiver full of arrows.

'If we are attacked run and hide. Shoot only if you think you will hit an enemy and keep your shield at your side at all times.'

Fatherly advice in ancient Gaul.

We were not attacked. Either the raiders had lost too many men and were regrouping, or they had given up when they saw the wine being burned. Alexander didn't spare an amphora.

Chapter Twelve

We rode all night and didn't pause until late morning. Our ponies were tired. They weren't the cavalry ponies Alexander had on his campaigns, used to going long distances as fast as they could. After only a couple hours rest, Alexander moved us on. We took no chances and didn't stop again.

No other travellers crossed our path. I was starting to feel panicky, surrounded by so much quiet and wilderness. I kept imagining our attackers hiding behind trees. It made me jumpy. We didn't speak. We were exhausted and fearful. We only paused to water the horses and relieve ourselves.

Finally, just before nightfall, we saw the flickering lights of a village in the distance. We were just within reach of shelter! The road was little more than a well-worn track through the trees. Clouds moved sullenly across the sky, hiding the wisp of a moon. Our horses plodded onward. Alexander had long ago stopped trying to urge them into a trot. Paul slid sideways, and Axiom caught him just before he fell.

'I'm so tired,' Paul said.

I gave him an encouraging smile. 'We're almost there.' To Alexander I said, 'We have to tell the authorities what happened. Maybe they'll know who did it.'

'I doubt it,' he said, 'unless there have been other attacks.'

One thing bothered me. 'Why didn't they wait until we fell asleep?'

'Because of the guards,' said Alexander. 'They would have been posted around us and more alert for danger. As it was, they were sitting to the side, eating.'

'Still, it seems odd,' said Axiom. 'A surprise attack while we were sleeping would have been more efficient.'

We rode in silence for a while. Then Axiom spoke again. 'I thought perhaps it was because of the darkness. They attacked well before the moon rose. But it was a sickle moon, and cast no shadows.' He shook his head.

Nearchus uttered a startled oath. He reined in so suddenly that his horse staggered and nearly fell.

'What is it?' cried Alexander, leaning forward.

'What is it?' I echoed, frightened by the look on Nearchus's face.

'The moon,' he said. 'I didn't think of it before. But when Axiom mentioned the moon it occurred to me. They attacked before the moon rose because they were afraid the Child of the Moon would be protected by his mother. Don't you see?'

'No,' I said dryly. 'I am the boy's mother.'

'But Orphics wouldn't know that.' He insisted. 'They must have been looking for Paul. Somehow they know he's here, with us.'

'Orphics?' It was Alexander. 'Where did you hear about them, Nearchus?'

'In Crete, where I grew up. The moon cult is tied with the worship of Orpheus and Dionysus. It is a strange and mysterious sect. They believe that the moon's child will destroy the earth.'

Alexander tipped his head back and gave a strangled cry.

'What is it?' I asked, worried.

He looked at me, his eyes bleak. 'My mother was an adept of the cult of Dionysus,' he said harshly. 'Do you remember what they said in Nysa? "If the moon's child left the valley, the whole world could be destroyed." The Orphics predicted that.'

I sputtered. 'That's utter nonsense!'

'It is written in the stars. I don't know how to read them, but perhaps people here do. They didn't want the wine. They were searching for the Child of the Moon.' Nearchus broke off, and we all looked at Paul.

I sighed. 'Tomorrow, Paul, we dye your hair black.'

Chapter Thirteen

We followed the lights to the village and arrived after everyone had gone to bed. Luckily, the gatekeeper was still awake and said there was room for us in the inn. Well, there *was* space in the dining room. I shared a bench with Paul. The men slept on their cloaks in front of a small fireplace.

In the middle of the night, Alexander had one of his nightmares, and woke the entire inn with his terrified yells. We sat up in our blankets, our faces pale with fatigue and shock. The innkeeper and the other guests thought they were being attacked. They stumbled out of their rooms, some clutching weapons.

Alexander crouched in the middle of the floor, his body covered with a sheen of sweat, his hair practically standing on end. He was shaking, his knees knocking against the wooden floor. Nearchus, murmuring softly, leaned over and draped a blanket over his shoulders.

When he was fully awake, Alexander apologized. He gave a crooked grin, his eyes huge in his haggard face. Most of the people simply nodded and faded back to their rooms.

The owner was harder to appease. He started forward with a stern expression, perhaps to tell Alexander to be more careful with his dreams or something. Whatever he wanted to say we would never know, because he stepped on Cerberus who was still sore, and the hound's screech woke up half the village. The innkeeper's scream woke the other half, as the dog sank his teeth in the man's bare calf.

The innkeeper threw us out after the dog bite, and we ended up spending the rest of the night in the stables. I snuggled down in the straw, bone-weary, and fell straight to sleep.

Nearchus woke up at dawn. He went to the market to buy dye for Paul's hair and to hear the latest news. Alexander went to apologize again to the innkeeper and to see how his leg was.

I slept soundly. Then Alexander was bending over me, his hair tickling my nose, telling me to get up and get ready to leave.

'Can't I sleep just another hour?' I moaned.

Alexander shook his head. He'd been chafing at our slow pace ever since we'd left Massalia, and now he was back in battle mode, fifty kilometres a day at a fast clip. He looked almost happy. I sighed. 'So much for tourism,' I said sourly.

'I'm not a very good tourist,' he said with a glimmer of humour. 'I get this urge to conquer everything I see. But right now, I just want to get Paul to safety.'

'Do you really believe that they attacked us to take Paul?' I asked. 'I mean, we *were* travelling with a cargo of wine that was worth its weight in solid silver.'

'It was worth more than that,' said Alexander, 'but Paul is priceless. Whoever has the moon's child can control the fate of the world.'

I stood up and picked straw out of my hair. 'Can I just wash myself before we set off?'

Alexander pointed to a stone trough. 'Hurry up.'

I eyed the horse's watering trough with distaste, but I knew it was all I was going to get. I was still bleeding. I had nothing but wet rags left. Alexander saw me staring dismally at my supply. 'I'll try and find something for you,' he said softly and went back into the inn.

I hoped that the innkeeper would have a sympathetic wife. I hadn't seen one, but perhaps she was a very deep sleeper.

I stripped and washed in the icy water. Alexander came back with a handful of clean cotton cloths. The sun came out from behind the clouds. Birds starting singing. Things were looking better.

And Paul looked fascinating with black hair. Actually it was more of a navy blue. I couldn't help comparing him to the teenagers of my time, the rebels who slashed scars on their arms and dyed their hair improbable colours. Paul had no scars except one, a crescent moon on his left shoulder. I had no idea where the scar had come from. I wondered if it weren't a pale, silvery birthmark.

Alexander stepped back and studied his son with a cocked head. 'You look like a cousin of mine,' he said finally.

'Oh? Who was he? Did you know him well?'

'No,' Alexander shook his head. 'He lived in Epirus, in my grandfather's kingdom.' His voice tapered off.

'What is it, Father?' Paul reached over and took his hand.

'Millis,' he sighed. We were silent after that. We all missed Millis. Axiom kept turning around, as if he were looking for him. I couldn't get used to not having him standing next to Paul.

'It was his fate,' declared Nearchus.

'I can't believe that his fate was to come all the way to Gaul just to die in the middle of a road,' I said. My voice broke.

'His fate was to save Paul from human sacrifice,' Nearchus said with conviction. We stared at him. He nodded. 'I went to the marketplace this morning. There is an important moon cult here in Gaul. We should have been more careful. They still have human sacrifices.'

'Who told you that?' I asked.

Nearchus shrugged. 'The shopkeeper.'

'How far are we from Lutetia?' Axiom straightened up from where he'd been checking our baggage.

'Three days. Two if we hurry,' Nearchus replied.

Alexander frowned. 'We have to get faster horses.'

Chapter Fourteen

There was a stiff wind, but it kept the sky clear. The sun warmed our shoulders. The new horses were fresh, and Alexander managed to push us along quickly. We stopped every three hours to rest and to let the horses graze. When we passed a stream, we watered the horses.

We first heard the drums while we were standing next to a stream.

I thought it was a woodpecker. The sound was like that – a fast, sharp tapping. However, Alexander and Nearchus both paused what they were doing and grew still. They didn't have to speak; we could see they were concerned. We mounted our horses and moved off at a fast trot. Now we didn't dare stop. Alexander kept us trotting until the sun was so low it was simply a thin, glowing red line on the horizon. Even then he didn't stop. None of us knew what the drums were saying. We suspected it was some sort of message, and perhaps it was about us. Danger was making us paranoid.

But, as Alexander succinctly pointed out, 'Better flee than be outflanked.'

'Is that another one of your Macedonian maxims?' I asked. 'One of the ones that would never make it to posterity such as: "the falling rock looks out for no one";

"water doesn't flow fast uphill"; and "wolves can't eat the caged goat"?'

Macedonians were full of sayings, some of them better than others. Today, Alexander wasn't in the mood to joke, so he just looked at me sourly and said, 'If time does away with wise sayings, it's because no one's listening any more.'

We left the road and entered the forest. Alexander led us deeper and deeper until we came to another stream. Night had fallen, and I could hardly see a thing. We splashed into the water and waded downstream. We moved slowly. The stream was wide and shallow, and the banks were low. Tree branches twisted overhead in an impenetrable canopy. Our horses picked their way carefully along the stream's bed, their hooves splashing quietly. It seemed hours passed before the stream wound into a reed-choked swamp, and we finally climbed out of the water.

As we left the cover of the trees, two stags bounded across the meadow. The moon had just risen, making their antlers gleam. One of the deer stopped and turned, facing us. I caught my breath. There are few things as majestic as a huge stag in the moonlight. His breath left his nostrils in white puffs, and his eyes were deep, liquid pools of darkness. His coat was ticked with silver, making him look like a statue cast in metal. Time was suspended as we stared at each other. No one moved. Then Cerberus woke up. He'd been dozing on Paul's lap. He saw the stag and scrambled down off the horse, landing with an *'ooof'*. Then he pointed his nose at the deer and bayed.

It broke the spell. The deer spun around on slender legs and leapt gracefully into the darkness, and we climbed wearily off our horses.

With a sigh, I unsaddled and brushed my mount. I hobbled him, making sure he couldn't run away. Then I helped Paul with his pony. Axiom made a fire in the cover of a small thicket and we dried our boots. We gnawed on strips of salted meat and shared some dried figs and apples. We were well hidden, so we left the fire burning to dry our clothes. Alexander, Nearchus, and Axiom took turns standing guard all night. I felt secure knowing they were there.

Chapter Fifteen

We left before the sun had fully risen. Sparkling white frost covered each blade of grass, and the air had a pale, blue look to it that promised snow. We made our way back to the road and set off at a gallop. Each time we stopped, we would hear the drums. The sound hurried us along. We reached the top of the highest hill just before midday. We could see the plains below us, chequered with farms and criss-crossed with paths and streams. The forest was behind us now.

Snow began to fall. Great white flakes floated in the air like dove feathers settling slowly on the ground as if making themselves comfortable.

Alexander made us gallop until we reached the foothills, then we slowed to a walk. The snow made visibility poor, but Alexander seemed to be looking for something in particular. Each time he passed a farm or settlement, he inquired as to who lived there. Most of the time he just nodded and motioned to us to continue. The farms were rare and the settlements too small to be called villages.

By the time evening came, I felt exhausted and numb with cold. We rounded a bend and arrived at another farm, its entrance marked by stone pillars. Alexander reined in his horse and stared at the stone marker in the road. A symbol was carved in it. I thought it looked vaguely familiar.

We passed between the pillars. On the ground was an antique cattle guard consisting of a large ditch with iron rods laid over it at wide intervals. Boards leaned up against the fence. Axiom climbed down from his horse, placed the boards over the rods so the horses could cross, then put them back. The road was straight and led directly to the farm buildings. A slave ran out to meet us, and led us to his master.

The owner of the farm was a wealthy Roman who had settled permanently in Gaul. He traded in wine, and the shipment we'd burned was partially his property. To prove it, he showed us the wax seals on the amphorae stored in his barn. They were the same symbol I'd seen on the stone gatepost and matched the wax seal from one of the amphorae of wine we'd burned, and that Alexander had kept with him.

The Roman invited us into his house and sent his slaves to fetch us some hot, spiced wine. As I sipped it, I glanced around the living room. It was lit by oil lamps, and the walls were covered in beautiful frescoes. The house had Roman and Gallic features; the main part of the downstairs was taken up by a kitchen and a living room. The living room was comfortable, with low, Roman-style sofas and rich rugs on the floor. The house had mica windowpanes, but the wooden shutters were closed against the darkness and the cold. Inside, it was warm and cosy. I noticed the floor was warm beneath my feet, and I realized that the house was heated Roman-style. Underneath the tiled floor were clay pipes carrying hot water. I turned my attention back to Alexander and the Roman, who were discussing the attack and our escape.

'It's a pity about the wine, to be sure,' the Roman said. 'I invested heavily in that shipment. But you say you managed to save the silver?'

'Yes, and I'll give you instructions to lead you to the place we buried it,' said Alexander.

His wife was sitting quietly in the corner of the room. Next to her was a basket made of finely woven birch branches full of skeins of multi-coloured wool, and she was busily sorting them. A young girl was helping her, and I wondered if she were a daughter, until I caught sight of the telltale gold bracelet around her ankle. A slave. I turned back to the Roman who was telling Alexander that he'd always been afraid of raiders.

He insisted that we stay the night.

'I have a bathhouse that rivals anything in Rome,' he said proudly. 'You are more than welcome to sleep in our guest quarters. We have plenty of room.'

I sat up straight. I was already imagining washing the grime from my hair and body. Sheer bliss. A smile started to curve my lips, and my eyes grew starry.

'No,' said Alexander firmly. I uttered a shriek, making the Roman and his wife jump, but my husband didn't even glance at me. 'I would leave my tired horses here and take fresh ones. If you could spare some bread and cheese, we could leave in half an hour.' I stared at him, my mouth hanging open. I thought I'd probably cry in a minute. The tiled floor was so warm beneath my feet!

Surprisingly, the Roman's wife stood up to protest. 'You can't leave before morning. Look at the boy; he's exhausted. If you set out now he'll fall and hurt himself,' she said reasonably. 'How old is he? He looks to be about ten. A handsome lad,' she added. 'Is he your slave?'

'He's my son,' I said angrily, then winced. Alexander's warning look hit me too late. Paul's hair was jet black, whereas mine was white-blonde. He looked nothing like me any more. Nearchus had even smeared walnut juice over Paul's face and arms, turning his skin tan. He looked like an exotic Persian boy with bright blue eyes, black hair, and smooth brown skin. Even his eyebrows and eyelashes were dyed black. Axiom proved to be an expert at dying hair. It was a shock every time I looked at Paul, but hearing him called a slave had made me forget my caution.

'Your son?' The woman's eyes widened. She was too tactful to say anything else about the matter. 'I propose you stay for the night. Tomorrow morning you can leave with fresh horses. I'll give orders to the cook to prepare a meal.' She looked at me and smiled. 'I suppose you would like to use the bathhouse?'

That did it. I practically threw myself on the ground in front of Alexander. 'Please, don't make me go outside again in the cold tonight,' I begged. 'We can stay just for the night, and leave tomorrow, early. Please? We'll be safe here,' I added.

'Of course you will!' The Roman stood up and clapped his hands. 'Yovanix, take our honoured guests to the bathhouse and prepare their rooms.' A slave came in and motioned us to follow him.

'Our baggage …?' said Axiom nervously.

'Will be taken care of. You'll find it in your rooms. I'll prepare a hot meal for you, come into the dining room when you've finished bathing.' The woman spoke with such a warm voice that I felt welcome right away. She was about my age, I guessed, younger than her husband. A second wife perhaps? Her hair was dark brown and intricately curled and braided. Her figure was lissom and, when she stood, I could see a little round belly. Four months pregnant, I guessed. She caught my glance and her smile widened. 'In five months we shall be blessed by the Mother,' she said, her hand cupping her belly.

I nodded, although I was unfamiliar with that expression. *Blessed by the Mother?* I forgot everything, though, when I saw the bathhouse. It consisted of a sauna, a changing room, a cold bath, an exercise room, *and* a warm bathing pool. Bliss!

First we stripped. Slaves took our clothes, and I hoped I'd never see my dirty linen shift again. Then we went into the sauna and got sweaty. There was a bucket with a dipper to put water on the hot rocks and make steam. Soft soap was there, and we rubbed it all over our bodies. It was lye soap, so I used it sparingly, preferring the clay from another bucket. Then we rinsed off with buckets of warm water. After, we stepped into the cold bath, then went into the heated pool. The slaves poured perfumed oil in it, making us smell like lavender sachets. We sat, soaking in the pool, our knees touching as it was crowded with all six of us. We couldn't stop grinning, though. It was *wonderful*.

I felt human again.

Alexander and I were the last to leave the pool. Everyone else had left when the smell of roasting meat came to our nostrils.

Alexander smiled at me. His eyes, half-closed, looked decidedly sexy. Wet hair curled around his face in ringlets. In the light of the lamp it looked nearly dark. Only a few bright strands of gold gave away its true colour. He needed a shave. For three days he'd been without one, and there was rough stubble on his cheeks interrupted here and there by the odd scar.

We circled around each other, drifting closer and closer, until our bodies were touching. I shivered as our thighs brushed. His hands cupped my face and we leaned into each other. The water buoyed us up. Weightless, I wrapped my legs around his hips. We made love slowly, with hardly a ripple, our eyes closed, each movement languorous. I put my mouth on his shoulder and bit gently. There was a moment of intense pleasure, when my muscles seemed electrified, and a pulsing was all I could feel. Nothing else existed. Alexander grasped my buttocks and held me tightly. His breath quickened and he moaned softly, thrusting into me.

Afterwards, he let his head tip backward until it rested on the side of the pool. I felt myself slipping into a boneless relaxation. There was a moment when I needed quiet, when my body was still caught in the glow that comes after sex. I loved to feel Alexander's arms around me then. Alexander always fell asleep for a few minutes. I kissed his mouth and eyelids. Our bodies were half lying in the water, half on the stairs of the pool. The warm water was black in the darkness; flames from the torch tipped the ripples with bright gold. The shadows were very deep. We lay in one. Only the water droplets sparkled in our hair. Alexander's lashes fluttered and he opened his eyes, his magnificent parti-coloured eyes, and grinned at me.

'I would give you the world,' he said sleepily, 'if you asked for it now.'

'I'm too tired to ask for anything,' I replied. 'I think I'm even too tired to crawl out of the water. Maybe I'll just sleep here on the steps, with my head on your chest.'

He chuckled, tickling my ear with the sound. 'I'm too hungry to stay here, and besides, I'm getting wrinkled.'

'I feel so blessedly clean,' I sighed.

'Inside and out,' he agreed with a leer.

If I'd had any energy left at all, I would have dunked him.

We ate dinner with the Roman's wife. I inquired after her husband, and she told us that he had been tired after a long day and had gone to bed. He would see us in the morning before we left.

We nodded, thanking her for waiting up for us, but we were so weary our conversation lagged. Paul left the table early after stuffing himself with roast goose. Axiom followed; he was yawning widely and could hardly keep his eyes open.

Nearchus fell asleep with his head in his plate, getting gravy all over the tablecloth and in his hair. I wasn't sure what to do. Our hostess seemed as much at a loss as I was. What *was* the polite formula for waking up a guest who fell asleep at the dinner table?

A slave trotted over with a basin of warm water. The woman leaned over and gently tapped Nearchus on the shoulder.

'*Arrgh*, what is it?' he cried, leaping up, tipping over his chair, and staring blindly about. His knife was in his hand. He blinked at it before putting it down. The slave washed the gravy off him, and Nearchus apologized profusely to the Roman's wife. 'I think I was a soldier too long,' he said, and staggered off to bed.

I turned to the woman and, dredging up the last of my energy and manners, asked her what her name was. I remembered her husband was called Julius, but I didn't remember hers. 'I'm so sorry,' I added, 'I usually have a good memory.'

'My name is Seleninonvorax,' she said with a little laugh. 'But my husband calls me Selena, as do all my friends.'

'Selena, the moon,' said Alexander.

The woman twitched. 'That's right.' She smiled then. 'You look very tired,' she said to Alexander. 'Why don't you let me show you to your room?'

He looked at me and frowned. All the colour was slowly draining from his face. 'I feel odd,' he said, a little breathlessly. He stood up shakily. 'Ashley?'

I tried to focus on his face, but my vision dwindled to a pinpoint of light, and I felt the floor hit me on the side of my face. 'Hey, not fair ...' I heard myself saying in English, and then all was darkness.

Chapter Sixteen

I woke some hours later. I blinked, trying to remember who I was, where I was, and what had happened last. There was a pool of light near my head. I craned my neck and managed to see that it came from a window. The sunlight was pinkish and gave no warmth. It was the cold light of an early winter's morning.

For some reason I couldn't move. This perplexed me. Then I realized my hands were tied behind my back, and my legs seemed to be bound to my hands. I arched backward, thanking every god I could remember for my limberness. My hands fluttered like bird's wings behind me, searching for the knots on my heels. I found them and started to worry them loose.

I struggled to get free, all the while frantic about Paul, Alexander, Axiom, and Nearchus. Where was everyone? Why was I alone? Where was I? The knots were tight, but I was patient and managed to hook my thumb under a loop. It was just a matter of time until my legs were free. Then I untied my hands.

I walked over to the window and looked out. The sun had just cleared the horizon. A man carried a load of firewood toward the kitchen. A woman tossed grain to geese in a pen. Another woman swept last night's snowfall from the porch. I tiptoed to the door and tried to open it. It was barred from the outside. I pushed, but it didn't budge.

I went back to the window. The tiled roof was steep, there was no windowsill, and the ground below me was a flagstone terrace, newly swept clean of snow. There was no mattress in my room to use to break my fall, but I did have a long piece of rope that had been wrapped around my wrists and ankles. I tied the rope to the stout wooden door and lowered myself down the roof. It was a scary descent. I'd waited until there was no one in sight, and now I slithered as quickly as I dared to the ground. The rope wasn't long enough so I had to drop the last few feet. I landed in a crouch and looked around. Then I bolted for the hedge I'd spied from my window. I hid in the bush and peered back at the house. No one stirred.

I looked at the ground. My footprints in the fresh snow led straight to my hiding place. *Damn!* I went back to the house, walking backward, placing my feet in my footprints the best I could. When I reached the house, I looked for a way in. I had just passed the corner when I heard a voice. I pressed myself close to the wall. It was the Roman, and it sounded like he was just over my head. I risked a glance upward. There was a balcony above me, and though I couldn't see him, I could hear him perfectly.

'Selena, did you see our guests this morning?'

'No, I believe they left at first light.'

'Did they leave their address? I must dispatch Antonis to see if the silver is where the man said it was. I would have wished to see him again before he left.'

'You should have made an effort to stay with us for dinner.'

'I know,' he sounded sheepish. 'But I was so tired I couldn't keep my eyes open. I would have made a pitiful spectacle of myself falling into my soup.'

'That's all right. The man left his address, so you can send him a message if you so desire.'

'A handsome group they were too,' said the man reflectively. 'I thought the shorter man was quite beautiful.'

Alexander would have hated to hear himself referred to as 'the shorter man'.

'I did think he was handsome,' said the woman. 'But I thought the woman strange, didn't you?'

'Strange? In what way?'

'I don't know, nothing I could really tell you about, exactly. Perhaps it was her eyes. They were so cold.'

'Yes, I see what you mean. But a lovely face and stunning hair.'

'Anyone can get that colour, it's quite unnatural, I assure you,' said Selena with a little laugh.

I wanted to cry out, 'Hey! It's my real colour!' I didn't. I wondered if the man knew that his wife had deliberately put drugs in my food to make me sleep, and if she had done the same to everyone else, including him.

I poked my head around the corner and saw the front door. It was standing open. With a quick look inside to make sure the servants were all in the kitchen, I darted in and ran silently up the stairs. There was only one door with a bolt on it, mine. The three others were simply latched shut.

I opened one door, and looked inside, searching for my companions. The room was furnished Roman-style with a bed, a low couch, a large trunk, a dressing table with a bronze mirror, and nothing else. I checked all the other rooms; they were all empty except for the furniture. By the time I'd closed the last door behind me, my heart was pounding painfully. I was standing in the doorway of a small bedroom, when I heard the Roman calling to his wife, 'I'm going to send Antonis and Claudius to fetch the silver. I'll see you for the noon meal.'

'I have to go to town, you won't see me until tonight,' she answered.

'Until tonight, my love. Selena, a little kiss before I go?' He sounded like a lovesick teenager.

'Of course, Julius.' She spoke coolly. I could picture them in bed. She would be thinking about where to plant the herb garden while he groaned and panted on top of her.

I slipped back into a room and peeked out. I wanted to trust Julius, the Roman, but I was afraid that he would hesitate to believe his wife had done anything wrong. I was a stranger.

Julius walked downstairs, glancing once more at his wife. She didn't leave until the front door closed and his footsteps had faded away. Then she swept out of her room, robes billowing, and disappeared into the room where I'd awakened.

She was a cold one. She only uttered an exclamation of annoyance when she saw I was missing. She leaned out the window and studied the ground, then went downstairs. She called loudly to someone as she descended.

'Yovanix, come with me.'

I heard a man running from the kitchen to join her. I moved to the top of the stairs and looked down. Yovanix was a young man. He wore a bronze slave bracelet and his light brown hair was cut short. He had a moustache but no beard. He was handsome, maybe a few inches shorter than Alexander, and well made. His arms were bare; Gauls were as impervious to cold as the Macedonians apparently.

As soon as they left, I ran into her bedroom. I searched for some sign of Paul or Alexander ... but there was no one. Nothing but a typical, messy bedroom with a rumpled bed and clothes scattered around.

From outside came the sound of low voices. I went to the balcony and listened.

'She walked into the bushes from here.'

'There's the rope.' Yovanix had a melodious voice.

'I see that.' Selena tapped her foot on the terrace with annoyance. 'Go and look in the bushes, will you? See where she's gone.'

Then it suddenly hit me. They were not speaking Gallic. If they had been I wouldn't have understood a word. They were speaking Greek. Who were these people? I'd assumed the woman was Gallic. I listened carefully as Yovanix walked slowly toward the bushes.

He walked in my own tracks, which raised my spirits considerably. Now it would be harder to see that I'd come back.

'The footprints come to this spot,' he said, standing up in the bush and waving at the woman. 'But they stop here, and then vanish.' Fear made his voice high.

Selena's face was a study in emotions. Anger, fear, disbelief, scepticism, all twisted her features. She stamped her foot. 'That's impossible,' she cried.

'If she was who you said ...'

'Be quiet, fool!' Her breath made white clouds in the air.

Yovanix looked around nervously. He kept pulling at his moustache. 'I think you'd better tell Anoramix,' he said.

Selena shook her head. 'You can't be serious,' she said.

They looked at each other and finally her shoulders slumped. 'All right. I'll tell him, but I can't go in person. Julius expects me here tonight to entertain his guests. I'll have to send a message.'

'You picked a fine time to have a dinner party!'

'It can't be helped. You will be my messenger. He won't dare harm you, you're his brother.'

'I'm a slave!' he cried. 'I'm no more his brother than the moon is.

'Silence!' Her rage was a palpable thing. 'You will go to Anoramix and tell him the goddess has escaped. But the Child of the Moon has been taken to the sacred grove. The men can be the sacrifice.'

'Will the druids accept strangers as the sacrifice?' he asked. 'After all, we know next to nothing about them. Except for the woman and the child, the prophecy was vague. Anoramix may punish us.'

'He can't punish us for trying to obey him. How can one capture a goddess? It's not my fault if the rope was not properly blessed!' She started to gnaw on her fingernails. 'Come into my room. We'll speak of the message.'

I darted into a closet and hid behind a large purple cloak. The closet had a lattice door, so I could see and hear everything. I was sweating and my head felt light. I wondered if it was nerves, hunger, or learning that Axiom, Nearchus, and my husband were slated for execution.

Chapter Seventeen

Selena and Yovanix closed the door behind them. I'll say this for them, they didn't waste any time. He tore off his breeches; she lifted her robe, baring a round belly and white thighs. Her pubis was shaved, Persian-style. Now I was even more confused. A Gaul, speaking Greek, with Persian habits? Who was she? Yovanix didn't ask. He took her from behind, bending her over the bed and grunting as he thrust into her. Her face flushed pink. Her breath came in gasps in rhythm to his movements. I closed my eyes, embarrassed to be caught in a delicate situation.

The noises intensified. Selena was moaning and begging him to go faster, deeper, and harder. I peeked. Yovanix was trying. His face was red and his eyes bulged. His arms tightened around Selena, and he started to shudder against her, groaning deep in his throat.

I nearly started to giggle and bit hard on my wrist. It was nerves, surely. It wasn't nice to make fun of people in the throes of passion. I looked at the floor and invented a grocery list, and when I glanced at them again, Selena was lying on her back and Yovanix was busy fulfilling her with his hands. I thought that was nice of him. So many men just roll over and go to sleep. Selena arched her back and started to pant. Then she gave a satisfied cry and sank back onto the bed. Yovanix flopped down beside her, and for a few moments there was a deep silence.

I wanted to knock on the closet door and say, 'Hey! Keep talking about where you've taken Paul and the men!'

The quiet didn't last long. Selena got up and stretched like a big cat. 'Yovanix, wake up. We have to talk.'

'Mmmm.' He raised his head. His eyes were dark brown, I saw now, and rather sleepy. His moustache trembled. '*Must* I go to see Anoramix?' His voice was resigned though.

Selena didn't even bother to answer. 'You tell him that the goddess vanished. I only hope he didn't need her for a specific reason. He didn't tell us why he wanted her, he only said to bring her to the sacred grove. The boy is already there, and you will fetch the men, is that clear?'

'Am I to bring the men there as well?'

'You're going to see Anoramix, you might as well take them.'

'But in broad daylight?'

'Hide them well in the straw.'

'Will Sesterix give me the hay wagon?'

'Tell Sesterix that you have orders to fetch a new couch for me, and the straw is to protect the fragile wood.'

'Very well.'

'And don't forget to remind Anoramix you're his brother.'

'By the sacred oak, Selena! I'm just a slave.'

'I cannot free you.' Her voice was sad. 'Perhaps if our parents hadn't been so poor …'

'Our parents sold us in order to save us from starvation.' His voice was bitter. 'But I sometimes think it would have been better to have starved. At least for me.'

'When I saw you in the market in Massalia, did I hesitate an instant?' Selena's voice cracked.

'No, you didn't. You begged your besotted husband to buy me for you, and he did. Now I am my own sister's slave.' Yovanix sat up in the bed and pulled on his clothes.

Sister? I raised my eyebrows. Well, in these days incest didn't have quite the same connotation it had for us.

'I'm sorry. I try to make life as pleasant for you as I can.'

'And I do the same for you,' he said, with a meaningful look at her nakedness.

'Soon you will be free. I promise.' Selena stood up and draped her arms around his shoulders, pressing her forehead to his. When they were so close together their resemblance was striking.

After they left the room, I breathed a deep sigh and crawled out of the closet. My legs were stiff, and I needed to pee. I looked around for a toilet. There was a metal chamber pot on the floor. It wasn't very stable, and when I sat on it, it rocked. The newest rage from Rome, I thought, and then sighed with relief. I didn't bother to empty it; the slaves would do that when they cleaned the messy room.

I sneaked out of the house and made my way through the barnyard to the stables. I had to find the cart with straw in it and hide.

Chapter Eighteen

It was easy. Everyone had gone to do various chores. The buildings were deserted. Selena and Yovanix were in the kitchen. Julius had left. Our horses were missing, I noticed. I found the wagon and crawled into the deep straw. It was warm and almost comfortable.

Faintly, from the house, I heard furious yelling.

'Who pissed in my helmet?' It was Yovanix. He wasn't having a good day.

It got worse.

For one thing, it started to snow in earnest. The white feathers that had floated gently to the ground yesterday were replaced by buckets of white confetti.

'Zeus snows,' muttered Yovanix, as he hitched the horses to the wagon. I nodded in satisfaction. He was Greek. Only the Greeks said 'Zeus rains', or 'Zeus thunders'. That could mean that he was a member of the strange sect of Orpheus, which originated in Crete and had spread to Gaul to become a new religion.

The snow meant the wagon skidded down the driveway. The horses snorted and slid trying to pull it. When we reached the cattle guard, Yovanix jumped off the wagon and started to place the boards across the stones.

One of the boards slipped and fell on his foot. He started to curse. I could see everything from my warm hiding place.

For a minute, I thought he'd broken his leg. That wouldn't have suited at all; I wanted him to collect Alexander, Nearchus, Axiom, and Paul. However, after wiping the tears of pain off his face and rubbing some feeling back into the bruised limb, he managed to limp back to the wagon and drive the horses through the gate.

The horses found better footing on the main road. The cattle guard stayed open. The cows would probably escape. I hoped so. I was so angry with Selena and Yovanix that I hoped that every single animal on the farm left.

We arrived at the village after a short drive. I shrank as far back into the straw as I could as Yovanix made a few stops. At one stop, a man put a large basket in the wagon. I peeked inside. Dried dates. My mouth started to water. I was famished. With a quick look around, I reached my arm over the back of the seat and grabbed a large handful.

I had eaten half the dates from the basket by the time Yovanix came back. There was a pause when he climbed into the seat. He picked up the basket and looked.

'What the …?' he muttered. I could hear him shifting his weight, searching in every direction. Finally he said under his breath, 'If I catch that filthy thief I'll …' He didn't get any further. A man called to him.

'Hail, Yovanix. Where are you bound? May I have a lift?'

I heard a deep sigh, then he said, civilly enough, 'I'm going to see Anoramix. But first I have some errands to run for the Lady Selena.'

'Well, just drop me off at the three crossings.'

I caught sight of the man's cloak and raised my eyebrows. It was deep red wool, lined with fur, and embroidered with eagles. This must be one of the Roman generals Marcus Quintus mentioned with such reverence. At the trivium he climbed out of the wagon and waved. 'Thank you, Yovanix. Tell your master I will see him tonight. He kindly invited me for dinner.'

'I won't forget.' Yovanix clicked his tongue and the horses moved off. Then he sighed. 'Bloody Romans. Now I'm late.' He didn't dare hurry though, as the footing was precarious. The road wound along the side of a gorge, and I swallowed nervously as we started down a steep hill. Luckily, the brakes held. We made it to the bottom in one piece and took the left-hand fork in the road, the one leading along the riverside toward a large forest.

When he stopped, I risked a peek. We were parked in front of a temple built along a flowing stream in honour of a nymph.

I raised my head in time to see Yovanix coming out of the nymphaeum with a figure slung over his shoulder. I held my breath. It was Nearchus.

Yovanix half shoved, half heaved him into the wagon. Nearchus landed on me. By the time I could speak again, it was Alexander's turn to be dumped unceremoniously into the straw, and a few moments later Axiom was added to the growing pile of unconscious men.

Alexander was breathing badly. The men were tied hand and foot, but Alexander also had a rope around his neck that seemed to be strangling him.

I wished all sorts of evil deaths on Selena and her brother and set about easing his bonds. The knot was tight and my fingers were cold. After pulling fruitlessly on it, I leaned forward and started gnawing. I could loosen it with my teeth. The knot began to give and I sighed with relief. Alexander gasped, and some colour came back into his cheeks. His eyelids fluttered, and he opened his eyes. Snowflakes landed on his long lashes. He blinked.

'Am I going blind?' he whispered.

'No, why do you say that?' I kept my voice low.

'Because there are white spots in front of my eyes.' He frowned. His handsome face had a puzzled expression. 'Where am I?'

'Shhh, we're being kidnapped.'

He sat up so fast he smacked me in the nose with his head. The inevitable happened, my nose started to bleed freely. I tried to staunch it with my hands, but the scarlet flood splashed through my fingers and onto Nearchus's face. It woke him up.

'AarrghhHHH!' he yelled, sitting up and trying to struggle. Finding himself tied hand and foot caused him to panic. He thrashed about, kicking Axiom in the groin, which made the poor fellow bleat with pain, although his eyes stayed shut.

Yovanix hauled on the horse's reins, stopping them, and he turned around, a horrified expression on his face.

'So much for the element of surprise,' I said resignedly.

I leaped up. Flinging my arms wide, I bellowed in English, 'I hope you realize how lucky you are because if I had a sword right now you'd be a shish kebab!'

Blood spattered off my hands and flew onto his face and chest. The effect was pretty much what I'd hoped for. His eyes rolled up and he keeled over.

Alexander sat up straight and stared at me. 'Shish kebab?'

'A spur of the moment curse,' I said, shrugging.

'Well, it worked. You killed him.' Nearchus, his hands still tied behind his back, leaned over to look at my handiwork.

'He's not dead, but he's going to wish he were.' I acted fast. Faints only last a few seconds. I took the rope that had been around Alexander's neck and tied Yovanix, like a dog, to the wagon. Then I tied *his* hands behind his back.

'Poor fellow.' Alexander was busy unbinding his own knots. 'He's got a nasty cut on his leg.'

'Serves him right.' I turned to Alexander and flung myself into his arms, knocking him over backward.

'Oooff.' It was Axiom. He woke up and glared at us. 'May I ask what you're doing in my bed ...' He broke off and looked confused. 'Who tied my feet together? Hey! This isn't my bed!'

I started to cry. 'You were on your way to be sacrificed! All of you were! They still have Paul! I have no idea what they will do to him, but I'm frightened. Oh, Alex, hold me!'

He did. He was sweet, he didn't quite laugh at me, although I heard him chuckle. 'You are a funny woman. Always brave in the face of danger and then bursting into tears when it's all over.'

'Look who's talking. Who always faints when the battle's finished?'

129

'My wounds are usually being cauterized.' He sounded tetchy, but he grinned. 'At any rate you're here, I'm here, and we'll find Paul as soon as the slave wakes up.'

Yovanix was having a *very* bad day. He woke up and found himself tied to the wagon. Three angry men and one furious goddess stood over him. He wouldn't answer our questions. All he would stutter was, 'I c-c-can't tell you.'

'Well let me tell *you* something,' I said, patience exhausted. 'First of all, it's not nice to make love to your own sister.'

Axiom made a disapproving noise. 'That's quite disgusting,' he said. He was a Jew, and they had strict laws about that sort of thing, even back in those times.

'Secondly,' I went on. 'If you do not lead us directly to Anoramix, who, as I happen to know, is your brother, you will regret it for the rest of your very short, extremely pain-filled life.'

'How do you *know* all this?' he shrieked.

'That's what I'd like to know,' murmured Alexander, with a puzzled look in my direction.

'And thirdly, you're going to tell us all about your religion, the druid, and the sacrifice.'

'Anything else?' he whispered.

'Most important of all,' I said putting my face very close to his. 'I want to know where my son is, and how I can get him back. And he had better be in perfect health, or I promise you the most horrible, dreadful torture …'

'Uh, that's enough, Ashley,' said Alexander, pulling me away. 'He's going to faint again.'

'Put his head between his knees,' I said. Then I smiled wickedly. 'Your hair smells awful, did someone piss in your helmet?'

He fainted.

When we finished untying Nearchus and Axiom, they stretched their legs, got their circulation going again, then urinated against a tree. I gave them the rest of the dates which they devoured.

Yovanix woke up again and had a few moments of the shakes before finally consenting to all my demands.

'We must go to the sacred wood,' he said.

'Where is the boy?' I asked.

'He's safe, I promise. No harm will come to him. Anoramix thought that with the moon's child, he would be able to control the stars ...' His voice trailed off.

'What will Anoramix do now?' I asked.

'I don't know, but the sacrifice must be tomorrow night.'

'Why then?'

'There is no moon that night. The child of the moon will be helpless. The prophecies will all come true. The signs have been many ...'

'How many men does Anoramix have?' asked Alexander, interrupting. 'How are they armed? Is his cave on a slope or on level ground?'

I recognized the army leader and sank back in the straw with a contented sigh. I had confidence in Alexander's ability to lead men and to fight. I closed my eyes. He would be talking tactics for a while yet. Now was a good time for a nap. I was exhausted.

When I woke up it was late afternoon. The cart was still moving. I was warm, straw tickled my nose, and snow made a thick blanket over me. I didn't want to stir. The snow-covered straw insulated against the cold so well that I was perfectly toasty and comfortable. Therefore, I snuggled deeper and dozed some more. I hadn't had a decent sleep since the night poor Millis had been killed. Poor, beautiful Millis, he had looked so much like his father.

I remembered the first time I'd seen Darius, king of all Persia. He'd been sitting on his throne, and when he stood, he'd taken my breath away. Tall, with black hair, smooth skin, and golden eyes like a lion. He had been naked except for a gold chain around his neck.

It had been in Persepolis, the sacred city Alexander had destroyed in a fit of rage. I could recall the day the city fell. The spring breeze had been soft as a kiss. Bright sunlight sparkled on the white marble, dazzling me. A dead slave sat in Darius's throne with his throat cut, while two of his generals hung above him, their skin flayed. The only colours had been the sparkling white of the marble, the empty blue of the sky, and the scarlet blood as it ran across the hot stone.

All that, because Paul had been kidnapped by Darius. Now Anoramix had Paul, the Harbinger of Destruction.

I wondered if Anoramix realized just what the Harbinger of Destruction's father was capable of when he got angry.

Chapter Nineteen

We arrived in the sacred woods at sunset. Yovanix started to tremble. He looked so ill that I took pity on him.

'What is the worst thing that could happen?' I asked him.

He looked at me, the whites of his eyes showing all spooked.

'The worst? The worst thing will be that Anoramix will realize that the men that are supposed to be sacrificed have escaped, and he'll insist on sacrificing me instead.'

'Won't that be a great honour?' I could hardly keep the sarcasm out of my voice and he blushed.

'You know I'm not Gallic,' he said.

'I don't know what you are.'

'I do.' It was Nearchus. 'You're from Crete. I know. I was born there, and I recognize your accent. You're an Orphic.'

I frowned. 'Is Anoramix an Orphic too? What would happen if the Gauls living here find out that your brother isn't a real druid?'

Yovanix shook his head. 'He *is* a real druid. The Gallic druids took many of the Orphic beliefs.'

'How strange,' said Nearchus. 'A sect in Crete that never got off the ground becomes a powerful force elsewhere.

'But, what is this sacrifice about?' I asked.

'It's something to do with the moon's child. I don't really know.'

'But, wouldn't a nice fat sheep do just as well?' I asked.

He shook his head. 'No. Only humans are worthy.'

'Great. And Anoramix not only wants to sacrifice three humans, he wants to be the most powerful druid in Gaul, right? That's why he has the Child of the Moon. But how did he hear about him?' I asked.

'Signs have been appearing all year. In the spring, three pure white fawns were born of one hind. Everyone knows that's a direct sign from Artemis, the moon child's guardian. Then, a rain of silver fish fell. It was a perfectly clear day, not a cloud in sight, and suddenly a cold wind bent the trees nearly to the ground, and small fish fell from the sky. They were intact, but covered in ice.'

'Do you swear to that?' Alexander asked, his eyes wide.

'Alex!' I cried. 'There's a perfectly logical explanation to that.'

'Go on,' he said, ignoring me. 'What other signs?'

'The moon was red for three months, after that, and then the sun disappeared at midday, swallowed by the moon. When the druids started casting the horoscope, they discovered that the moon's child had arrived in Gaul. News came a week ago that the moon's child was *en route* to Lutetia. We simply waited. The signs were clear. He

134

will come, and then three men must be killed, and their blood used to wash the child.'

'Holy shi …'

'Ashley!' Alexander clapped his hand over my mouth.

'You don't believe all that crap, do you?' I was furious.

'Well, not exactly.' He frowned.

Nearchus gaped. 'Frozen fish falling from the sky?'

'It's a natural meteorological phenomenon,' I cried. They ignored me.

'We have to figure out a way to save Paul, that's all that counts right now,' said Axiom. Luckily, he was a Jew and couldn't care less about frozen fish.

Alexander gave a start. 'Of course, you're right.' We had been sitting in the wagon, the horses stopped, while we spoke to Yovanix. Now Alexander clucked and the horses moved on. 'How far to Anoramix's cave?' he asked.

'Over the hill and through a narrow gorge. Then ford the stream and look up and to your right. His cave is in the hillside. Usually we tie the wagon to a small tree near the stream, but today, since I'm supposed to be bringing the sacrificial victims, I'm to drive all the way to the sacred grove.'

'We'll do just that,' said Alexander. 'Will Anoramix be waiting for you?'

'Of course. Selena sent a pigeon telling him that I had news for him. He's so excited about the goddess and the moon's child, he'll probably be outside waiting for us.' His voice was glum.

'You'll have to drive the horses then.'

Yovanix drove with a knife pressed to his side.

Hating slavery and meaning to help him, I said, 'If you get us out of this mess and help save Paul, we'll buy you from Julius and set you free.'

'Paul?'

'The moon's child,' I said angrily. 'Do you agree? Or else I'll turn you into a frog.'

'How can I refuse?' he cried, tears running down his face. 'I'm so scared I pissed myself.'

'By Poseidon, he's right,' said Nearchus, moving quickly backward.

'Will you please let me handle this from now on?' asked Alexander reasonably, pulling straw over my head and pushing me down to the wagon bed. 'Hush. We're approaching the stream.'

I moved to the other, drier side of the wagon and huddled in the straw. Evening was falling and visibility was poor, but Alexander had eyes like a jaguar. He peered through the straw and the dusk and murmured to Nearchus, 'There are three men by the sacred oak: one by the left side; two around the back. One man is down by the stream. I see another man in a tree; he's cutting mistletoe from a high branch with a small golden sickle.'

'That's Anoramix,' said Yovanix between his teeth.

'I hope he falls out of the tree,' I said balefully.

At that moment we heard a loud crack, and the branch holding the druid fell down. The golden sickle tumbled out of the tree in a bright arc, landing on a rock with a clang. The man caught himself, and swung easily down from the tree.

'You forgot to add, "and breaks his neck".' It was Axiom, awe in his voice.

'Damn.' I was impressed. 'It wasn't me. Honest.'

'I know that,' said Nearchus. 'Paul must be somewhere close.' His voice was high. I glanced at him sharply. He was making the sign against the evil eye.

'How's Yovanix?' I whispered.

'He's fainted again, but I don't think anyone will notice. I'm holding him upright.' Alexander kept his voice low. 'I don't see Paul, but Nearchus's right, he must be close.'

'How can you tell?'

'Because two of the three men have fresh bandages on their calves.'

'Paul can't really make accidents happen,' I said, getting cross now.

'No, but Cerberus bites, remember?' He chuckled.

Anoramix hailed the cart and came over. 'Yovanix?' he spoke sharply. 'Are you all right?' Yovanix was coming out of his faint and he groaned. Anoramix stepped closer. 'By Persephone's icy heart, you're ill!' he cried.

Yovanix opened one eye and moaned, then he leaned over and vomited on his brother, which cheered me up, and made Axiom shake with laughter. The straw rustled.

Anoramix took off his soiled robe, and tossed it on the ground. I widened my eyes. He was very young, maybe younger even than Yovanix. He didn't look at all like his siblings. He was swarthy, with straight black hair and grey eyes. He had a bony face, a strong chin, and high cheekbones. His torso was long, with flat muscles like a wrestler's. He had black curly hair on his legs, arms, and pubis. A line of black curls snaked up his flat belly. He stood, naked and barefoot, with snowflakes whirling around him. He didn't seem to mind the cold. It gave me goose bumps.

'Yovanix, where are the prisoners? Are they hidden in the straw?'

Yovanix just nodded, his lips clamped shut. Sweat shone on his forehead.

'Drive the wagon to the cave. I will meet you there when I finish collecting the mistletoe.

We drove to the entrance of the cave. Alexander was grimly satisfied. 'There are two men inside,' he whispered. 'But it's very dark, and I may have missed someone. Be prepared, Nearchus, we have to subdue them before Anoramix gets back.'

As Yovanix stopped the wagon, the two men inside the cave wandered over. Alexander waited until they were close. Then he and Nearchus levitated out of the straw and landed on the men. The fight was over in minutes.

They quickly tied and gagged the two men and shoved them under the straw. I sneaked out of the wagon and stepped into the cave. 'Paul?' I called softly. 'Cerberus?'

There was no answer. Discouraged, I sat down near the fire and watched Alexander and Nearchus. They hid behind the wagon, waiting for Anoramix. Axiom was still lying in the straw. Yovanix was leaning over, his face in his hands. He looked like he was about to faint again.

Anoramix came up the hill carrying his soiled robe and a basket of mistletoe. He peered into the wagon, nodded in satisfaction, and then said, 'Come into the cave and give me your message.'

Anoramix was naked, unarmed, and carrying a basket of plants. Not a great weapon.

'Who are you, and what do you want?' he asked coldly, when we were all sitting in front of the fire. Nearchus held a knife to Anoramix's ribs.

'I want my son,' I said, my voice like ice.

His head snapped around. He hadn't even looked at me, women being beneath consideration, I guessed. 'The goddess,' he breathed.

'I see you recognize me.' I didn't smile. 'Where is my son?'

'He is safe, I promise. He is in the centre of the sacred grove. The purification ceremony is for tomorrow night. When he has been washed with the blood of the three victims, then he will be stripped of his powers. I have been chosen to do this.' Even with a knife poking his ribs he sounded confident.

'You're sick,' I said.

He looked shocked. 'I have been chosen to save the world!' he insisted. 'All the signs have pointed to me since I was born: the earthquake on the day of my birth, the white crow who perched on my shoulder one day, and the white hind struck by lightning underneath my sacred tree. All those portents belong to me. The moon's child is mine now. With his power I can save our world.'

I was speechless with indignation. 'He's not the moon's child, he's *my* son. And no one can own him; he's not a slave like your poor brother.'

His mouth dropped open. 'You know he's my brother? Did he tell you that?'

Yovanix started panicking again. 'I didn't! I didn't, I swear. But she knows more; she knows about Selena. And the helmet. And she escaped from the room and disappeared! Then she flew into the wagon and bewitched me!'

I felt sorry for him, but I wasn't about to admit to hiding in the closet yet. 'I only want to get my son back and continue our voyage in peace.'

'There is only one way we can let the moon's child go,' said Anoramix.

'What?'

'We must go ahead with the ceremony. When his powers have been stripped, no one will try to capture him. Otherwise, each time there is a moonlit night the world will be in danger.'

'I refuse!' I cried. However, Alexander reached forward and grasped my wrist. 'I agree,' he said in measured tones.

'What?' I struggled, but he was absurdly strong. His eyes bored into mine. 'We have to agree,' he said. 'Will you feel safe knowing that all the Orphic druids in the world want our son? If everyone knows his powers have been shorn, they will leave him alone.'

'No.' Tears started leaking from my eyes. 'How can you agree to be sacrificed?' I was shaking, my teeth chattering.

'I won't be sacrificed,' said Alexander gently.

'Who will be?' I whispered.

Alexander pointed his chin toward the wagon. 'There are two already there. And the third man is in front of us.'

Yovanix jerked like a hooked fish, but his brother put a hand on his arm. 'No,' he said. 'He's speaking of me. I misread the signs.'

'But who will take your place? We can't leave the sacred grove without a druid!' Yovanix protested. 'No, take me. I will offer myself to the moon's child and to the winter.' He looked so noble as he said that; I felt perfectly horrible for making him suffer so much.

'Don't be dramatic,' I heard myself saying. 'Can't you understand that human sacrifices are an abomination?'

Anoramix smiled thinly and pointed to the back of the cave. 'Look,' he said.

I turned and gasped. Whorls, waves, spirals, and curlicues were carved deep into the rock. However, what held my attention was a huge arched doorway. Set into the rock around the door, hundreds of skulls grinned at us.

'May I?' Axiom walked over to the skulls. He touched one gingerly. 'How are they set into the stone?' he asked. 'It looks as if the stone melted and they were pushed into it. There is not the slightest space between bone and rock.'

'What does it mean?' I asked Anoramix.

'That our gods and your gods are not the same. Our gods want human blood. Blood and bones from sacrifices have filled the earth's belly since the beginning of time, and soon, perhaps, she will be replete. But for now, she is still hungry. If we do not satisfy her hunger, she will make us suffer.' His voice was sad. 'When your son was born, the world trembled. For ten years he was hidden from the moon. However, he grows, and soon he will call her down to him. I have been chosen to save the world. That is what the portents were trying to tell me. Not just any three men would do. My blood will wash away his powers.'

'But, but …' My hands fell to my sides. A terrible lassitude filled me. Tears pricked my eyes. 'I don't understand,' I said finally.

'But we do.' Anoramix's voice was gentle. 'We have been initiated into the mysteries. Now you are here, and now the ceremony can be brought to its very end.'

'What is the very end?' I asked.

He looked at me, and a smile quirked the corner of his mouth. 'Kid, I fell into the milk.'

I gaped. 'What? Kid? What kid? What milk?'

'The goat's milk. It's the last sentence in the initiation rite. You are the goddess. Tomorrow night, we will say the proper words, and I will pass into the green meadow where singing is heard and the sun is always bright. Where flowers bloom for ever, and men and women live in peace.'

'You believe in heaven?' I was stunned. In Greece, in any religion around the world at that time, you died, and then you disappeared, disintegrated, reincarnated, or you went into a horrible underworld and whirled like a leaf. This was the first time I heard mention of a paradise. 'Explain.'

'For those who have undergone the initiation, death is a doorway into another world,' he said. 'We Orphics believe that Persephone has reserved a special place for those who die. We go to a glorious meadow filled with music, song, and dance.'

'How amazing,' I heard myself saying.

Nearchus leaned forward, his hands on his knees. 'Have you been initiated?'

'I have.' Anoramix shrugged.

We all sat back and looked at each other. I was trying to come to grips with the sudden merging of the druids' bloody sacrifices and an afterlife in paradise.

'I still don't understand why you have to die,' I said finally.

'We don't die, really.' Anoramix said.

Axiom saw me opening my mouth, and he shook his head at me. Alexander put his arm around my shoulders, and I leaned into him.

My eyes met Anoramix's over the fire. His were strangely innocent. 'Who were the men who attacked us four nights ago?' I asked him.

He looked surprised. 'You were attacked?'

'Before the moon rose, we were set upon by raiders. They killed almost everyone.' Axiom answered. His eyes were dark, and in the firelight they glittered. He looked angry for the first time that night.

Anoramix shook his head slowly. 'I didn't know, but it doesn't surprise me. Any druid who hears about the moon's child will want to capture him. What does surprise me is the bloodshed. We don't kill unless it's for a sacrifice. It's against our beliefs.' He looked outside where a sliver of a moon had started to rise, barely visible through the trees. 'The moon has come. We can fetch your son now.'

'But, don't you understand that sacrificing and killing are the same?' I asked.

'No.' Anoramix stood up. 'Come, we'll go before he catches cold.'

'You mean he's outside in the snow?' I scrambled to my feet. 'He'd better not be cold,' I hissed, 'or you won't live to die tomorrow night.'

'That sounds very profound,' Alexander told me, patting my arm. 'Why don't you stay here out of the cold? Nearchus will take care of the horses. Yovanix and Axiom will fetch the men in the wagon, and Anoramix and I will get Paul and Cerberus.'

I did as he suggested. I didn't want to leave the relative warmth of the cave and go into the forest, where at least twelve centimetres of soft snow blanketed the ground. The rising wind sent flakes whirling and falling through the air. The tall trees were nothing but black shadows now, and low feathery clouds nearly hid the moon.

Chapter Twenty

I decided to cook dinner. I filled a large caldron with fresh water and set it to boil. Then I inspected the cave. The sleeping quarters were next to the fire. Sacks of dried peas, lentils, a crate of apples, onions, garlic, flour, and an earthenware jar of honey were in the storeroom. Salted hams, sausages, and salamis hung from the ceiling. A large amphora of wine stood against the wall. The wine inside it smelled like pine. The Greeks had weird taste in wine, sometimes they salted it, and sometimes they sweetened it with honey. At times, they grated cheese into it, added handfuls of flour, and boiled it into a sort of primitive fondue. I put lentils, onions, and a slab of fatty bacon into the boiling water and added a handful of dried thyme and some garlic.

I stayed away from the doorway with the skulls. Their eyes seemed to follow me as I walked around the cave, so I sat by the fire, my back to them.

Axiom, Nearchus, and Yovanix came back with the other men, stomping the snow off their boots and shaking their cloaks off outside. Yovanix sat as far away from me as possible, but he did murmur something nice about the smell of the lentil stew.

Nearchus went to examine the skulls. I heard him tapping them with his fingers, trying to dislodge them. 'These skulls are certainly set in the stone tightly,' he said admiringly. 'Who did this work?'

Yovanix shrugged. 'No one knows. They have been like that since the cave was discovered by the first of the old ones. The carvings were here too. All was as you see now.'

'What do the carvings mean?' I asked.

'I don't know. Many believe they are necessary for the initiation. When you drink the wine and inhale the sacred smoke, the carvings seem to move. It's as if they become the sea, the wind, the grass moving, snakes, or even smoke spiralling up to the heavens. Everyone sees something different. However, all say the carvings lead you through the doorway.'

'And then?'

'And then you are initiated.' He made a face. 'I am but a slave, I have never taken part in the rites.'

'Have these men?' I asked, pointing to the two men sitting cross-legged by his side.

'Yes, they are both druids. And the three men who are guarding the moon's child have been initiated also.'

'Can a woman take part in the ceremonies?' I asked.

'Women are not druids, nor are they priestesses.'

'Are women sacrificed?' I asked.

'Of course! Every summer a virgin must die.'

'Oh?' I raised my eyebrows. 'Is she initiated so that her soul may go to the green meadow paradise as well?'

'Yes, the rites last nearly all year. The girl goes through the whole ceremony.'

'And then she's killed.' My voice was raw. 'How awful. I can't imagine anything worse than knowing you're going to die on a certain day.'

'There are far worse things.' Yovanix tried to explain. 'The girl is treated with great respect. She is the most important person in the village. And in the spring she goes to the green meadow.'

'Bullshit,' I said in English.

Nearchus, who'd learned that word, winced. 'My Lady, I think we should speak of other things. It is wise to let the beliefs of others alone.'

I was chastened. Nearchus rarely spoke, and he never contradicted me, but his navy-blue stare was implacable. *'Be quiet,'* it was saying, *'you're not going to change anything.'*

The stew started to bubble. I stirred it. The aroma made my mouth water.

'Mummy!' Paul flung himself into my arms, and Cerberus rushed around, barking and making a mess with his snowy paws.

'Are you all right?' I grabbed his shoulders, looking intently at him. His nose was pink with cold, but otherwise he seemed fine.

'Of course.' He drew a deep breath. 'Oh, that smells wonderful, when can we eat?'

Anoramix took a ham from a hook and cut off slivers of smoked meat for us to nibble on while we waited for the stew.

Three other men came into the cave and stood shyly in the entrance. I was glad I'd made plenty of stew. Anoramix motioned them in, and we crowded around the fire. There was only one chair, but animal skins covered the floor, so we were comfortable. Baskets held cloaks, blankets, eating utensils, and bowls. The fire burned in a large fireplace, and the smoke went up the chimney and didn't swirl around the cave. When we were all inside, Anoramix went to the entrance and pulled a heavy leather curtain across it, shutting out the cold and the snow. In a few minutes it was very warm in the room, and I felt my muscles relax.

'That's better,' said Paul, sitting cross-legged in front of the fire. Cerberus had his head on Paul's lap; his yellow eyes narrow slits as he stared at the flames. 'I was kept in a cage! I think they believe I'm a monster.' He shook his head. 'It was scary at first. When I woke up, I was in a wagon. Luckily, Cerberus was with me, otherwise I might have cried.'

I thought the trails of tears down his dirty cheeks argued poignantly for crying, but I didn't say anything. I just leaned over and gently wiped his face with a damp cloth. 'You must have been terrified,' I said.

'I'm mostly hungry,' he admitted. 'Besides, I knew that my father would save me.'

'Well, he did save you,' I said, smiling at my husband.

Alexander tried to look modest, but although his face was the most eloquent one I'd ever seen, modesty wasn't one of his expressions. 'I had some help,' he told Paul.

'Shall we eat?' I asked, lifting the lid off the pot and letting the fragrant steam escape.

We ate from clay bowls with spoons carved from bone, and I didn't ask whose bones. I was too hungry.

Afterwards the Gallic men played a game of knucklebones.

I had to go to the bathroom, but I was reluctant to leave the warmth of the cave. The toilets were outside, of course. Before going to sleep, I made my way through the dark and the snow to a small outhouse. At least there was an outhouse.

Anoramix went to a large wooden chest and pulled out an armful of fur rugs that were to wrap up in to sleep. Most of them were from sheep, a couple looked like wolfskins, and all of them smelled like the animal they'd belonged to first. I put my face into Alexander's neck and tried to breathe as shallowly as possible. Everyone was snoring loudly, even the dog, and everyone smelled awful, especially the dog. He must have rolled in a dead animal. I wondered if I could find a bunch of dried thyme in the dark and sleep with it crushed to my nose, but I was afraid I'd step on someone.

Morning finally came, and Anoramix opened the curtain and let a draft of icy air into the cave. I took a deep breath. It was the first one I'd taken since the night before. I felt stiff, dirty, cold, and I longed to take a bath. Why couldn't we go back to Julius's farm and float a while in his heated pool? I wondered if Alexander would consider that. I made the mistake of asking him within earshot of Anoramix.

'No,' the druid told me firmly. 'You must prepare yourself for the ceremony tonight.'

'I won't take any part in a ceremony that ends in bloodshed,' I told him. 'I refuse. You can't make me,' I added defiantly.

149

'You must. Please. We need you.' His voice was incredibly seductive and gentle. I could see where he wouldn't have too much trouble convincing people to follow him.

'Don't make me a part of your sacrifices. I don't believe in your religion or in killing. I have no powers.' My voice was strained. I meant what I said. I was starting to feel nauseated at the thought of watching men die.

'You must learn the chants. You were sent to us because you are the only one who can sing them.'

'What chants?' I asked. But my skin prickled. I remembered what Apollo had told me, far away in a smoke-filled temple in Siwa. 'The Chants to Persephone,' I whispered. And I knew I was beaten.

'Let me show you something,' he said. 'Come with me.'

I put on a warm cloak and pulled on my boots. Paul and Alexander were playing on the slope, making a snow fort. Cerberus was barking at a squirrel. Axiom was speaking to Yovanix, and Nearchus was busy helping the other men gather firewood.

Anoramix and I took a narrow path through a grove of huge pine trees. The path led to a brook, which we crossed on a stone bridge. Then we continued through the woods.

This was part of the primeval forest, uncut since the beginning of time, sacred to the druids and gods of Gaul. There were pine, oak, ash, and beech trees, and all were taller and more massive than any I'd ever seen. We followed the path uphill through the giant trees for nearly half an hour before reaching an opening in the face of a cliff. Anoramix disappeared within, and I could hear his

150

footsteps become suddenly amplified. 'Come,' he called. His voice boomed.

Chapter Twenty-one

I stepped inside. The cave was immense. From outside, its enormity couldn't even be guessed. I found myself in a vast cavern.

There was light. Torches flicked from sconces on a wall. Anoramix took one and held it above his head, showing me size of the place. Then he pointed to his right.

I had never seen original cave paintings. I'd only seen photographs in glossy pages of books. What I was seeing now had nothing to do with photos. Vibrant and alive, the animals seemed to leap off the walls.

I stared, losing all sense of myself as I followed Anoramix through time, back further than any of the Time-Travellers had ever gone. Back to a time when man and nature were so close, that with simple handfuls of clay and charcoal, our ancestors had created a masterpiece. The paintings made me shiver. They were so true to life and full of raw energy that the animals seemed to say, *'See us? We were here before you. We existed before any of you even dreamed of us. We are still alive here on this wall, and we will be here long after you're gone.*

The beauty of the paintings amazed me. Nothing I'd ever seen compared to the power of these animals. They leaped, galloped, and breathed with nostrils flaring. Their eyes blazed with life.

We walked slowly toward the back of the cave. There were horses and bison, bears and lions, wolves and rhinoceros ... and handprints. Human hands. Shivering, I raised my own and pressed it against one that was eye level. The hand was slightly broader than mine, the fingers somewhat shorter, but it was a powerful, graceful hand, and it had created a masterpiece.

I pressed my hand to the stone and closed my eyes. I would have given anything to be present while the artist had been at work. I tried to picture the man painting, his bare shoulders gleaming in the torchlight, his hands deft as they wove their magic. However, there was a deep secrecy about the paintings. I was filled with a sense of disquiet and awe. The man had worked alone, and the images were not for all eyes. Perhaps only the chosen ones could see them, the priests and priestesses of that ancient time. Or were they decorations for a ceremony? I didn't know. The paintings spoke, but in their own tongue, and it was a language more akin to the snarls and whinnies of animals than of the words we used. I stepped back and looked, holding my breath, trying to hear the sound of hoof beats.

Anoramix took my arm and led me further, and there he showed me the bones.

They had been carefully arranged. The skulls sat on top of crossed femurs and placed over the rest of the bones, which were stacked in a strict order. At least twelve layers of skulls stared at me. The ones at the bottom were yellow with age, the bone turning brown around the eye socket and jaw. The skulls at the top were white and gleamed faintly in the dark. They seemed to be grinning happily at some secret joke they all shared.

I felt no sense of horror. It was strange, really, but I felt completely dislocated from place and time. I felt separated from the living; like the bones, sitting and staring for all eternity at the paintings. For that was what they were doing. Lined up in perfect rows, arms folded beneath their chins, they watched the wild animals galloping across the cavern. Smiling dreamily, eyes vague, seemingly lost in tranquil contemplation of a stunning masterpiece, I almost felt as if the bones would answer if I spoke to them, or that they were speaking to each other.

'Nice artwork. I love the rhinoceros.'

'My favourite one's the doe, with the fawn at her side.'

'I like that one too, but she had better watch out, there's a lynx above her, on a branch.'

'Oh yeah, I didn't see that!'

I smiled; my imagination running away with me.

'Hush, there's a stranger in our midst, can you feel the shift in time?'

I jumped. 'Did you say something?' I whispered to Anoramix.

In the torchlight, his face had deep shadows and resembled nothing more than one of the skulls. 'It is the old ones. They speak if you listen. Soon I will join them.'

'This is no green meadow,' I said, my voice wavering.

'It is a doorway. From here one can go back and forth. The meadow is beyond utter darkness and unimaginable fear, but for the initiate the journey is easy. So easy that one can come and go at will. From the gate, the old ones can see who is coming next and welcome them. It is the

154

same principle as the doorway in my cave. The skulls set in the stone are guardians, if you like. They pass the message back and forth from the afterworld to the newly dead, helping them find their way.'

'And they can admire the paintings,' I said faintly.

'Let me tell you what happened when I was initiated,' said Anoramix. 'It happened here, in this cave, with the old one whose name I will not say. You can see him now; he rests on the top over there, the closest to the wall. You can greet him if you like.'

I looked at the pile of bones and saw a new skeleton, still pearly white and shiny. 'Hello,' I said. My voice cracked.

Anoramix looked amused. 'On the first night we were in the darkness. No light showed us the way, the paintings were hidden, the bones too. I drank *kykeon*; a ritual beverage made of water, barley groats, and pennyroyal. Afterwards, I was shown the sacred objects hidden in the basket. I was allowed to touch them.'

'What were they?' I asked.

He smiled. 'The sex of man and woman, made of baked, glazed clay. I was told they were made by the first old ones for the rites, and I have no reason to disbelieve this. Then I put the sacred objects back, and said these words; 'I fasted, I drank the *kykeon*. I took the objects from the basket again and after accomplishing the deed, I put them back. Then I placed the basket in the hamper and took it out again. Then I put it back.' We have to do everything in just the right order. We chanted, sang, and then I was led out of the darkness of the cave.'

'What deed did you accomplish?' I asked. There were some parts of the ceremony he'd left rather vague.

He looked sideways at me and shook his head, a grin on his face. 'I think you can imagine what one does with sexual organs. I don't need to show you, do I?'

I caught a trace of laughter in the air. I imagined the skulls chuckling too. 'Were you initiated then?' I asked.

'No, not yet. The second night we came back. As before, the darkness was complete. I was surrounded by fear that time. I was pushed roughly into the cave and all around me were the chants of evil. There were malevolent beings in the cave that night. They sought to frighten me away. Even the bones took part in the ceremony. They would suddenly glow with an unearthly, greenish light that came straight from Hades.' He shuddered with the memory. 'I thought my heart would burst or that I would shame myself. Deep terror filled me. Death, I thought, could be no worse than this. Finally the fear passed. When I stopped feeling anguish and stood up straight, a torch lit up, and the light was like a revelation. In the centre of the cave was the torch burning, but not held by any mortal hand. It lit up one perfect, golden ear of wheat. Your mother's sign. The other torches were lit, and the old ones invoked Demeter and Persephone. Listen now to what the old ones told me.' His voice dropped several tones and became low and mysterious.

'"The soul, at the moment of its death, feels like those who are initiated into the Great Mysteries. At first it wanders, lost, through detours and endless dark windings, frightened and alone. Before the end, the terror, the shaking, the cold sweat, and the horror are at their* *greatest. Then, suddenly, a golden light appears. One passes through the darkness to an endless meadow where singing is heard, where dancers can be seen, and sacred words are spoken. A deep respect and reverence is felt. Thus man, now initiated and perfect, becomes free. He has celebrated the Mystery; he is crowned and lives with pure men and saints. He watches as the uninitiated toil through the mud and the darkness, afraid of death. They struggle to escape their fate, rather than believing that death can set them free. The only true happiness comes in the afterworld.".'*

His voice stopped but there were strange echoes, as if a chorus had spoken with him.

I shivered from the intense cold. It leached through the stone walls, and I noticed a faint sparkle of frost on some of the bones. I was silent, but not because I had nothing to say. Questions jostled for position in my mind. I wanted to know so much more. 'What about women?' I asked finally.

'What women?'

'Is your paradise only for men? You speak of initiates; can initiates only be men? What about women? Aren't we good enough for an afterworld?' I asked.

He raised his eyebrows. Surprise made his eyes round. 'Women don't need to be initiated,' he said. 'You, who make life, must understand death better than we can *ever* hope to. It is through women that the chain of life continues. Backward in time, however far back you go, it is by women that the link is forged. And forward, through you and your daughters. Can you feel it? The initiate enters the past, the present, and the future, and he finds it through the woman. You are made of the same clay we men are, but there is something already sacred about you. You have the power to make life. Nothing we can ever learn can equal that.'

There was something touching in the way he was looking at me. I felt his faith in a way I'd never felt anyone else's. Yet he was so young. Why did he want to die? His muscles moved smoothly under his skin as he raised the torch. Light fell on his upturned face. His grey eyes, so uncanny in the daylight, turned to pools of silver in the firelight. I stepped toward him. My foot slid over the rough stone and touched something soft. I looked down. A bear stared up at me, its pelt spread over the floor. I nudged it with my foot. My chest was growing tight. Firelight flickered on the walls of the cave; animals and bones stared back at me. They all seemed to be waiting for an answer. An answer I didn't think I could give.

'Why does anyone have to die?' I whispered.

'Because the earth wants blood. It leaves us our bones to see, our soul to feel, and our memory to hear, but it drinks our blood. It has done so for all time and will continue to do so. Does the earth not drink blood in your world, Queen of Darkness and Ice?'

'It does.' I shuddered and took a deep breath. If anything, the earth gorged on more blood in my time than it ever had. Blood tainted with radiation. Blood spurting from bullets. Blood oozing from bodies broken by bombs. Mass graves still existed.

'I don't want you to die,' I pleaded.

'I won't.' He reached his hand out and touched my belly. The caress ended with his hand on my breast, cupping it tenderly.

I jumped backward, startled. 'I understand now, you want to …' I choked on the words. 'But I can't, I won't. I'm married, and I love my husband. You'll have to find someone else. I knew this was going to be a mess, why did you have to choose me? It's not going to work,' I said hastily, backing away from him. 'I'm sorry, I can't make love to you.'

'You don't have to. Three virgins from the village have already been chosen, one for each of us.' There was a definite chuckle in the cave now. I felt my cheeks redden. 'But I need your blessing. Tomorrow night I will lie with a woman and my seed will be sown. Whether it grows or not is the choice of the Mother. But the earth will drink my blood, my bones will be set here in the cave to see the sacred paintings for ever, my soul will be free to go to paradise, and my memory will linger. My words will be heard until the end of time like those who have spoken before me.'

'I don't want you to die.'

'I want to die. I want to feed the Mother.'

'I won't take any part in a ceremony that kills you,' I cried. My voice echoed around the cave, booming loudly then fading suddenly.

'Please, I need you.' He said the words simply. He didn't try to touch me. He held the torch face level and stared at me. Tears sparkled on his lashes.

I bowed my head and wept. My own tears were an acceptance. The skulls behind me breathed a sigh of relief.

159

Chapter Twenty-two

I walked back to the druid's cave as if in a dream. The ritual was explained to me, but I only heard a third of what Anoramix was saying. His words rattled in the empty air and shredded in the bare branches of the trees.

When we were nearly in sight of the others, I whirled around. My breath made white clouds in the air. 'I don't want anyone to die,' I said. 'I want you to know that I don't believe in any of this. For me, you're just throwing your stupid, short, vain life away.' I was gasping now; my chest was so tight I couldn't take a decent breath.

'I understand, but please, nothing you say can change anything. I will die tonight. Two men will die with me. They believe. *I* believe. Whether you do or not, is unimportant. But if you insist on claiming your disbelief, you will only confuse and hurt the people coming to assist and take part in the ceremony.' His voice was gentle. A slap couldn't have stung more. 'I truly believe we have been chosen to save the world. So do the people who are coming. They will venerate us for the rest of their lives.'

'How many people will come?' I asked, wiping my tears away.

'There are six villages in this valley, four more on the plain. Nearly two thousand in the region.'

'But why is the ceremony in Greek? Why? What happened to the real druids here?'

'There still are some, but the ways have changed dramatically. Ours is a people of nomads. We have adopted customs from all over the world. We have changed. Perhaps you think that the sacrifice to be held tonight is horrible, but let me tell you what happened before. Young men and women died violent deaths without even being initiated. Their blood was poured into the earth, and their bones were put into a great pit dug behind the oppidum's sacred grove. Four times a year the earth drank blood. Now we only usher in the summer solstice with blood.'

'You said a young virgin would die, that she had been prepared all year long. Is this the sacrifice for her?'

'No, she dies just before the harvest.'

'How lovely.'

'The tone of your voice belies your words.'

'It's called sarcasm.' I was tired. I wanted to sit in front of a blazing fire and sip a hot cocoa. Chocolate wouldn't get to Europe for ages. After the Dark Ages, the Middle Ages, and the Golden Ages. I would have a long while to wait for hot chocolate. I sighed. 'What is *this* sacrifice then, if it's not for the summer solstice?'

'This is for the moon's child. We would take away the power he has to destroy the world.'

'But, why now? Why not in the sacred valley? I don't understand.'

'Because the valley protected your child. Now he is in the open, and the world is in danger. If an evil person found him, they could use your son's powers for their own ends and change the world. Three men must die and their blood be used to wash the power from the child.'

'I simply don't believe it.' I kept shaking my head. 'It's monstrous to ask me to think that three men must die because of my son.'

'He is not your son yet, he is the moon's child. Only when he has been washed with the blood, will you be able to claim him.' He was firm. 'Three men must die. It is written.'

'It is *terrible*.'

'I'm sorry you feel this way, but you cannot change the world. Yours is not the power to change anything.'

I looked at him sharply. I'd heard that before somewhere, far away in a smoke-filled temple. 'What is that supposed to mean?' I asked, but he didn't answer, he just stared at me.

The snow contemplated falling again. The sky scraped its grey belly against the treetops. Clouds looked as soft as a baby owl feathers. Anoramix's eyes were that colour.

'I'm sorry too.' I couldn't look at him. My misery was too sharp. 'But I would ask something of you.'

'Ask.'

I took a deep breath. 'You said that the uninitiated wandered around, lost. When you find yourself in the winding corridors of the afterworld, in the dark, I want you to find someone named Millis and lead him to the meadow.'

'Millis?'

'He's a eunuch and a mute, so he won't be able to answer you if you call him. Tell him I sent you.'

'He won't be a eunuch in the afterworld, and he'll be able to speak. When we reach the light, we will sing together.'

I blinked, sending tears down my cheeks. 'Please find him.' I whispered.

He looked up at the sky. The wind whirled through the clearing, lifting the snow off the ground in a biting swirl of ice particles. Anoramix's cloak flapped around him, and a flurry of snow sparkled on his shoulders. He took my hand. 'Come, daughter of Demeter. The ceremony is long, and we have much to do before I can search for Millis.'

If he felt my shudder, he didn't say anything.

Chapter Twenty-three

The blessing was easy. I poured ritual wine into a cup and gave it to the three men and three women standing in front of me. We were in the cave, just the seven of us.

Torches lit the scene. The painted animals were still vibrant and beautiful. That night they seemed tense, like wild animals before a storm. They raised their heads and pricked their ears, listening, nostrils flaring, scenting the wind.

A wind of change was blowing. I felt it because I came from the tail end of it, three thousand years in the future. I felt it because I had read the history books that told about the Romans conquering Gaul and killing all the druids as they cut down the sacred groves. The oak that had grown for nine hundred years was cut down, and a straight, Roman road was laid upon it. The last generation of druids was here before me. The seeds planted that evening would grow, but they would not prosper. My hands shook as I poured the wine.

Anoramix looked at me with something akin to pity. The woman at his side was silent. She was as tall as he was, dark-haired and willowy. Her eyes were wide with what could be awe or just the effects of the wine. There had been a great deal of it flowing before the ceremony. I gave her a reassuring smile, but my lips were stiff. I tried to calm myself, but I couldn't. Anoramix and the two other men were completely relaxed. I would have thought that it was inhuman, but I saw the size of their pupils. They were drugged with something strong.

Anoramix stood in front of me. His eyes were *all* pupil. The girl standing next to him was flushed. Her breath came quickly and her chest rose and fell, her breasts showing beneath her linen shift.

I wasn't sure what to do. Anoramix had bade me serve them the drinks, but he didn't tell me at what point he wanted me to leave. The two men who were to die with him had curious blank looks. One girl kept licking her lips, a strangely erotic gesture. The men had erections, I noticed.

'Do I do anything else?' I asked Anoramix in a whisper.

'Just say the ritual blessing with me, and then you can leave. Go to the sacred oak and wait.' His voice was as clear as cut glass.

We recited the blessing together. I was trying to speak calmly but my voice kept breaking. I ended the blessing in a whisper. Then I pulled my cloak tightly around my shoulders and left. The three couples stayed in the cave. When the night was nearly over they would join us.

'Us' was the two thousand people gathered in the sacred forest that evening. Most of them built fires and sat down to wait with their families. Women held children in their laps, and men talked in loud voices. They grilled meat, ate, and drank hot spiced wine. It was like a huge picnic, with a show at the end. The hours went slowly.

Paul wandered around as he liked. The ceremony, although supposedly about him, had so far ignored him.

'Best not to call attention to the moon's child, moon or no moon,' explained Yovanix.

I wished Alexander were with me, but he had been busy all day long with Nearchus and Axiom, helping the druids organize the ceremony. I'd been so occupied I hadn't had time to talk to him or Paul about the coming sacrifice. I'd been stuck with the three victims, learning the chants, and I had a bad case of nerves. I fingered the flask of wine at my hip. Well, it couldn't hurt. I took a huge swallow and then coughed as the wine coursed down my throat. *'Whew!'* I gasped. It was warm, spiced with pine, and something else I couldn't identify. A glow settled in my stomach, and I decided to drink more. Getting drunk started to appeal to me. I would miss the slaughter. No, the sacrifice. *Damn, this stuff was strong!* I peered at the flask. Well, bottoms up. I finished it, then made my way to the crowd near the oak tree.

Selena was there, but not her husband Julius. She was startled to see me, of course, and even more shocked when she saw Yovanix speaking to me. She rushed over.

'Where is Anoramix?' she asked.

'Well, hello again,' I said angrily. 'Thanks a lot for getting us into this mess.'

She shot me a strange look that was completely devoid of regret. 'I had to,' she said. 'It was either give you to Anoramix or let you be captured by Voltarrix.'

'Who?' I asked.

'A powerful druid from the land of snow and ice,' she hissed. 'He has come to this region in search of the moon's child, and he means to take him to the land of the Eaters of the Dead.'

'What?' I took a step back, shocked. 'What does he look like?'

'He has pale hair like yours. He wears a helmet with horns.'

'I saw that man the night Millis was killed,' I whispered. 'He's a druid? But I thought druids couldn't kill, except for sacrifices!'

'Voltarrix is *not* a Gallic druid. I just told you. He wants to take Paul to his land. And they sacrifice children there.' Her impatience showed. 'Where is Anoramix?' she asked again, staring past me.

'In the cave. He has decided to sacrifice himself.' Yovanix spoke in a low voice.

Selena gasped. 'What about the three men we captured? I sent a message telling him not to sacrifice himself!' Her voice was shrill with pain. 'He can't die!'

'It's too late,' said Yovanix.

'No, I won't believe it! I must stop him!' She pushed past Yovanix and me, running toward the hillside.

'You had better stop her,' I said.

'Me?' his voice hit the stratosphere. 'Are you mad? Begging your pardon, My Lady, but I am a slave, remember? I don't have the right to touch her.'

'You're kidding, right? You make love to her and you say you can't touch her?' I was struck by a sudden thought. 'Do you think the child is yours or Julius's?'

'It's not mine, I swear. Now catch her before she does something foolish! Please!'

I sighed and then started after Selena. I arrived just in time to see her duck inside the cave entrance.

'Damn,' I muttered, and then I followed her.

I entered the cavern and saw Selena standing, as if transfixed, before the paintings. 'Selena!' I hissed.

She jumped, but didn't come back. Instead, she headed toward the rear of the cave where some heavy breathing was making it rather plain what was going on.

I trotted after her. When I grabbed her robe she turned on me. 'Leave me alone,' she said angrily. 'I must see Anoramix.'

'If you go back there, you'll probably see more of him than you expect,' I said. 'Wait at the entrance and you can talk to him as he leaves.'

She hesitated. The groans were coming closer together now. A woman whimpered, then gasped. I swallowed hard. A wave of sexual desire submerged me. There must have been an aphrodisiac in the wine. The women and men had been aroused. I was starting to feel my own legs trembling.

'Let's get out of here,' I said. This time she listened to me and turned, but her face was streaked with tears.

'I love him,' she said.

'I know, he's your brother,' I said gently. 'I'm sorry.'

'The babe is his.' She put her hand on her belly.

I gaped. 'Did you sleep with all your family?' I asked stupidly, before realizing I sounded rude. 'I apologize, it's none of my business.'

'He's not my blood brother. His parents were killed in a great earthquake. His mother was our slave. My mother had just lost a child, so she took him in to raise. He looks nothing like us,' she added.

'I did notice that,' I admitted.

'When we left Crete, we brought him with us. He was the first one my parents sold, and then they sold me. I was bought by a Roman who fell in love with me. He cannot have a child though. His first wife died barren, and I didn't become pregnant until I took Anoramix as my lover.'

'What about Yovanix?' I asked.

She looked at me, her eyes hooded. 'A woman with a child in her belly wants a man. I feel a strong need. Julius is not enough.' She shrugged.

I didn't say a word. Who was I to argue? Besides, I had two lovers: Alexander, my husband; and Plexis, Chiron's father. Thinking about Plexis made my face twist in sorrow. I missed him terribly. I missed the way he looked at me, his eyes mocking, and his hands deft and gentle. I missed the way he would arch his eyebrows and grin. 'Plexis,' I whispered. The wine and the longing made my breath short. Plexis could rouse me with a look.

Selena was close enough to touch. Tears glistened on her cheeks. I put my hand on her arm. 'I'm sorry,' I repeated.

She turned and pressed herself against me. I could feel her whole body under her cloak. It was full and generous. As if I were half asleep, I felt myself pulling her close. Her cloak slid off her shoulders. Her tunic was fastened with a pin. I pulled it out of the wool, and she stood naked before me. Her eyes were heavy-lidded with the same desire I felt. My breath was coming fast. Her breasts were heavy, her belly round and smooth. I cupped her breasts, then ran my hands over the slope of her belly.

She sighed then, and unhooked the pin from my own cloak. My tunic fell to the ground in a heap. She leaned over and touched my nipples with her lips. I gasped at the feeling. Her arms went around my back, and she pulled me toward her, our thighs touched.

Underneath our feet, the bear skin was thick and soft. We found ourselves lying on it, kissing, our legs entwined.

It felt odd to embrace a woman. Her mouth was soft, her lips yielding. There wasn't the roughness of whiskers, only softness. Our breasts were soft, our legs as they rubbed against each other were smooth, and our hands, as they roamed, encountered only curves and slopes. Her pubis was shaved, mine had curls blonde as pale wheat. The tightness in my belly was so intense that as soon as her hand touched me I was shuddering, my breath coming in deep moans, my nipples hard nubs against her chest.

I'd never made love with a woman before. I wondered if Selena had. She seemed to know what she was doing, but any woman knows what she's doing, when you really think about it. Her body was the same as mine. I knew every sensitive spot, every dip and curve that raised goose bumps, every place that could kindle a cry. To run my hands over her body was to stroke my own, and I was familiar with my own body. I had made love to myself often enough to know. Right now my breasts felt heavy and full. I leaned over, took one of Selena's nipples in my mouth, and tugged gently. Her moan told me that I was right. Her hand reached between my legs again, and I arched my back. The places I knew belonged to her as well.

Her fingers found me and thrust, and I did the same, taking her with me. She gave a soft cry and tipped her head back. She wrapped her legs around me, her hips moving in an age-old rhythm. Then she cried out again, and I felt the waves rushing through her; I felt them with my hand and it brought me to the edge and then pulled me over. An answering throbbing filled my sex, and I held onto her as our breathing became harsh, then eased. I couldn't stop trembling. The fur beneath me was warm, but I shook anyway. Then Selena wrapped her arms around me, and I fell asleep.

Chapter Twenty-four

I don't know if we woke because of the cold or the silence, but whichever, we both sat up and looked around. The torches had burned nearly to embers. No more heavy breathing came from the back of the immense cave. Selena leapt to her feet. 'They've gone,' she cried, and her voice chilled me.

We dressed and rushed out of the cave into the darkness. Selena wept. Her feet slipped as she scrambled up the snowy slope. When we reached the clearing, the night erupted with thousands of voices. In the firelight, I saw everyone standing. On the far side, there was a high stone altar with three men on it. Anoramix was one. He raised his arms and cried, 'Make way for the goddess!'

The people saw me coming and parted. A wide aisle opened, and I walked down it, Selena at my heels. I climbed onto the altar. Ten steps that felt like ten hundred. Anoramix took my hands and pulled me to the centre of the stone altar. I felt groggy, dazed from the wine, and frightened. The ceremony became suddenly real.

Selena stayed at the foot of the stairs. She looked up at us, face twisted with grief, hair unbound and streaming in the wind. 'Anoramix,' she cried.

He froze. The colour drained from his face. 'Why are you here?' he whispered. Only I could hear him. His lips hardly moved.

'Please, don't do this,' she begged.

'I must.'

'The babe is yours,' she said, stepping closer to the stairs and holding her robe tightly to her belly, showing him the round curve.

He smiled. Two spots of colour appeared on his cheeks. 'Then it is true,' he said. 'I *will* live for ever. Take care of him. I will look for you in the green meadow when your time has come.' Without another glance in her direction, he went to take his place next to the other two men.

Paul stood nearby. He was naked and tied by his hands to a stout post. The crescent moon scar on his shoulder seemed to give off a light of its own. His face was white beneath his dyed hair, and his mouth trembled. His eyes bulged with fright. I gave no more thought to Selena or Anoramix; in two steps I crossed the altar and took Paul in my arms.

'Anoramix said I mustn't be afraid,' he said, his voice quivering. 'And that I must close my eyes, because the blood will burn. When it's over, you can untie me and wrap me in those furs. Father will carry me to the cave.'

'Where *is* your father?' I asked.

'I'm not sure. When the ceremony started he was with Nearchus. He'll be here soon, I hope.' His voice dropped to a whisper, 'I'm so scared.' Tremors shook his arms and legs.

'You won't be hurt,' I said. My eyes were drawn to the scar on his shoulder. Why was it glowing? Part of my

173

mind wanted to know the answer; another part refused to think of it.

'I'm not scared for myself,' Paul said, tears in his eyes now. 'I don't want anyone to die because of me. Don't you understand? I know perfectly well that if it wasn't for me, these men wouldn't have to die.' His words tumbled over each other.

'I wish there were something I could do to stop it,' I told him. 'But, Paul, they're adults, and they know full well what they're doing. I don't want you to feel responsible for anything that happens to them, please?' I saw that my words had no effect on him, so I took his face in my hands. Looking into his eyes, I said clearly, 'It is *not* your fault. Do you understand me?'

He nodded, his cheeks, wet with tears.

Someone tugged on my arm and I turned. A druid stared at me. His beard sparkled with snow crystals, and he held a sharp knife made of gold. 'We must end his power now,' he said.

I blessed the sacred grove, the altar, and the knife. Then we spoke the ritual words from the Chants for Persephone.

Anoramix stood before me, a slight smile on his face as he recited the chant.

' *"I come from a virtuous people, O Queen of Hades, for I believe I belong to your kind. But destiny struck me down. I broke free from the circle of pain and sorrow and leapt lightly toward my chosen crown. I take refuge in the arms of the Lady, Queen of Hades.".'*

' *"O blessed one, O fortunate one",'* I said loudly, trying to put my heart into it. ' *"You have become a god from the man you once were.".'*

174

Anoramix looked at me and gave a sweet smile. ' *"Kid, I fell into the milk"*,' he said. Then he embraced me, holding me tightly against his chest. I felt his heart thudding with painful slowness. Mine was pounding madly. He let go of me and stepped away. Two druids caught his wrists and laid him backward on the stone altar.

He didn't take his gaze from mine as they cut his throat. His smile didn't fade. Only his grey eyes became strangely opaque as his life left him in a scarlet fountain.

'Thank the gods!' screamed the watching thousands.

I fainted, thank the gods.

Druids collected the blood and poured it over Paul. I came to when Nearchus picked me up and slung me over his shoulders. Then Alexander wrapped Paul in wolf skins and picked him up.

The crowd fell silent. I could hear my breathing, Paul's sharp sobs, and Cerberus growling at the druids who got too close to the boy.

'I'm awake, put me down,' I whispered.

Nearchus nearly dropped me. 'Sorry, I'm nervous,' he said, setting me on the ground. His hair clung to his brow damply and his eyes were nearly all pupil. His hands shook.

The crowd parted to let us through. I didn't look at the three bodies. I didn't want to faint again. I felt like vomiting and gritted my teeth together.

I saw Selena and tried to speak to her, but she pushed me away. 'Because of you, he's dead,' she spat. 'I didn't get to speak to him in the cave. I could have stopped him. I would have saved him.' Her voice was raw with sorrow, and hatred blazed in her eyes.

I didn't say anything; I knew how she felt. I too had wanted to save the one I loved from certain death.

She turned her back to me and pushed her way through the crowd. Yovanix went to her side, and she buried her head in his chest. I saw her shoulders shaking.

There was a bitter taste in my mouth. Hot tears scalded my cheeks. I bent my head and stumbled after Alexander. He was easy to follow; blood dripped from the bundle in his arms and stained the snow. In the torchlight, the blood was black.

When we reached the druid's cave, Alexander put Paul in front of the fire and unwrapped him. The stench of blood was overpowering. I ran, retching, from the cave. I fell on my hands and knees outside and threw up in the snow. The wine I'd drunk was making me sick. I already had a hangover from the stuff. My stomach heaved and I vomited again. The snow was cold, but it felt wonderful against my hot forehead. I rubbed it over my face and felt better. My head spun, but I was upright and my stomach was empty now. I took a deep breath and went back into the cave.

Paul was mostly clean. Alexander had filled a caldron with hot water, and he'd sat Paul in it. I was brought to mind the cartoons I'd seen of explorers in a cannibal's soup pot. My laughter died in my throat. Alexander was staring at me with the strangest expression.

Then Alexander turned back to Paul and started washing the sticky blood from his hair. Axiom was sitting nearby. In his hands were clean and dry clothes for Paul. He glanced at me, then quickly looked away. He too had given me an odd look. I looked down at myself. I felt my cheeks flame. 'Damn,' I said in surprise.

I had left my tunic in the cavern. I wore my woollen cloak, and nothing else. Ribbons of blood, splashes of mud, melted snow, and deep scratches covered me. And on my left breast, a lovebite was clearly visible. I frowned. This would not do. I turned and left the cave. The cold was biting; dawn was just beginning to grey the sky. I went to the river to bathe. Too bad if I froze to death. I wasn't sure I'd feel anything anyway. I was numb, in body and mind.

The crowd hadn't left. Rather they seemed to be having a picnic. They were eating something. I went closer to have a look. They were eating raw meat. The bodies were gone, but their whitish-pink bones were starting to appear on the stone altar. The sacrificed men were being devoured. The druids were making quite a show of cutting them up into tiny pieces and passing the bits around on a golden plate.

The people lined up as if going to Communion. *"This is my body ..."* The Orphics were eating their sacrificial victims. I fainted for the second time that evening.

Chapter Twenty-five

I didn't wake up until the following morning. I was lying next to the fireplace. It was warm near the embers. I sat and looked around. Cerberus slept curled next to me, his back pressed against mine, his head on Paul's legs. I searched for Alexander but didn't see him. With a groan, I struggled out of the furs and got stiffly to my feet. My mouth felt like something had died in it during the night, and I was filthy. Blood stuck my fingers together. With strange detachment I pulled them apart, rubbing the little black flakes of dried blood off my hands as I walked outside.

The snow was nearly all trampled away by the night's festivities. Most people had left, but a few remained. They were now packing their belongings and getting ready to leave. Spirals of smoke from campfires looked like blue tissue-paper streamers reaching for the sky. The snow had been turned to muddy slush on the paths. I walked down to the river's edge and stripped off my dirty cloak. I looked at the blood caked on it, then I tossed it into the river and watched as the swift water took it away. I shivered.

'That was a strange thing to do.' Alexander looked at me from across the river, where he'd been standing beneath the trees.

'I don't want it any more. It was covered in blood.'

'So was Paul, but I washed it off.'

I didn't smile. There was nothing to smile about. I was tired and unhappy. My stomach hurt, my head ached, and I didn't know what I felt any more. Alexander walked over the bridge and took my hand.

'I'll help you bathe,' he said softly. I just nodded.

There was a crude bathhouse near the stream. In it stood a tub of hot water. Alexander had anticipated my every move. I climbed in. When I'd washed my skin and hair, I took a small birch twig and brushed my teeth. Then I dressed in the clean clothes he'd brought for me.

Alexander had been silent, sitting in the corner, but now he spoke in an odd voice. 'What did you do last night in the cave?'

My hands, I saw, were steady now. I held them out in front of me and frowned. Then I let them fall to my sides, and said, 'what do you think happened?'

'I would prefer you to tell me.' He spoke evenly. There was nothing in his voice to hint at what he felt.

I started to laugh. It was a low laugh that shook me. An embarrassed laugh, because I was not proud of myself. 'I'll tell you what happened,' I said, wiping tears out of my eyes. The laughter had turned sour suddenly. 'I got drunk on the ceremonial wine, and I made love with the Roman's wife. I didn't want anyone to die, and a man was killed in front of me while looking straight at me with a smile on his face. And then they ate him.'

'What?' Alexander sounded shocked. I didn't know what he was 'what-ing' about. The fact I made love to a

179

woman, the fact Anoramix smiled at me, or that he'd been eaten.

'What "what"?' I asked crossly.

'They *ate* him?'

'Didn't you know?' I said tiredly. 'Where did you find me last night? I remember going to rinse off, seeing them eating the raw meat, then I woke up next to Cerberus. Where were you?' My tears were falling faster now. I brushed them away. 'I needed you yesterday, and you were nowhere to be found. I looked and looked. I wish …' I stopped, hot blood flooded to my cheeks. 'I'm sorry. I apologize. It wasn't your fault. I lost control of myself. I'm ashamed.'

'You wish what?' his voice sounded odd too.

'I wish we could have avoided all this. It seems to have changed so many things. My perception of death, of love, of fear.' I started to tremble, so I shut my eyes tightly. 'I'm afraid that nothing will ever be the same, and I was so happy before all this. Tell me, Alex, do you still love me? Are you shocked about my making love to Selena? Tell me the truth, I can face it.' I turned to him and opened my eyes.

His face was still. But a curl at the edge of his mouth betrayed a smile. 'I love you still. I will always love you. Didn't you tell me one day that love was not something that could be given and taken away like a treat?'

'You remember everything,' I said, shaking my head in wonder.

'Well, except the day Barsine knocked me unconscious.' His smile grew. He looked down at his feet then back up at me, his parti-coloured eyes half-serious, half-mocking. 'I was hurt. You know how jealous I get. When I saw you with Anoramix, I was sure that you'd made love to him.'

'Would you have forgiven me?' I asked.

'I don't know. I was ready to hear you tell me about it. I was even ready to try to forget. I wasn't sure how I would react. I think I love you too much. I'm not shocked. You were drunk on ceremonial wine, shattered with nerves, and frightened for Paul.' He tilted his head. 'Will it happen again?'

'No. What about Nearchus?' I asked. As long as we were getting everything out in the open.

He blinked. 'Oh.'

'Oh,' I agreed. 'I know where you were last night.'

Two red spots appeared on his cheeks.

'Did you do it for revenge?' I asked, curious.

'Actually, I drank the wine too.' His laugh was brief.

'I wish I'd found you before I'd gone in that cave. I think I'd feel better this morning. Selena won't want to see me again. She loved Anoramix, did you know? They were lovers; the babe is his. She wanted to save him last night, and that's why she went into the cave.' My smile was wry. 'I've seen Nearchus watching for his chance for ten years now. Are you in love with him?'

'I was, once. Last night Nearchus held me anchored to the earth. I needed you, but you were gone. I didn't know where to search.'

'I must have been in that dreadful cave. At least you found me when I fainted,' I said.

'It wasn't I who found you, nor Nearchus. It must have been Axiom. He looked after Paul as well. I think we're lucky to have him.'

'We're lucky to have each other,' I said.

'Nearchus is afraid you'll be angry.'

'Do you want me to act angry? Will it make it easier?'

'Easier?' His laughter was warm now. I felt his relief washing over me. My own body suddenly relaxed. The knots in my neck and belly dissolved.

I smiled and shook my head. 'No, forget what I said. I'll talk to Nearchus. It's a conversation long overdue. We've known each other too long to walk on eggs around each other.'

'"Walk on eggs"? What kind of ceremony is that? Do you do that in your time when you speak to someone?'

'Only if the conversation promises to be exceedingly difficult.' I stepped toward him, and he met me halfway. His body fit into mine, and I sighed. I felt the familiar flat muscles and bones beneath my hands, the strong neck to bury my face in, with the pulse beating in the base of his throat. I smiled. 'I feel like I've come home,' I whispered.

We stayed for three days in the druid's forest. We had to wait until the replacement druid came. He was an older man, with a long beard and unbleached woollen robes. He looked exactly how I imagined a druid would; he carried a large woven basket over his shoulder, and a golden sickle in his right hand. In his left hand was a long staff, and a hound dog trotted at his side, tongue lolling. The dog pulled a travois with the rest of the druid's luggage on it.

182

Paul immediately set about making a harness for Cerberus, which took his mind off the ceremony and kept him busy for the rest of the time we were there. He woke up screaming every night now. Between Paul's nightmares and my cold – I had a fever and chills from walking through the snow barefoot – I couldn't get any sleep. The new druid took one look at me and cooked up a steaming hot potion. The drink smelled like lemons and spice and made me sleep nearly a whole day, but when I woke up, I felt much better.

The cave needed to be cleared out. Anoramix's things were sorted into two piles: the things the druid wanted to keep and those he was throwing away. We all worked hard. We knew that we'd be able to leave once everything was organized, and none of us wanted to stay a moment longer.

Around noon on the second day, a horse and wagon pulled up. In it were Selena and Yovanix.

I looked up from my work and felt my cheeks burn. I wanted to run and hide at the back of the cave. I thought that facing the doorway of skulls would be easier than seeing Selena. Yovanix helped her out of the wagon. She stood for a minute in the mud, then straightened her shoulders and started toward the cave.

Cerberus saw them coming and barked, but his tail was wagging so hard his hind legs kept slipping out from under him. He bounded happily toward Yovanix, skidded to a halt, then jumped up and planted muddy feet on his chest. 'Greetings,' said Yovanix, staggering. He cleared his throat. 'We've come to see you, My Lady.' He'd shaved off his moustache and now looked about seventeen.

I sighed and put down the clothes I'd been folding. I'd folded one shirt eight times since Selena had arrived, and it still looked like a crumpled rag. I stood and wiped my hands on my tunic, then nodded toward the hearth. 'Come in, get warm. Will you have a bowl of soup?'

'Yes, please.' Selena wouldn't look at me. She and her brother stood awkwardly in the doorway.

I was glad when Axiom came to my rescue, taking their cloaks. I hastily found two clean bowls and filled them with the broth that was always simmering in the iron soup pot in the wintertime. My hands were shaking badly, but I managed to serve the soup and not spill any.

Alexander came over and sat next to me and put his arm around my shoulders. It made me feel better. I hadn't had time to talk to anyone so far. Neither to Paul, who was still as pale as chalk, nor to Nearchus, who avoided looking at me as assiduously as I was avoiding looking at Selena.

The whole situation was getting uncomfortable and out of hand. Something had to be done. I took a few minutes to talk sternly to myself. Strangely enough, whenever I did this, it was my mother's voice I heard. *'Ashley! Sit up straight! Get hold of yourself! Stop snivelling! Stop running away from your problems! You'll never get anywhere, mark my words. You always get into the worst trouble. What am I going to do with you? You're such a failure!'* My mother's voice had always grated in my ears.

Yet, as cold and unfriendly as her voice was, her eyes had been worse. Mine were warm and inviting compared to hers. A journalist had once written about her in these terms:

184

"Mrs. Vladimir de Fontanov went to the charity ball wearing a floor-length gown made of pure-white silk, a tiara with five hundred carats of diamonds, and a platinum and aquamarine necklace. She looked as if she'd just stepped out of a freezer, and if she had, it probably warmed up after she left!"

My mother called her old friend, the owner of the newspaper, and had the journalist sacrificed on her own personal altar. She despised journalists even more than she scorned rock stars, drug addicts, homosexuals and failures. She was sure I was going to turn out to be a failure, no matter what I did, so she married me to an older, brutal man when I was barely out of childhood. My childhood had been miserable, my marriage a torture. But the thought that my mother was three thousand years away from even being conceived, calmed me. I had *not* turned into a failure. I *had* become a journalist. I would get over this.

When the soup was done, and some colour had come back into their cheeks, Selena and Yovanix put their bowls down and turned to me.

'We have come to ask a favour of you, My Lady,' said Selena, studying her hands.

'Selena?' I wished my voice were stronger. I frowned and tried again. 'Selena, please look at me. I'm glad you came, I wanted to speak to you.'

Now her cheeks were flaming. 'I'm sorry I was angry with you that night,' she said.

'I know how you felt,' I told her. 'I'm sorry too. But not about everything. What happened between us was an accident, but I don't regret it.'

She glanced at me quickly. My expression must have surprised her, because her eyes lingered. I thought for a second she would smile, but her sorrow was too great. 'I know not what you mean,' she said curtly. 'I have come because I want you to take my brother, Yovanix, with you. I bought him from my husband last night. Here are the papers proving it. I will give them to you.' She handed me a small parchment, carefully rolled and tied, and then she got to her feet. 'I must leave now. I return to my husband and our farm. Do as you wish with Yovanix; he's honest and a hard worker.'

'And, he's your brother,' I said. 'Would you like to say goodbye in private?'

'We said our goodbyes in the wagon, on our way here. Nevertheless, one last thing I would tell you. The Celts have a legend about the Thief of Souls. I heard a story about Voltarrix, the blond druid with the horned helmet. They say he steals souls. If it is true, you must be very careful.'

When she left, she didn't turn around, but her shoulders shook. I thought I knew why. Yovanix sat as still as he possibly could and watched her leave. His mouth was set in a thin line, his eyes bleak. When the wagon disappeared around the bend, he jerked once, then he was still again. The stillness of a slave in the shadows. I sat there, trying to make sense of her last words, then I sighed and looked at Yovanix.

'What are the formalities for freeing a slave here in Gaul?' I asked. Having already seen the amount of official documents that were needed just to enter Massalia, I feared the worst. Yovanix simply shrugged.

'There are no formalities. You take off my slave bracelet. I am freed.' He held out his leg and we saw the thick bronze circlet on his ankle.

Alexander nodded once, sharply. Axiom took a hammer and a chisel and cut the bracelet off. I tossed the parchment into the fire and we watched it burn. No one spoke.

I went back to packing. Axiom and Paul disappeared into the storeroom, and Nearchus left the cave to fetch firewood. The new druid went to his caldron and stirred it. A sharp, minty smell floated in the air. On the fire were three large iron pots. One held steaming water, one had soup, and one held the druid's 'potion of the day'; some sort of cold remedy, from what I gathered. He was getting ready to strain it through cheesecloth and take it to the nearest village. Yovanix rose uncertainly and went to help the druid. His arms were strong and he easily tilted the caldron while the druid held a bucket underneath it. The druid's beard kept slipping out of his belt and dipping into the bucket. I made a mental note not to let him stir the soup.

After helping the druid, Yovanix stood nearby, hands dangling at his sides, looking forlorn. He kept glancing at me. I didn't want to be rude, but I didn't want to take him with us. I was uncomfortably reminded of Selena each time I saw him. Maybe the druid would like to keep him around to help.

I sighed and tucked the last shirt into the bag I was packing. I'd taken an hour to do a chore that should have taken me ten minutes. We had next to nothing in the clothing department. It was my nerves, I decided. I was still frazzled by the fact I'd gotten drunk and seduced a woman. I put my face in my hands and tried very hard to think of something else. Thinking about the night of the sacrifice made me feel ill. I wished I could either accept what I'd done or forget about it. I dug my fingers into my scalp and squeezed my eyes shut. Why couldn't I? Because … because, if I were honest with myself – and I was always honest with myself – I'd admit that the mere thought of that night was enough to make my knees get weak and my nipples stand at attention while a heat I was ashamed of grew in my belly.

I raised my head and saw Yovanix staring at me. With a muffled curse, I got to my feet and ran out of the cave. I took the path leading to the river where smoke from the chimney in the bathhouse told me that there was hot water waiting. I would have bathed in ice-cold water at that point, though. Anything to wash off my shame and sorrow. I'd been unfaithful to Alexander. That's all I could think about.

I bathed until my skin was so wrinkled I looked like *I* needed ironing. Then I climbed out of the tub and slowly dried off. I thought of our voyages. I missed travelling with the army. And taking a bath surrounded with twenty or so soldiers in peak physical condition. I would lie back in the tub, my hands straying to my nether regions, as I watched them slather their bodies with clay and then rinse off. Sometimes helping each other. My heart fluttered, and I tilted my head back, considering. Was what I'd done any different, finally? Was it simply a question of lust, and nothing else? Perhaps I was making too big a deal about the whole thing. I squeezed the water out of my hair and leaned nearer the fire to dry it.

My thoughts kept going back to the difference between love and lust. I was not a philosopher. I didn't have an answer for everything. Was lust so bad? Why did it make me feel, well, so dirty? My fingers twisted in my hair, braiding it. Maybe if Selena hadn't looked at me with such hatred, I would have felt better. I was surprised to find tears trickling down my cheeks. I looked up at the hole in the ceiling where the smoke was leaving in a thin spiral. Some questions simply had no answers; I would never understand what happened that night, or why I felt so badly about it. The thing was, I eventually learned to live with it.

However, it was a sobering lesson. How could Alexander come to terms with what *he'd* done? All I'd done was make love to someone who had no feelings for me, and whom I didn't love. Alexander had been seduced by his own mother, he'd killed his best friend, and maybe he'd had a hand in his father's murder. His nightmares took on a new, more profound meaning for me. Was it really his soul that was missing? Or was it something more sinister? Was it because he could never live with what he'd done? Would his melancholy madness come back and this time destroy him? He was like a fabulous gemstone with a flaw. He had a fissure that could shatter him.

I finished braiding my hair and walked slowly back to the cave. Night had fallen. I looked up at the stars. I hoped that we would find what we were seeking in the land of ice and snow, where the sun never rose and never set, and where the Eaters of the Dead gnawed on the bones of their sacrificial victims. Where the Thief of Souls waited for us.

Chapter Twenty-six

Yovanix joined our group. The men decided that an extra pair of strong arms could be useful in case of an attack or simply to help push our cart out of a deep mud puddle, which is what happened often between the druid's sacred forest and the city called Lutetia.

The road was winding, muddy, snowy, and windy. We were wet, cold, and miserable. Rain came down in sheets, washing away the snow and most of the road. We were soaked through by noon, and didn't find a settlement before night fell. We were pathetically glad to reach the cheerless huddle of huts and barns that marked the edge of a village. Once on the main street, we realized that the village was a large, prosperous one, and we found good lodgings.

There was an inn, and a real stable for the horses. The inn had two bedrooms free, and a huge fire roaring in the dining room. We changed into dry clothes and ate a rich pork stew.

The Gauls' staple food was pork and pork products; salt pork, bacon, smoked ham, salami, sausage, pâté, pickled pig's feet, ears, and anything else you can think of starting with 'pig'. I was surprised that Axiom ate the meat. As a Jew, he was supposed to shun pork. But he only shrugged and said, 'When in Gaul, eat like the Gauls do, or starve.' He had a point.

Axiom, Paul, and Yovanix shared one room. Alexander, Nearchus, and I shared the other.

I think Nearchus was startled when Alexander organized the rooms, but after a quick glance in my direction, his face became carefully blank. I hadn't had a moment alone with him to talk, and I wondered, too, what Alexander wanted. He never did anything without carefully thinking through all the consequences.

Alexander left us alone together while he went to bathe. I sat on the bed and unbraided my hair, brushing it slowly while I tried to think of something to say. Nearchus walked around the small room, tapped on the shutters, held his hands toward the fire, then sat on the low stool in front of the fireplace.

'My Lady,' he said, 'Iskander has left us here together, so obviously he wants us to speak. But I am at a loss for words.'

'Me too.' I admitted. 'Alexander told me that you and he spent the night of the sacrifice together, maybe he wanted you to tell me about that.'

'Oh. He told you?' A blush spread to his cheeks.

'I know you've loved him for years,' I said. 'In the beginning I was more jealous of you than of Plexis.'

'Do you mind?' He looked curious.

'No, I love him, so I can easily imagine anyone else loving him.' I said. 'I believe that love is something that can be shared. However, I don't think sex has any part in real love. I learned that lesson the hard way.'

192

He spread his hands. 'I have no claim on him. He is your husband. But I do love him.'

'I know. That's why I don't mind.' I frowned and looked at my hands. 'At least, I don't *think* I mind.'

He looked startled. 'Plexis and I often spoke of you,' he said slowly. 'In the beginning, when I thought you were the goddess, I understood you more than I do now. Plexis never pretended to understand you. He simply let himself go, he told me, like a feather in the wind, and the wind took him to you. But I have always followed Iskander, and I will follow him to the ends of the earth.'

'Nearchus, I'm glad for Alexander that he has a friend as faithful as you.'

'Plexis used to say that we were in love with the sun god,' he said sadly.

'And the sun gives his warmth equally to everyone,' I agreed. 'Plexis was right in some ways, but wrong in others. The sun has no need for us, but Alexander does. He needs us very much.'

'We will always be here for him, won't we?' Nearchus said. 'At least, if you want.'

'I do,' I said firmly.

'There is a saying from Crete. It goes, "what woman wants, the gods want". I'm beginning to see that it is true.'

'Aren't you glad it is?' I finished combing my hair and I left it loose on my shoulders. We were silent as the fire crackled in the hearth. The rain battered the window. I loved hearing the sound of it. It made me feel even more warm and cosy. I snuggled into the covers and blinked drowsily. The bed was soft and warm. In a minute I would fall asleep. However, before I did, I had to do something. I shrugged off my tunic and motioned for Nearchus to join me. He hesitated, then slid into the bed. His body was long-muscled and tall. He had no desire for me. And I had none for him. I'd learned my lesson well. I kissed him once, on the lips, then I turned over and went to sleep. When Alexander came back into the room I didn't wake up, and nothing woke me until morning.

There was a patch of milky light on Alexander's cheekbone. It made his skin look nearly white. His forehead was touching my shoulder, and his legs were thrown over mine. Nearchus was sleeping on the far side of the bed, on his back with his left arm trailing over the side. His head was turned toward Alexander, his hair spilling onto his shoulder. In sleep, their hands were touching.

The sun had just risen. There were quiet, early morning noises coming from downstairs, telling me that the innkeeper was awake and lighting the fires in the kitchen and the great hearth in the dining room. We were in a modern village; the Romans had left their stamp on the architecture already. There was a real bath.

I eased out of bed without waking anyone and grabbed my toiletries. I would bathe and dress, then I would go shopping in the village. I needed a new cloak.

I took a nice long bath. The innkeeper's wife had soap that smelled like roses. I asked her for the recipe, and she told me where I could buy some in the village. My spirits were lifting as I dried my hair and dressed.

I went back to the room to get money. As quietly as I could, I opened the door. Nearchus and Alexander were not sleeping. I quickly backed out and shut the door. I waited a few minutes. Then I knocked. This time I waited until I heard a muffled 'come in'. Two flushed faces stared at me from the depths of the bed. I cleared my throat. I had thought I wouldn't be jealous, but seeing my husband in someone else's arms was a shock. 'I need money for a new cloak,' I explained.

'I'll get it for you.' Alexander said. He started out of bed, before realizing the state he was in. Now my face was flushed as well. I went to the small box where we kept our coins and fumbled it open. I took what I thought was enough and left hurriedly. Once outside, I leaned against the door and took some deep breaths. My brain was jealous, but my body was betraying me. Alexander aroused was like an electric shock. I closed my eyes. My legs were trembling.

From inside the room came the slow, telltale creak of the bed and the soft moans and cries I knew so well. I felt as if someone were driving a knife into my stomach. I ran down the stairs. The cold air outside was a welcome relief. I wandered about blindly for nearly an hour. I didn't know where I was going; I'd forgotten everything, the soap, the cape, shopping. All I could think of was the feeling of bitter disappointment. I didn't mind when he made love to Plexis, because Plexis and I made love. But Nearchus loved only Alexander. I was shut out of their relationship, and it hurt.

I had never been jealous of his other wives. He'd made it clear they didn't mean anything to him, and I'd actually liked Barsine very much. However, I was confused about Alexander and Nearchus. Confused, and maybe a little angry. Angry with myself, first, for not knowing how to handle the situation, and angry with Nearchus who had thrown himself at Alexander the first chance he got. Finally, I admitted sadly to myself, I was angry with Alexander.

I found the shop selling soap. I bought a few bars and some perfume, but my heart wasn't in it. I should have been ecstatic. Real shampoo at last. But I simply let the woman marvel over my hair and sell me what she wanted, then I went to search for a warm cloak.

I found what I needed. It cost eighteen silver sesterces. Gallic coins were minted by the tribes – each had its own money, but all coins were called sesterces. Gold ones were beautifully worked and came from Lutetia, minted by the Parisii. They were a rich and powerful, and I was eager to see their city. I'd known Paris well, three thousand years in the future, but I didn't think I'd recognize it now: no baguettes, berets, or swearing taxi drivers.

I was feeling no better by the time I got back to the inn. Everyone was having breakfast. I hugged Paul and asked if he'd slept well. His cheeks had more colour this morning, and he gave me a real smile. I was glad to see his appetite had returned; his plate was nearly empty. Alexander and Nearchus were sitting in front of plates full of sausage and eggs. Axiom was eating porridge.

Yovanix was sitting at the very end of the table. He still looked as if he wanted very much to be invisible.

I nodded politely to everyone and went back upstairs. I wanted to be alone for a while.

I put the new soaps and perfume in my bag and made sure everything was packed and ready for us to leave. I lay down and buried my face in the pillow. If only time could

196

go backward. *Ha!* That thought made me give a strangled scream. Time could only go backward from the future. I was stuck here, in a time not my own, with people I'd grown to love, but didn't understand.

Alexander had grown up with *The Iliad*, where Achilles and Patroclus share a bed with two women – I bet you'll want to read it more carefully now, huh? He'd been seduced by his own mother who was an adept in bacchanal orgies, and he took his pleasure wherever and however he felt like it. It suited him, although it wasn't a perfect example of these times either. In these times, women were supposed to remain faithful, but men could have harems.

'What is the matter?' Alexander came into the room and sat on the bed with me.

I opened my eyes and sighed. 'I'm jealous of you and Nearchus.'

'Oh?' His eyes widened. 'Then I will not sleep with him again.' He shrugged.

I narrowed my eyes. 'Are you serious?'

'Yes.'

'But, but …' I sat up. 'Don't you love him?'

'Yes, but not the way I love you. He's been begging me for years to make love with him. We did. He should be happy now, for a few more years at least.' He shrugged.

'Will his feelings be hurt?'

Alexander spread his hands. 'I doubt it. He will do as he likes, I do as I like, and you do as you like. Isn't that how it's always been with us?'

'Yes, but now I'm afraid.'

Alexander looked at me sadly. 'So am I,' he admitted.

'Why are *you* afraid?' I was confused.

'Because I feel the wind in my bones. There is something about you I don't understand. I can tell when you go back to your own time. It is so different from mine that the very air around you changes. Your voice changes, your face, your words. It makes me afraid. Afraid that you will never accept living, here and now, with me, and that somehow you'll find a way to return to your own time.'

'Even if I had the chance now, I wouldn't take it. I won't leave you, Alexander, unless you ask me to.'

Alexander turned to face me. 'If you are afraid I will leave you for Nearchus, you are wrong,' he said.

I blushed. When he said it aloud like that it *did* sound silly. 'I'm sorry,' I whispered. 'I never wanted to ask anything of you.'

Alexander smiled then. His eyes softened. 'I know. I know that. You are like a man I once knew in Macedonia. He was considered very strange by the people in the village.'

I bristled. 'Oh, thanks a lot, you're making me feel better already.'

'No, let me finish. He had a herd of horses. His horses were the most beautiful in the kingdom. The horse he loved the most was a pure white mare. Everyone wanted her, but he never sold her. It made the people around him crazy, because not only did he never sell her, he never even rode her. He never put a bridle on her or touched her in any way. He left her free. He would climb into the high meadows and watch her for hours, but he never tried to own her. That's what your love has always been for me. You left me my freedom, all the while loving me.' His smile was blinding. 'O, Ashley of the Sacred Sandals, of all the people I have ever known or loved, only Plexis and you love me for myself, and not for what I am. Now, kiss me and tell me you love me. Don't be afraid of anyone else.'

'The same goes for you,' I said shakily, when I could speak again. His kisses were as sweet and slow as honey.

'I feel like making another little baby.' His voice was almost teasing. 'I miss Cleopatra so much that my heart aches some days.'

I giggled and swatted his hand away. 'No, not now. I don't want to get as fat as a hippo right now; I want to make a good impression on my ancestors.'

'Well,' he said philosophically, 'I'll just have to assuage my needs with Nearchus. He won't be having babies.'

'In my time men *can* have babies,' I told him.

His eyes widened. 'Really? By Zeus and Aphrodite, that sounds so strange.'

'It seemed natural to me. The babies are born in artificial wombs. A real pregnancy and birth are rare. That's why my mother didn't realize she was pregnant until I was nearly ready to be born. Although it's a good thing she didn't realize it, or she would have aborted me.' My voice was forlorn.

Alexander shook my shoulders. 'Come back from the future,' he ordered me. 'Stay here, with me. My world is yours now. You have my love, for what it's worth; Paul, Chiron, Cleopatra, and Plexis are all yours.'

'Mine too are the blisters from walking, the sore butt from riding, the itching lice and the biting fleas. Mine is the cold that freezes and the lye soap that burns.'

'It's not all bad, is it?' he asked worriedly.

'Mine are the nights spent in my lover's arms beneath a starry sky, with his voice whispering in my ear telling me all the wonders of the universe. Mine are the ancient cities that were buried beneath the dust for centuries, and that I saw as new and shining bright. The blue, gold, and green enamelled walls of Babylon were mine to behold, as was the new city of Alexandria in all her white and gold splendour. I saw lovely Ecbatana with its silver roofs and rose-coloured bricks. Mine too the lazy days spent swimming in the Euphrates with the date palms casting blue shade over curly-haired goats. The snow-covered mountains of the Himalayas and the mightiest river in Asia, the Indus, were mine. I slept with you in the palace of a rajah with the steaming jungle looking in. I held you in the desert sands, on a storm-tossed sea – with you seasick and an interesting shade of green, by the way – on an island surrounded by a night-time sea glowing with phosphorescence, and in a sacred oasis. Each time you took me in your arms, my heart sang with joy. All *that* is mine, Alexander. *You* gave it to me.'

He started crying. He cried easily. His emotions were so strong they often overwhelmed him. I took him in my arms again and crooned into his ear, telling him all the reasons why I loved him, and why I would never leave him. After ten years I had so many reasons I could hardly remember them all but, if you love your husband, I think it's important to tell him these things now and then. He rewarded me in his own way, and we didn't leave the bed until dinnertime made our stomachs growl like impatient lions.

Nearchus never slept with us again. He went back to being Alexander's faithful admiral. A serious, canny-eyed man of above-average height with hair as blond as dark wheat. He polished his helmet, and taught Paul how to use the stars to navigate. He sat next to Alexander, but his hands never strayed toward him. His eyes still held the love they'd always held.

Alexander was the sun blazing in Nearchus's sky. But I was no longer the small dark cloud on the horizon. Nearchus thought of me now as a friend, and our relationship became easier. He even asked me to play chess with him sometimes, real proof that he liked me. He was a consummate chess player, and I was only mediocre, at best. Playing with me must have been a bore. Usually he played chess with Axiom. Usse had been more on his level, but Axiom could sometimes surprise him.

Axiom was a quiet man. Years of slavery had made him incapable of sitting still and relaxing. He always had something to do and if he wasn't working he was praying. Alexander had freed him ten years ago. He was free to go where he pleased. Alexander had given him gold for each year of service. I knew he had a large amount in a bank in Alexandria. Plexis and I had gone with him to open his account.

Sometimes, I wondered why he followed Alexander still, when he could have stayed in Alexandria, or gone anywhere he wanted. I never asked him. I had been raised in a society where personal questions were considered as rude as a slap in the face. No wonder my mother hated journalists. No wonder I had trouble relating to people who laughed when they saw someone trip, or cried when they heard a sad story.

Axiom and Nearchus were my friends, but there was still a wall between us, and they felt it. They had learned to respect it, though. It hurt them no longer. Where they might reach across the table, grasp each other by the wrist and even kiss each other fondly, to me they limited their show of affection to a sideways glance, a quirk of the lips, or a touch as light as a feather on the shoulder. Even that sometimes made me jump. Three thousand years is a formidable barrier.

Only Alexander had reached across the immense gulf of time that separated us. Was that the secret of his timelessness? The gift that made men wonder about him and create legends and stories about him three thousand years after his death?

I caught him looking at me and blushed. He smiled, and in that smile I saw all the ambiguity of his character written in his face. He sipped his beer, not taking his eyes off me, looking supremely sure of himself. At a word from Nearchus he put his beer down and turned away, but his hand crept onto my thigh under the table, and I smiled.

Chapter Twenty-seven

I wondered why no one ever recognized him. His picture had been painted a hundred times, his profile was on coins, and his likeness was everywhere; on statues, plates, even mugs. Nearly two years later, people were still talking about his death. But no one had ever pointed at him and cried out, 'Why! It's Iskander of Macedonia! As I live and breathe! By Hades! How did you escape the underworld?'

The voice boomed across the room, startling everyone.

I spilled my beer onto my plate and gaped up at the mountain of a man who was striding over to us.

'Iskander! By Zeus and Hades! Don't you recognize me? Say something! You remember me, don't you?'

'By all the gods,' breathed Alexander, putting his beer down very carefully. 'Is it you? Is it really you?'

'Afraid so.' The man spread his hands out in front of him almost apologetically.

'But, I thought you were dead?' The question hung in the air, rather comically.

'Well, I thought the same for you. Perhaps this is Hades' underworld, and all that I've believed for twelve years is just dust.'

'Has it been twelve years already?' Alexander shook his head.

'Time is a strange thing,' said the man.

'More than you'll ever know,' murmured Alexander. He took a deep breath. 'You never met Nearchus. He is, no, *was* my admiral. This is my lady wife, Ashley. This is Axiom, and this is my son Paul. And this is Yovanix.' He added. Yovanix blushed. 'Everyone, this is Charidemus.'

The man bowed. I raised my eyebrows. *Charidemus*? The name sounded familiar, but I'd never seen him before.

'What have you been doing?' asked Alexander, making room for him between us. I shifted over obligingly. The man sat down slowly, like old warriors tend to do when half their bones have been broken and limbs bend with some resistance. He appeared to be around forty-five, give or take a decade. It was hard to tell. His hair was long and brown, with silver streaks. His face was clean-shaven. He had dark eyes, pale skin, and a nose that had been broken too many times to tell what shape it had been to start with. His size was his most obvious feature. He towered over all of us, even Nearchus, and he would have made Millis seem slight. He saw me staring at him and grinned. His teeth were mostly all there, but the ones that were missing had been replaced with gold.

'Don't you mean how did I manage not to be killed by Darius?' he chuckled. 'He condemned me to death, but I managed to escape. I had one or two friends in the prison. Then I travelled. I went to Carthage, to Iberia, and then started trading with the Gauls. It's a good life. I miss Athens, but I go back now and then. What about you? It seems impossible to see you here, but I suppose there is an explanation. Would you give it to me? Why did you abandon your new kingdom?' He cocked his head. 'No, don't answer that one. I lived with Darius; I know what it must have been like. You weren't made to be divine, were you?' he chortled. 'The news came regularly. I was in and out of Athens during your campaign against Bessus, and then when you went to India and came home again. I heard Demosthenes ranting in the market place that you'd set yourself up as a god.'

'I'm sure that's not all you heard,' said Alexander quietly.

'To be sure it wasn't. I nearly went to join you at least a dozen times. But I thought you wouldn't want me.'

'It's a good thing for me that Darius didn't want you. You and Memnon were perhaps the only two who could have defeated me in the beginning.'

'The gods decided otherwise, didn't they? At least they didn't make me sicken and die like poor Memnon. What a general he was, eh? The best tactician the Persian army ever had. If Darius had listened to me, and taken up Memnon's plans, you would have been finished before you'd even started.'

'But he didn't, did he? He had you executed.'

'Darius always was a fool,' said Charidemus thoughtfully.

'I've heard that before,' Alexander said. 'But I loved him, silly fool that he was. I would have saved him from that traitor Bessus.'

'I know you would have.' Charidemus put his arm around Alexander's shoulders, nearly hiding him. 'So, tell me, what brings you to this place? Granted it is a nice village, as villages go. But you're used to cities, and to opulence.'

'I'm used to everything by now,' Alexander said. His voice was growing stronger. He looked up at the man and grinned. 'By the gods, Charidemus, it is good to see you.'

'Call me Demos, everyone here does.'

'They don't really. They probably call you something like Charidemus-big-guy-vix.'

He grinned back. 'Probably, but not you. Ah, Iskander, so many years. I never thought to see you again or that it would be like this. I thought I would be begging for my life at your feet. A mercenary in front of a king. And I would have begged, yes, begged to be allowed to fight with you. By Zeus, what an adventure you must have had!' His voice grew dreamy. 'Travelling seems to be in your bones, though, to have brought you all the way to the land of the savage Gaul. Where are you heading?'

'To the land of the Eaters of the Dead,' said Alexander.

There was a silence. We all looked at each other. Charidemus spread his fingers on the table like nine fat sausages – he was missing one – and frowned. He looked at Alexander, then at Nearchus, Axiom, and Yovanix, and he seemed to be weighing each man against the hordes of savages in the far north. Finally he sighed deeply. 'Well, Iskander, it looks as if the gods have put me in your path again, but this time I won't ignore them. I missed my chance before; I won't let it go by again. If you'll have me with you, I'll come. I have a few more grey hairs, and it takes a few more minutes for me to get up in the morning, but I can still wield a sword and lance, by Ares, and against the best I'll still win. I'll stand between you and death. See if I won't.' His voice was gruff, but his words were clear.

Alexander was too choked up to speak, but he managed a smile.

The big man clasped Alexander to his chest and bellowed for another round of beer. Tears as big as raindrops rolled down his cheeks. 'A toast to the adventure!' he cried, and we all raised our auroch horns and drank the honeyed beer.

Our heads were swimming by the end of the evening. We were full of that strange magic that happens when old enemies meet after a lifetime and become fast friends.

The stories went on all night. Alexander and Nearchus told of their adventures, and Demos told of his. He'd travelled to the land of ice and snow, and he'd seen the northern lights. He'd visited Carthage, Rome, and Iberia. He'd searched for Atlantis with pirates, sailed to the Canary Islands, and went as far as Iceland, a place he described like 'Hades on Earth', with volcanoes and icebergs side by side. We listened, our eyes as round as shiny coins.

When the beer slurred the men's words into unintelligible sentences, we shook ourselves awake and crawled upstairs. Axiom picked up a soundly sleeping Paul and carried him to the room he was sharing with Yovanix. Alexander and I made it to the bed, but Nearchus and Demos fell like toppled trees to the floor and snored loudly for the rest of the night.

In the morning, I opened my eyes before anyone else. The light hurt my head. Too much Gallic beer. Those auroch horns held a litre, and I'd drunk at least three. I had to pee so badly, I thought I'd explode. Carefully, I crept out of bed. Nearchus was sleeping rolled up tightly in his cloak next to the fireplace, but Demos was flat on his back, snoring, his arms flung wide, his legs splayed. In the morning light he looked almost harmless, a friendly giant snoozing on the floor. I eased one leg over his and held my breath. I didn't want to wake anyone.

There was a sort of *'whump'* as the air was displaced. Demos rolled over and grabbed my shin, jerking my feet out from under me. I found myself with a knife at my throat and a growing puddle of urine under me. My teeth were chattering. I didn't dare breathe. Then Demos opened his eyes and saw he'd saved Alexander – from me.

He blinked. He looked at me, at the knife, and at the closed door.

'I'm sorry,' he said contritely.

'Me too,' I said heartily. 'Believe me!'

'I usually sleep alone, I forgot where I was,' he explained.

'May I get up now?' I asked. 'Not that there's any more need to hurry.'

'Sorry.' His face became bright red as he realized my predicament.

'If you really want to help, you'll let me up and then mop up the mess before it runs all over. It's heading toward Nearchus now.' I said helpfully. I was past being embarrassed. Demos was embarrassed enough for both of us.

Alexander woke up and looked over the side of the bed at us. His handsome face was marred by a frown. 'Ashley, you should go bathe,' he said finally.

I got up, and with as much dignity as I could salvage, grabbed a towel, my bath things and some clean clothes, and stepped over the puddle.

I left the room before Nearchus woke up. If there were any justice at all, he would think that Demos had done it.

Chapter Twenty-eight

After breakfast, we left the village. We were only three days from Lutetia. I was impatient to get there. Somehow, I guess, I had imagined a city like the ones I'd seen in Mesopotamia. The cities there were more beautiful than any in my own time. Grey cement and stone can't compare to bricks enamelled all the colours of the rainbow and roofs covered in gold, silver, and copper.

We travelled quickly. We had sturdy ponies and carried little baggage. Demos had given a snort of approval when he saw our outfit.

'No tent, no slaves, no maids in waiting. Good idea. Travel light and fast. I like it.'

After three days and three nights of riding and camping, I was glad to arrive in the valley of the Parisii and catch my first glimpse of the future city of Paris, built on an island in the middle of the river Seine.

At first, I was disappointed by Lutetia. It had a hidden charm that wasn't evident. Then I started to see the careful way the city had been laid out to make the most of the river, the island, and the small hills. The bridges were clever, made of stone and wood, and functioned like drawbridges. The island could be easily defended.

That was my husband speaking. Alexander dissected the defences and wondered how long it would have taken him to conquer the Parisii.

I thought about pushing him off the bridge. To make him happy, I told him that he'd have defeated them in three weeks, tops.

'Tops?' He tilted his head and considered. 'Three weeks, maybe four,' he conceded.

We walked over the bridge and went into the main part of the city.

The Parisii were a rich tribe. They were goldsmiths and masons. They did excellent work and were often hired elsewhere, but they always came home with their wages, making the city of Lutetia a prosperous, busy, riverside town.

The women dressed in fine robes of soft wool, and glittered with gold jewellery. They wore make-up, like the Persian women, and lots of perfume. Perfume seemed to be the Parisii's answer to fewer baths, although there were public baths. There was a Roman theatre, Greek baths, Turkish saunas, and a large Roman sports arena. The Parisii were adapting to the changing world.

The first night we were in Lutetia, we saw a play in the open -air theatre. It was a Gallic play, and I'd never seen anything like it. It was mysterious, beautiful, and totally incomprehensible. The music was almost modern. It was heavy on the drums with lots of wailing harps and wind instruments. The beat was fast and heady, and the dancing was fascinating. I couldn't follow the story, which seemed to be about a druid and a woman falling in love, and her being sacrificed, of course. The spectators sobbed loudly.

After the play, we were invited to a banquet by the people sitting next to us. They were very friendly and didn't seem to mind that there were five of us, including one who looked like he could probably eat an entire roasted boar by himself.

At the banquet, a woman asked us where we were travelling. The question came from a red-haired Celtic lass about twenty years old, buxom and freckled, with a hand – that she was about to lose – on Alexander's arm.

'Why to the far north? Are you trading?'

Alexander caught my look and tried to shrug her hand off. 'We are going to search for my soul,' he said. As if that's what he did every year for the summer holidays.

I didn't think she was listening. She'd been flirting with Alexander since we'd arrived at the banquet. She had attached herself to his arm, despite my frosty glances. Now she was practically purring into his ear. 'That sounds so interesting, why don't you tell me more about it in private?'

'Excuse me,' I said. 'He's mine, *sweetie.*'

She looked nonplussed then shrugged and disappeared into the crowd.

Alexander looked at me reproachfully. 'You scared her away.'

I narrowed my eyes. 'You seem to forget you're married, *buster.*'

'Buster?' He looked pained. 'It's when you speak in your future tongue the troubles start. It's as if the gods find it unbearable to their ears. "Sweetie", "buster". The earth should start shaking soon.'

'Alexander, you hate it when men flirt with me. Why should I be any different?'

'I know, I'm sorry.' He leaned back against the wall and took me in his arms. 'The river is very beautiful. It is quite romantic here.' He pointed to our reflections in the water. 'Look at the river, it glides past the island as it goes to the sea. Do you think we should take a boat north? Nearchus and Demos seem to think it would be best to avoid the Peatbog People.'

'Who are they?'

'A strange tribe who make human sacrifices all the time. They throw the victims into the peatbog. They believe the bog is alive, and that it eats the people they give it.'

'Sounds perfectly horrible,' I said. 'We should give it a miss.'

'We can take a boat then?' He sounded suspiciously meek.

'Yes, it's a good idea, why?'

'Well, you've already met the boat captain, so I guess it's settled then.'

'The boat cap …what?' I turned and pointed to the redhead, who was now draped over Nearchus. 'That … that *person* is a boat captain?'

'She's a member of the *nautae Parisiaci*, one of the most successful boatmen corporations in the world. She's got a very nice boat. You should pay more attention to the conversations going on around you at the theatre.'

'I was listening to the music.'

'And dreaming. I saw your eyes, you were in another world.' He laughed softly. His voice gave me goose bumps. He leaned over, kissing me. 'How would you like to leave the banquet early?'

'Where's Paul?' I asked, pushing him away.

'With Axiom. Yovanix and Demos are looking after him, as well. You worry too much. I told you that before, remember?'

'Yes, it was just before you got hit with a catapult, I believe, and spent three days in a coma.'

He took my hand and pulled me out of the doorway and onto the busy street. We walked through the city. It was lovely at night. Shops were still open and dancers and singers performed in the streets. People laughed and talked in silvery voices. The moon hung over our heads in a slender crescent, and the stars seemed to swim in the river. Underfoot, the street was cobbled but clean.

The forest was close. On the hill, where Montmartre would eventually be, vineyards had been newly planted. The Romans had introduced wine, and now the Parisii wanted to try growing grapes. A small herd of sheep bleated softly, and shepherds played music on reed flutes to quiet them. Alexander and I went back to our room at the inn and made love.

We left the window open. That evening, late March in Lutetia, spring blew in from the south.

Chapter Twenty-nine

The same wind filled the sails of the boat we took from Lutetia to the Atlantic Ocean. We sailed down the Seine. The current and the wind combined to make waves curl around the bow of the boat. A small statue at the helm of a boat represented a woman, lying on her side. When I asked, I was told it was Sequana, the goddess of the river Seine. She would protect our boat. I hoped she'd also protect those riding on it.

Paul rushed around getting in everyone's way. Cerberus barked at the people fishing on shore. Nearchus hauled in the sail and grinned. Demos strode around the deck and waved. Yovanix tried to make himself invisible and helpful at the same time. Alexander hung over the side and vomited.

I kept an eye on the boat captain, who seemed absolutely smitten with Alexander.

She was lovely in the daylight too. I wished I'd had more time in Lutetia to go shopping. I would have liked a miniskirt like hers that showed off my legs. Or a lovely sweater knit from green wool. It went with her green eyes.

Or Alexander's green face. After two days of seasickness, he looked awful.

The boat captain's ardour wavered. She started spending more time with Demos. Her name was Phaleria. She was always cheerful. She was an independent woman in a man's world. I became curious about her and forgot my animosity when she started flirting with Demos.

She had largely ignored me for the first couple of days, although it was not easy to ignore someone on a boat. I'd gotten to know the crew. There was a Gaul named Vix, and three Celts called Titte, Kell, and Oppi. Then there was Erati, the cook.

He had a large clay stove on deck, and cooked all day long. It was wonderful; you could eat whenever you were hungry. There was always a fresh loaf of bread or a pizza. There were shish kebabs of lamb and beef, and there were honey buns in the evening with soup. Erati was a very small, skinny man, forever hunched over his oven or busy kneading dough.

Vix, Titte and Oppi were the sailors; doing all the heavy work and taking care of the sails. Kell was the navigator. They took orders from Phaleria and didn't seem to mind that she was a woman.

I thought it was an interesting situation. In all my travels, I'd never met an independent woman. At first I was jealous. I hated the way she looked at Alexander, and the way she pointedly ignored me. Then it occurred to me, perhaps she thought I was one of those downtrodden Greek or Persian women. After all, I only spoke Greek or Latin; Paul did most of our translating, although Alexander, with maddening ease, had started speaking Celt and Gallic.

I decided to try speaking to Phaleria myself. Maybe she and I could become friends. Except for Barsine, I'd never had a woman friend, so I wasn't sure how to approach her. She intimidated me.

It took me four days to get the courage to speak to her. Four days spent caring for Alexander; who lay in his pallet, asking me over and over, 'Why did you agree to take the boat? Why? I would have preferred to die in the peatbog. Oh Zeus, where's the bucket, I'm going to be ill again!'

Poor Alexander. After four days, he felt slightly better. 'The best thing is the headache has gone,' he admitted, as we stood near the stern.

We heard a splash and looked up in time to see a seagull fly away from an osprey. The bird of prey swooped down and picked up the meal the seagull had dropped. Alexander cried, 'A sign!'

'A sign of what?' I was perplexed. I'd been with Alexander long enough to know that he was a fervent believer in omens, and birds could be important ones depending on what they were doing. Seagulls were good omens, I guess, if you were lost at sea. What did this one mean?

'It means that we'd better watch out for pirates.' Phaleria walked over to us and nodded toward the horizon. 'The seagull represents us, his meal is our cargo, and the osprey the pirates.'

'How interesting,' I said politely. 'Are there many pirates in this region?'

'Some. The worst are the Peatbog People. They have low rafts that hide in the swells. You don't see them until you're practically on top of them, and then they swarm onto your boat and take everyone prisoner. They don't kill the prisoners,' she added.

'Well that's good,' I said brightly.

'They wait until they get back to their land and offer them to the bog. The gods eat them alive as they sink into the mud. But the omen said quite clearly that pirates would attack us at sea,' she went on. 'I think we'd better prepare ourselves.'

'I'm glad the omen was so clear this time,' I said. Alexander elbowed me in the ribs.

'Are you any good in a fight?' she asked Alexander.

I choked, but my husband smiled faintly and said 'A little.'

'And you?' she asked me.

Before I could answer, Alexander said, 'She's only good for killing eunuchs. You can count on Nearchus, Demos, and me, if pirates attack.' I glared but he ignored me. 'Why don't you let Paul climb up the rigging to keep watch? He has the sharp eyes of youth, and he'll be able to see a raft low in the water.'

'Very well,' said Phaleria, shrugging. 'He can watch this evening.'

'And no lights at night,' Alexander went on. 'We'll have to practise one or two times together, so that everyone knows their positions. I'll see Nearchus.' He was starting to mutter. That meant plans were starting to form, tactics were being plotted, and strategy was being developed. Alexander walked slowly down the length of the boat, glancing upward now and then, on his way to speak to Nearchus. The two of them would probably turn the calm boat into an army camp within an hour or so; I had just enough time to see Paul.

Chapter Thirty

Paul had future lessons every day. The reason I was teaching him this was simple. To survive, my descendants would have to avoid major wars, plagues, and natural disasters. For example, I told Paul that Pompeii was a beautiful city. A nice place to visit, but not a good place to live.

I settled down to give Paul his lesson while Axiom, himself very interested in the future, listened attentively. Paul asked questions about inventions, whereas Axiom tended to be more interested in politics. Nearchus, when he attended one of my 'classes', wanted to know about geography, and Alexander was interested in *everything*.

Paul sat with his chin in his hands and listened. He always sat perfectly still. Only his eyes and mouth sometimes moved, as he grimaced or grinned. Now he twisted his mouth to the side and said, 'Phaleria says that the people in the far north are very wild, and that the women are the chiefs in some villages. She says we're heading toward one of those villages, and that she knows the woman in charge. She also says that they have dogs trained for war, and that the deer which live in the forests are bigger than the elephants my father had in his army.'

'How would she know?' I asked. 'She never saw an elephant.'

'I did so.' Phaleria strode over and sat down next to Paul. She tipped her chin at Paul. 'Did your father tell you that you must be watchman at dusk? We're counting on your eyes to keep us away from pirates.'

Paul shook his head. 'No, he didn't tell me.'

I was glad Phaleria was speaking Greek. Often she ignored me and spoke Celt with Paul.

'As soon as the sun reaches the sea, I want you to replace Vix. Be careful when you climb up the rigging. Don't slip and fall. Move only one hand and one foot at a time. Promise?'

'Promise.'

'Good fellow!' She reached over and ruffled his hair.

'When will we arrive?' Paul asked.

'In two weeks, if we keep on this tack and the wind stays strong. First, we'll stop in a coastal village to get supplies.' She looked out over the water thoughtfully. 'We will sacrifice a chicken tonight and pray. Nearchus says we should pray to Poseidon.' She made a doubtful face. 'I think we should pray to Odin, since we're heading north. But as we're still in the land of the Celts perhaps we'll be better off praying to Belenus.'

'Which god do you usually pray to?' I asked.

'Lug, the sun god, or and Epona. I pray to the gods who transform humans to animals. I have been asking for years to be able to turn myself into an animal, but only the druids have that power.' She gave a heavy sigh.

Paul and I looked at each other. I wanted to ask her which animal she wanted to turn into, but thought my voice would betray my scepticism. Since it wasn't nice to doubt someone else's beliefs, I just nodded and told Paul to go see his father. I wanted to speak to Phaleria alone.

'Are there really women leaders in the lands we're going to?'

She looked at me sideways. 'There are many. The village I trade the most with is called Orce. The people are fair, like you. The woman in charge is very old, almost a hundred. Her name is Orcina. She has worn the horned helmet ever since her husband died. The villagers agreed to let her keep it because she is so wise. For thirty years now, she has ruled them.'

'In Greece and Persia, the women don't have as much freedom or power. I prefer it here.'

'I imagine you do.' she gave an exaggerated mock shiver. 'Have you ever seen a harem?'

'I spent a few years in one,' I said. 'It was dreadful.'

'And your husband took you out of it? I thought the only way a women could leave was on her funeral pyre.'

'There was a war, and the king died, and we left Babylon in the confusion ...' I wasn't sure how much to tell her.

'Were you in Babylon, when Iskander died?' Phaleria sounded impressed. 'That must have been amazing. Did you ever set eyes on the king himself?'

I kept a perfectly straight face. 'A few times. He wasn't all that impressive.'

'Not as nice looking as your husband, eh?'

'Nowhere near as nice,' I assured her.

She nodded. 'I thought about marrying a few times, but I like my freedom too much. I inherited this boat from my father, and managed to keep most of the crew. I retained more clients than I thought I would. The world is changing.' Her voice was deep and could be vibrant when she wanted. She looked at me with green cat's eyes and said wistfully. 'But I do envy you your son. I would marry just for the joy of having a child.'

'You should marry Demos,' I said. I meant it lightly of course. I'd forgotten how the people of this time reacted to statements; they took them verbatim. Phaleria asked if I thought Demos were good looking.

I watched as the brawny man helped Vix haul in some sail. The muscles in his back rippled like waves.

'Yes, and he's strong,' I said.

'You're right. I'll marry Demos, and then he can help me out on the boat. He doesn't suffer seasickness like your husband does.'

'Alexander is more at home on a horse than on a boat,' I agreed.

'I like his looks, though.'

'He's mine, sister,' I said.

Phaleria shot me an amused look. '"Sister"?' she asked.

I blushed. 'It's just an expression.'

She took a lock of cinnamon coloured hair and wrapped it around her finger. 'I never had any sisters or brothers, and I grew up on this boat. You probably think I'm a barbarian. All the Greeks call us barbarians.'

'I'm not a Greek,' I said, watching as Paul slowly climbed the rigging.

'Don't worry about him, he'll be fine. If you're not Greek, what are you? Are you one of the descendants of the Celtic tribes that have crossed the mountains at the end of the world?'

'I have no idea,' I said.

'Where were you born?'

I winced. This was a tricky question. America hadn't been discovered yet. 'I don't know.'

She made a face. 'You lived in a harem. You don't know where you were born. Were you a slave?'

'No.' I smiled wryly. 'Unless you consider most women slaves. I wasn't anything, really.'

'Fine, you don't have to tell me anything.' She sounded hurt.

I plucked at a thread in my skirt. 'I'm sorry. I'm not used to speaking to anyone about myself. I never thought my life was of interest to anyone. If I sound curt it's because I'm jealous of you.'

'You're jealous of *me*?' She laughed aloud. The men turned to stare at us, their eyebrows raised. Phaleria was roaring with laughter now. Tears ran down her face. 'You, jealous of me?' she kept saying.

'What's so funny?' I asked.

'It's just that *I'm* jealous of you.' She wiped her eyes. 'I grew up on this boat and have no friends, only my crew. You seem so sure of yourself, so confident. And you have such a handsome husband and son.'

'I have two sons and a daughter,' I told her. Loneliness and missing my children made my throat hurt suddenly. 'I miss them terribly.'

'What are their names?'

'Chiron and Cleopatra.' I sighed. 'I want to find Alexander's soul and then go home.'

'Where do you live?' Phaleria's face was shadowed. The sun was sinking below the horizon now. An orange light filled the sky.

'Alexandria, near Egypt,' I said.

'How lovely it must be there.'

'It is. You're welcome to come and stay with us. You would like it there. You can bring your boat if you sail through the Strait of Gibraltar.'

'Where?'

'The Pillars of Hercules?' I ventured.

'Oh. Strong currents there.' She was pensive. 'My father and I sailed to Carthage once. That's a strange place. They sacrifice youths.'

'How terrible,' I said.

We sat in silence. Phaleria squinted at the setting sun, while I watched Paul on the crow's nest. It was little more than a plank. He sat on it and wrapped his arms and legs around the mast. The wind died. The lull usually lasted until the first stars came out, then a new gust of wind rose, and the night crew took over.

I sometimes woke and saw Kell, our navigator. He would stand by the bow and hold his navigational instruments toward the stars as if he were casting magic, as if the shining brass and silver instruments were offerings to the night and to the constellations.

Everyone slept together in the cabin: Alexander and I, Paul and Axiom, Nearchus and Demos, and Yovanix, who slept huddled in the doorway. There was no room for privacy, no room for making love, although soft, reassuring whispers rustled through the night. The stars and moon shone into the latticed windows, making small dappled squares on our faces as we slept. It had been a tranquil voyage so far.

The boat had a large deck, and there were the usual coils of rope, barrels of pitch, and blankets to sit on or wrap up in when needed. Laundry hung on a small clothesline and flapped gaily in the breeze. A pen full of chickens doubled as a bench along the port rail.

The wooden deck planks were unvarnished, smooth, and scrubbed with caustic soda so the wood was white as bone. The sails were made of linen; they were heavy, large, and unwieldy, but the rigging was simple. The boat wasn't particularly fast or manoeuvrable. It was a trading ship, with oars for everyone in case of a dead calm – and for when we arrived in port.

Chapter Thirty-one

'Row, row, row, your boat,' I sang gaily. Alexander made a face at me, and Nearchus grinned and chimed in. He remembered the words. Alexander did too, but I'd forbidden him to sing. His voice could curdle milk, and we were too close to shore. I told him we should try to make a good first impression.

We rowed more or less in unison. Alexander beat time with his foot while the rest of us sang *Row, row, row your boat!* Paul and Phaleria were on deck with Kell, and everyone else was pulling their oar.

Mine splashed into the water, and I jerked it backward to avoid tangling with Axiom's. Cold salt water splashed into the porthole and soaked my arm. I shivered. The water was green and icy. In a little while, we would arrive at the first of our stops, a small village on the shores of modern Denmark. As I peered through the wide porthole, I saw tall trees and a rocky shoreline where the bustling city of Esbjerg would one day spread. I pulled at my oar ineffectually, and managed to splash Vix, who was sitting right behind me. He didn't seem to mind.

The waves were choppy in the bay. We hadn't yet reached the shelter of the little island, and the wind was coming off the land, making the sails useless. Little white caps crested on the top of the green waves and foam decorated our oars with lace. I managed to row correctly for a while, then my mind started to wander and I lost my rhythm.

We headed directly toward a large stone pier. From what I could see, three other boats were tied to it and looked like Roman trading ships. Fishing boats bobbed further out in the harbour; they were coming back in before the sun set. We'd timed our entrance with the tide, and now our boat seemed to be pulling a whole flotilla in its wake. As soon as we were close, Phaleria's men took over, and Alexander, Nearchus, and I clambered onto the deck to get our first view of Denmark.

It wasn't called Denmark back then, of course. It was part of an ancient iron age civilization, and, aside from the obvious farming, trapping, and fishing going on, there was an important export of Baltic amber, wood, pewter, salt, and pine pitch.

They imported wine, vases, spices, and other luxuries, which was what Phaleria was trading. She had a hold full of wine from Italy, some lovely necklaces from the Parisii, and Greek vases. There was also a case full of the little lion-shaped oil lamps made of bronze. Phaleria told me they sold very well.

Paul, Alexander and I went into town, intending to sightsee. I was a typical tourist, and Alexander still wanted to conquer everything he saw.

The village was fortified, and had a medieval look that reminded me of some parts of Europe in the middle ages, still a thousand years away. It was strange, as if time had folded over on itself.

Alexander found fortifications quaint. He didn't think much of the town; the cities in Mesopotamia were so much more luxurious and the villages here seemed primitive. He walked carefully through deep mud, wondering aloud why the people didn't get some decent pavements.

'Like the ones in Gaul,' he said. 'Remember? They were perfectly adequate when it rained. This is dreadful. The rain is icy, by the way,' he added, pulling the umbrella closer to his side. Umbrellas haven't changed much over the centuries, though the ones here were rectangular.

Paul didn't mind. He was walking between us, but when Alexander moved the umbrella, cold raindrops ran down my neck. 'What I'd really like is a bath,' I said wistfully. 'There are some public baths on the other side of town. Phaleria said they were not too bad.'

'Let's go then.' Alexander was game.

'We'll just get muddy going back to the boat,' Paul said. He looked up at the castle wall. 'This is a big place.'

'It's small compared to the fortifications in Tyre,' Alexander began, getting ready to explain how he'd breached those walls, but Paul and I headed him off. We'd heard that story before.

'Father, look at that!' Paul pointed to a man leading a white ox. The ox pulled a large, covered wagon. Behind the wagon walked a donkey, heavily laden with bundles. A horse, wearing an old blanket and carrying two wooden chests, plodded next to the donkey. There was nothing odd about it, except for a monkey sitting on top of the wagon. The monkey was soaking wet and looked positively miserable. Every now and then he'd give a sharp cry, but the man didn't even glance at him.

'There's a monkey on your wagon!' shouted Paul.

'I know that,' the reply came in Greek and was tinged with amusement.

'What's he doing?' Paul wanted to know.

'He's being punished.' The man looked up at the bedraggled beast. 'I suppose you've learned your lesson. Get back inside, and next time you have to pee, you do it outside the wagon. I don't care how cold you think it is.'

The monkey gave a glad shriek and jumped down, landing lightly on the ox's back before springing to the man's shoulder. He gave the man a noisy kiss, then leapt into the wagon, lifting the cover in a strangely human gesture.

'What an amazing animal,' said Paul. 'I wish I had one.'

'No!' Alexander and I both cried at once. 'You already have Cerberus,' I reminded him.

'Besides, that monkey isn't an animal,' the man told us, his voice lowered mysteriously. 'He was a druid. He became trapped in one of his spells. Now he has to spend the rest of his life as a monkey.'

'How awkward for him,' I said.

'It could have been worse, I suppose,' the man said. 'He kept the ability to understand the language of humans, and he can write a little in Greek, but he can't speak any more, and he tends to forget himself and pee in the wagon. When he does that, I make him ride on the roof.'

We stared at him. 'He writes in Greek?' I asked, finally.

The man scratched his head. 'I know it sounds odd,' he admitted. 'The strangest thing about that is, he never spoke

Greek, and he was quite illiterate before he was stuck in the spell. However, I'm sure there's an explanation.' He shrugged. 'At any rate, come to my show this evening in the market place. It starts after sunset.'

'We'll be there,' Alexander promised.

'I'll keep an eye out for you.' He tipped his hat, sending a stream of water splashing to the mud.

We watched as he disappeared around the corner of the street, and then we went on toward the baths. I was cold and wet, and I thought a nice long soak in hot water would do wonders for my morale.

After days of sailing and no bathing except in cold seawater, I was longing to wash my hair, soak in a tub, and dress in warm, dry, clean clothes. My clean clothes were carefully folded in my waterproof bag. Alexander and Paul had their clothes with them as well, and I'd brought a bar of Gallic soap and some scented shampoo with me. I couldn't wait.

When we caught sight of the baths, I was disappointed. There were five or six wooden huts standing in a line in front of a large, black pond. Built slightly off the ground, the huts had steps leading to blanket covered doors. Steam escaped from the roofs, and I realized they were saunas. As I looked, a bright pink man shot out of the last building and tore across the open space separating the last hut from the pond.

The man leapt into the pond, and I imagined I heard steam hissing as he sank into the dark water. Then he climbed out of the water and disappeared into another hut. He was naked except for a brass armband.

231

Alexander said to me, 'When you come flying out of the hut like that fellow, don't trip. All the beneficial effects of the steam will be undone if you land in the mud.'

I looked at the first hut. A woman was beckoning me. With a heavy sigh, I shouldered the bag containing my clothes and patted Paul on the head. 'I suppose that's the ladies' room.'

Alexander and Paul went to the second hut where loud laughter was heard.

As I plodded through the mud, another bright pink man shot out of a hut with steam billowing off his naked body. He looked like a scalded lobster. He jogged down the narrow wooden dock before diving headfirst into the pond. He disappeared under the water and only ripples showed where he'd gone. Then his head broke the water like a seal's and he snorted loudly before swimming lazily toward the shore. He climbed out and jogged back to the buildings, being careful to stay on the plank walkway.

Raindrops spattered the surface of the opaque water. Ducks quacked loudly from reeds on a small island near the centre of the pond. I shivered. The water looked like black ice.

An hour later, I couldn't stand the heat another second. My whole body was scarlet, and sweat poured down my back and between my breasts. The woman next to me grinned and motioned toward the doorway. When I lifted the blanket, cool air gusted in. When I lowered it again, I felt as if I were suffocating.

The last thing I had to do was wash my hair. I took a dipper of hot water and poured it carefully over my head, then I took my small cake of solid shampoo and rubbed it in my hair, scrubbing hard.

'Well, here goes nothing,' I muttered and ran to the lake. The dock vibrated under my feet as I trotted to the very end, then, without dipping my toe in to see how the water was, I took a deep breath and jumped.

I sank below the icy water and came up sputtering. There was a fine coat of sleet on the surface of the pond, too sheer to see with the rain and the dark. It was like frozen tissue paper floating on the water. I closed my eyes and dived underwater, then slowly rose to the surface. Once in the air, my face was covered with a fine layer of ice that melted in seconds.

The water was like silk on my hot body and I was amazed to find I wasn't the least bit cold. However, I knew that to linger was to invite a chill. I rinsed my hair then clambered up the wooden ladder and ran back to the hut. I was tingling all over. My head was clear as spring water and I felt invigorated. I turned when I heard a shout. Paul and Alexander dashed toward the lake, their bodies glowing like embers in the dim light.

I watched as they plunged into the water, and heard Paul's surprised shout as he discovered the ice. I laughed when Alexander dunked him. Paul hurried out, but Alexander, never cold, took the time to swim in a huge, lazy circle, disturbing the ducks, who left the lake with a heavy flapping of wings and a chorus of angry quacks.

I dried thoroughly, braided my hair, and then put on my clothes, savouring each instant. I knew that I wouldn't be able to bathe again before we arrived at our next stop, a week's sail away.

233

When I was dressed and warm, I poked my head out. The rain had nearly stopped, only a few drops fell. Ducks flew overhead, their wings making a lovely jingling sound. Alexander paid the owner of the baths, and we made our way back to the village.

Our boots were muddy when we arrived in town, but we were clean. The rain had stopped, and watery, pale sunlight sparkled over everything. The colours were all metallic: pewter water, silver sky, and gunmetal shadows. Trees looked as if they were etched out of steel plate, and flocks of white gulls wheeled across the harbour, their eerie catcalls loud in the dying wind. A copper line on the horizon was all that showed of the sunset. Torches were lit all over the town, and soon the streets were dotted with gold.

Chapter Thirty-two

We decided to eat in town. Vendors sold grilled fish and steaming bowls of soup, with fresh bread and hot chicory drinks. We sat at a rough wooden table beneath an awning and ate our full. There was barley soup, salmon, and bread flavoured with herbs. Their chicory was unsweetened and burning hot, but it was cooled with long draughts of cold beer.

When we finished eating, we wandered to the market square where the entertainment was about to begin. The man with the monkey had lit torches next to his wagon and called loudly that the show would start shortly. He'd hung a curtain across his wagon, and lined up bales of hay for seats.

'Take your places everyone, the Great and Marvellous Sindi-Dan will charm and amuse you! Come one, come all! The show is free, free as the air you breathe. If you like it, you can donate a few coppers toward the care and feeding of the mighty elephant I have in the wagon. But otherwise, don't worry, don't worry if you have no money! I'll welcome bread and fish. I even accept fresh eggs, as long as you don't throw them at me!'

The crowd chuckled in appreciation and started to wander over. A small boy yelled 'What's a nelephant?'

'An elephant, my friend, is a mighty creature. Iskander the Great Conqueror used them to go all the way to the sacred valley! Why, he gave me one himself, just before he died. I also have a selkie, a mythical creature.' This was said in a half-serious, half-joking voice.

'I've heard of a selkie!' the boy scoffed, 'Where is he?'

'You'll see him soon, he's a shy beastie and won't come out until the night has fallen!' The Great and Marvellous Sindi-Dan spoke in a deep, mysterious voice.

I dug my elbows into Alexander's ribs. 'I always wondered what you did with the elephants,' I whispered. 'Now I know.'

He grinned. 'I wondered too.'

'Father, hush!' Paul tugged on his arm. 'Listen, he's telling everyone he knew you!'

He was. In a loud voice, he was proclaiming himself one of Alexander's magicians who had followed him on his journeys. As we sat and listened, spellbound, to his hyperbole, a deep voice tickled our ears from behind.

'Well, Iskander, it seems you've found one of your cronies!'

It was Demos, settling his bulk comfortably behind us. Axiom and Yovanix were not long coming to the show. Soon we were all in a group again, sitting on bales of hay, watching as the shadows grew deeper and longer, and the glow of torches and swinging lamps dappled the white show curtain.

When the last bit of light had faded from the sky, and a large crowd had gathered, the Great and Marvellous Sindi-Dan stepped into the middle of the clearing and opened his arms wide in a theatrical gesture. 'Men, women, children,

236

and spirits of the night, welcome to the show! Welcome to the mysteries of the Orient! Welcome, one and all!' He bowed, and a dramatic billow of smoke masked him from sight. When the cloud disappeared, a white ox stood in his place. There was a brief flurry of laughter and shrieks, then the ox slowly kneeled, giving a parody of the Great and Marvellous Sindi-Dan's bow. Gaily coloured ribbons fluttered around the ox's horns and neck. Another puff of smoke appeared, and the ox vanished, leaving nothing but a few scattered ribbons that settled on the ground. Before anyone could move, a loud shuffling noise came from behind the curtain. An invisible hand parted it, and a small elephant trotted out.

The crowd gave a cry, for most had never seen an elephant, and even one as small as this was a terrifying sight. The elephant stopped in front of the crowd. It wheeled around and around like a spinning top. Then it pointed its trunk to the sky and trumpeted loudly. It had perfect little tusks and beady eyes that reflected the torchlight like rubies.

Some people in the crowd jumped back with loud screams, but they were delighted shrieks. Despite the fear, everyone was thrilled. The elephant whirled around once more then darted behind the curtain. After a collective sigh of relief, the crowd eased forward again. I wanted another look at the elephant, which seemed to be a perfectly formed adult despite its diminutive size. I'd heard of pygmy elephants. I wondered if this were one, and how Sindi-Dan had obtained it?

Then Sindi-Dan appeared. Behind him was a dark shadow, undulating in a terrifying manner. Paul let out a frightened squeal and grasped his father's arm. 'What's that?' he cried.

Sindi-Dan held up his arms. 'Do not make any sudden moves and don't breathe a word!' he cried. The people fell silent 'Now, let all the women cover their faces! If the selkie sees a beautiful woman, he will change into a man and steal her heart!'

There was a ripple of nervous chatter. It soon hushed, and the ladies drew their scarves or cloaks over their faces, peeking out with wide eyes as the sea lion – I recognized the animal right away – flopped its way to the centre stage.

He was a huge sleek animal, with round eyes and a startled look on his moustached face. He opened his mouth, showing sharp teeth, and uttered a loud bark. The crowd jumped. Paul hid behind Alexander. I patted his arm, and whispered, 'don't be afraid, it's just a seal.'

The sea lion leaned backward, ponderously, and then reared up and clapped his flippers together. The Great Sindi-Dan patted his head and slipped a morsel of herring into the gaping mouth, and the sea lion obediently flopped down and started back to the curtain. But he suddenly stopped and reared up again. He uttered two or three sharp barks and turned, facing the crowd. Carefully the giant animal leaned forward, balancing on his front flippers, then lifted its back end completely off the ground.

'What's this?' Sindi-Dan cried. 'Oh no! He's seen a beautiful woman! Why did you not hide your face! In a moment he'll change into a man!'

The crowd held its breath and the seal barked once more. Then a puff of smoke rose again, this time bright blue. When it evaporated, a man stood blinking in the torchlight. He had black hair and black eyes, and his skin was a curious swarthy colour. He wore a sealskin loincloth, and an intricate silver torc ringed his strong neck. He blinked and rubbed his face, then made quite a show of looking at his hands, then lifting his feet up, one by one, and studying them. The crowd was absolutely still. You could hear the creak of the wooden sign swinging slowly overhead.

This man was a consummate actor. He made a huge show of being amazed at his human form. Fear, awe, joy, and then a sly grin crossed his handsome face, for handsome he was. He must be Iberian, I decided. The dark Spaniards sometimes looked like that, with eyes as hot as embers and a full, sensuous mouth. His skin had an odd bluish cast to it, and he had a thick mat of black hair curling from his chest to his flat abdomen. His muscles were strong and clearly defined. I looked at the crowd and saw that most of the women had let the corners of their cloaks fall and were staring with unabashed admiration.

The dark man hesitated, then took a faltering step. He was superb; he made it look as if he had never walked before. His hips swivelled like the seal's and he threw his arms wide, pitching forward onto the ground. A young woman gave an audible gasp. He raised his head and their eyes met.

The man rolled over and got to his feet in a fluid motion. Gathering himself, he leapt into the crowd, scattering the spectators. He seized the girl by the waist and tossed her over his shoulder. Then he jumped back into the middle of the open space, and another huge puff of smoke appeared, hiding both of them. The crowd cried out in surprise. When the dark blue smoke cleared, a black horse stood, snorting and pawing the ground. The girl sat on the horse's back, clinging with both hands to the mane.

With a whinny, the horse tossed its head and reared. The girl held on tightly. The crowd parted as the horse suddenly plunged forward and galloped through.

'He's heading for the harbour!' someone cried.

There was a moment of stunned silence. The horse's hooves clattered loudly on the cobblestone road. Then a great splash was heard. Silence washed back upon us like a wave.

'Now look at that!' It was Sindi-Dan, standing in the centre of the crowd, hands on his hips. 'Just look at that, will you? I asked you women to cover your faces, but someone didn't listen. And now what?'

We all held our breaths. No one had the faintest idea what would happen next.

'What happens is, I lose my selkie.' There was a teasing note in his voice. The crowd settled back to its place, murmuring appreciatively and looking expectantly at the Great Sindi-Dan.

'The selkie sees a beautiful woman and he changes into a man. The woman falls in love with him, and when she touches him, he turns into a horse and carries her back to his home in the sea. She'll live there for ever now, I suppose, in his castle below the waves. Did I tell you a selkie was an enchanted prince? I didn't?' He looked amused. In the firelight his eyes were as deep as black wells. 'Now I shall have to capture another selkie, and it's not easy, I assure you!'

He clapped his hands. 'Well, I suppose I shall have to entertain you some other way then. Ithobaal! Ithobaal! Come out and show yourself. Bring the tablet; you'll have to amuse the public while I think of something to finish the evening! Ithobaal! Oh, that lazy fellow. He's probably eating all my figs.' He snapped his fingers angrily and the curtain parted. A small shadow eased out, and the people started to laugh.

It was the monkey. He looked as if he were in disgrace. His head was bowed and he carried a wax tablet behind his back. His tail was low to the ground.

'Ithobaal used to be a druid,' said Sindi-Dan in a loud whisper, 'but he became entangled in one of his own spells.' He nodded toward the monkey. 'Now he pisses in my wagon and eats all my food!' The crowd whispered loudly. One person cried out something that sounded like 'bullshit!' and his friends laughed.

Sindi-Dan ignored the scepticism. 'Did you eat all the figs?' he asked the monkey.

The little monkey cocked his head and then took the tablet. With a sharpened reed he wrote something. He handed the tablet to Sindi-Dan.

'Who reads Greek?' he called out. Then spying Paul, he said, 'You! Young man, come here. I can tell you're well educated. Here boy, what does he write?'

Paul took the tablet and cleared his throat. 'He wrote, "Your figs are rotten".'

The crowd roared as Sindi-Dan made an angry face. 'Rotten are they? Well, you can have them all then.'

The monkey looked at the crowd and gave a huge wink. There was more laughter.

241

'If he's a druid, make him tell us our fortunes!' cried a man from the crowd.

'Very well.' Sindi-Dan rubbed the wax smooth and handed the tablet back to the monkey. 'O Wise and Wonderful Ithobaal, will you tell the people here their fortunes?'

The monkey wrote something on the tablet and handed it to Paul who read aloud, 'I will, O Big and Boastful Sindi-Dan.'

'Well, who is brave enough to ask first?' asked the magician, looking at the crowd and folding his arms across his chest. There was a hush. No one dared ask first. Then Demos stood up from behind us. 'I ask,' he boomed.

'A brave man,' approved the magician, nodding toward the monkey. 'Very well, Ithobaal, tell this man's fortune for him.'

The monkey jumped lightly over our heads and landed on Demos's shoulder. He peered into his eyes. Then he fingered his cloak, and patted his hair and shoulders with his little hands. He bared his teeth and gave a funny monkey screech. Demos chuckled. The monkey jumped back to the ground and took the tablet. He nibbled the reed thoughtfully, looking so much like a little scribe, I couldn't help but laugh. Then he wrote rapidly on the tablet, pausing now and then to stare at Demos' face. When Paul took the tablet to read, there was a supernatural silence hanging over the crowd.

Paul held the tablet up to the torchlight and read loudly, 'Your fortune is twofold. First, to seek an object unseen at the end of night. Second, to make your home on the endless sea. A great, strong man like you is made for adventure, but beware! Strong ropes may not tie you down, yet the softest lock of a woman's hair may hold you spellbound! Follow the Queen of Darkness to the land of her ancestors, then marry the woman with fire in her hair. True love shall triumph!'

The men applauded as the women sighed.

'Very romantic,' said Sindi-Dan, 'if you can figure it all out. Personally, I have never been able to understand prophecies, although ever since Ithobaal transformed himself into a monkey, he's much easier to understand.'

There was a ripple of laughter, and several other people called out to Ithobaal to tell their fortunes.

The monkey sat on Paul's shoulder and pulled on his bright hair. Without waiting, he rubbed his tablet smooth with his soft hand and wrote some more. He handed the tablet to Paul who read, 'If you want your fortunes told, you'll have to pay me directly. Sindi-Dan won't give me money, he only feeds me rotten dates.'

There were shouts of laughter from the crowd. The monkey jumped off Paul's shoulder and landed on Alexander's lap. Alexander scratched the monkey's chin and said, 'Well, Ithobaal, what's your price?'

The monkey bared his teeth and held up three fingers.

'Three? Three what? Dates?' Alexander laughed.

The monkey shook his head and pointed to Alexander's purse. Alexander sighed loudly and untied it. The monkey dipped an agile paw into the leather bag and came out with three bright coins.

'Hey! That's silver!' cried Alexander, but the monkey chattered excitedly and put the money into a little bag tied to his waist. He grabbed the tablet from Paul and wrote, then gave the tablet directly to Alexander. He jumped up and down, making impish grimaces with his expressive monkey face.

The crowd was roaring with laughter at the monkey's antics, but Alexander had grown very still. He looked at me, and I thought he would show me the writing, but at the last minute he passed his hand over the wax, smoothing it. He handed the tablet to the monkey and got to his feet.

'Aren't you staying to the end of the show?' I asked.

'It's over,' he said shortly and waded out of the crowd.

Paul and I looked at each other. We were torn between wanting to see more entertainment and following Alexander. We had been cooped up on a boat for so long without books or any games. Now, there was a promise of a night of magic and songs. I told Paul to stay with Axiom and Nearchus and went after Alexander. Maybe he'd tell me what was wrong.

As I walked through the streets, I heard music starting. Someone was playing a reed flute, and I heard what sounded like a bass drum. The music shivered through the air, making the torchlight dance on the black puddles.

Chapter Thirty-three

Back at the docks, there was the usual bustle. Slaves were busy loading and unloading the boats in order to sail with the first tides. Fishermen readied their nets and lines. Phaleria's boat was the only tranquil one. Two lamps burned in the galley, and I saw Alexander's shadow wavering through the latticed doorway.

Quietly, I stepped aboard. The boat rose and fell gently with the waves. My feet made no noise on the wooden planks. When I opened the door to the cabin, I saw Alexander sitting on his pallet, looking out the window. The lattice made a criss-cross of shadows on his face. Without turning around he said, 'Come.'

I slid into his arms. His body was warm. His neck was made to fit my face. 'What is the matter?' I asked.

'Don't you mean, "What did the monkey write?"' His voice held no clue as to what he was thinking. It was unlike him.

'I didn't ask you that,' I said.

'I know.' His lips brushed my hair. 'It was so strange. One minute I was a man. Just a man sitting in the crowd. I had forgotten everything. It's rare, you know. Perhaps you believe I never think about … before.' His voice hesitant, as if he were blindly feeling his way. 'The truth is, I think about it all the time. Not a moment goes by that my body doesn't stiffen, and I think that there's something urgent I have to do, someone I need to see, an order I need to give. I can't relax. I told you before, I feel hollow, as if the wind could take me away.'

I held him tightly. 'You had forgotten, was that it?'

In the dark, I felt him sigh. 'That's right. I had forgotten. Perhaps he really *is* a magician. Even the stories he was telling about the Great Iskander didn't concern me, they were so far-fetched they had nothing to do with … me,' he finished softly.

'The monkey reminded you of who you really were?' I asked.

'The monkey said that Aristotle was dead.'

'What? Are you sure? When? What *did* the monkey write?'

'He wrote that Aristotle of Stagira would teach no more, and that Craterus died in battle. The war still rages in Persia over my succession.' He shook his head. 'Why did you never let me designate an heir? Craterus. Do you remember him?'

'Of course I do.' I could picture Craterus perfectly. He had been tall and quiet, with a mournful smile and grey eyes as soft as a dove's feathers. He'd been a clever general and a valiant fighter. He'd commanded Alexander's phalanx for nearly all the years they'd fought together. 'I couldn't let you designate an heir because history says that …'

'History? History?' His voice rose. 'To Hades with history! Clio be cursed! I am here *now*. What is three thousand years to me? Why did I ever listen to you?' He nearly pushed me away, then he took a great gasping breath. 'I'm sorry.' He drew me into a hard embrace. 'It's not your fault. I was wrong to think that – even for a second. As you said, history is already written. How do you feel about that, you who have always refused to believe in fate?'

I was silent. All the beliefs I'd held tightly to since I'd arrived in this ancient time were crumbling like wet sand. Then I turned to him. For a moment his face held me enthralled, as it always had, by its pure lines and arresting eyes. I managed a smile. 'I don't care what you think,' I said. 'I don't care if you blame me for all the misery of the world. I saved you, and that's all that counts. You say you believe in fate, fine, but you can't lie to me. You only pretended to believe. Deep down inside, you know that you're free. And you always knew it.'

He didn't look away. The fierce look in his eyes softened. A twitch of the mouth told me I'd found my mark. His lips curled slowly into a smile. 'You told me you never believed in magic,' he said, 'so explain this to me.' He delved into his baggage and came up with Millis's wax tablet. He took the stylus that was clipped to the top and wrote, then handed it to me. 'That is what the monkey wrote,' he said.

I took the tablet and held it up to the light. Written in Alexander's careful hand, were three lines.

"Hail, Iskander, come back from the dead. Aristotle of Stagira will teach no more, his shade flutters in Hades in the eternal garden. Craterus has joined him there. The fighting continues. What happened the day your father died?"

I put the tablet down slowly. 'Why your father?' I asked.

He wouldn't look at me. 'I didn't have to write that,' he said finally.

'Unless you wanted to,' I agreed.

'I can't tell you yet. I'm afraid you'll see me as I really am.' There was something heartbreaking in his voice.

'When you're ready, you can tell me. I won't judge you. You know I won't.'

'I do know that. You never judge. It's almost as if you don't care. I know that's not true,' he added hurriedly. 'But I'm afraid to talk about that time in my life. When I think about it, it's like staring into a whirlpool that will suck me into its vortex.' There was a pause. 'I'm afraid of the look in your eyes afterwards.' he said simply.

'There's another possibility.' I looked past his shoulder out the window.

'What's that?'

'When you see that I still love you, perhaps you'll stop loving me. You'll think that it's impossible I could still care for you, so you'll push me away. You mustn't make up your mind for me,' I told him. 'You can't pretend to know what I'll think or feel.' The night was as deep as the ocean now. Stars blazed in the sky. Without electric lights everywhere, the constellations seemed close as the mountaintops.

I felt a soft caress on my cheek. 'Why are you crying?' he asked.

'Why? I don't know. I always hoped you'd fall off your pedestal. I love you, that's all that matters for me in the end,' I said, kissing him. I kept my eyes closed. I didn't want to talk any more.

He growled then, and took my head in his hands, his fingers slipping through my hair. My arms encircled him. We'd been travelling in close quarters with everyone for weeks now. Finding ourselves alone for once was suddenly intoxicating. My breath caught in my throat as he unfastened my tunic and pushed it off my shoulders. I sighed as he pushed me backward onto the hard floor, covering me with his body.

He was urgent, so was I. Afterwards, he slept deeply, the moonlight through the window striping his body. I covered him with his blanket and snuggled into his arms.

Chapter Thirty-four

Next day the crew was busy getting the boat ready to sail. I mostly tried to stay out of the way. At the back of the boat, Yovanix tended the chickens. He had been such a quiet addition to our band that I could sometimes forget all about him. I think, perhaps, I wanted to. Whenever I looked at him, I felt a sharp pang of something I couldn't define. Guilt? Sorrow? Pity? I didn't know.

He caught my glance and smiled. He had lost the habit of blushing every time our eyes met. I sighed. He was a nice person. Shy, unassuming, and clever with his hands. He whittled animals out of wood and gave them to Paul. He was making a chess set, and little pawns were forever dropping out of his pockets. There was one at my feet now. He must have lost it when he was feeding the chickens. I picked it up.

'Here, look what I found,' I said.

'Thanks.' He tucked it into his pouch and nodded at the horizon. 'It's going to be rough out there,' he said.

'Do you mind?'

'No, I don't get sick at sea.' He grinned briefly. When he smiled he looked so very young. I felt another pang. He didn't often smile.

'How old are you?' I asked.

'Eighteen.' His answer surprised me. It must have showed, because he blushed. 'You must think badly of me,' he said. 'I know what I did was wrong, but Selena can be so …so persuasive. And I was her slave.'

'I'm sorry.' I looked away. 'I don't think badly of you at all. I make no judgements. It's not my way. Besides, I only know about it because I was hiding in the closet. Oh, and I thought the helmet was a newfangled toilet from Rome.'

I saw his body stiffen. Then he chuckled. 'I always wondered about that.' His voice trailed away. We were silent a moment. The wind seemed to mock us.

Then I said, 'Now that you're free, what would you like to do? You don't have to stay with us, you know. We'll be glad to give you what you need to start a new life. Is there anywhere you'd like to go? Anything you'd like to do? You're young, handsome, and healthy. Why don't you take advantage of that?'

'Can I ask you something?' He sounded unsure of himself.

'Of course, please do.'

'Is it true that your husband is the great Iskander? No, don't worry,' he said quickly. 'I will never tell anyone, but I was there the night Demos came and heard everything. Just tell me, is it true?'

'It is.' I stared bleakly at the waves.

Yovanix took a deep breath. 'All my life I've dreamed of adventure, of being free, travelling, and becoming a great hero. You must think it's silly, I want to live a great adventure. You have to understand that I was a slave nearly all my life. Everyone told me what to do. I had no future. I heard about Iskander and his conquests. The Gauls were sure he was going to sweep through their land. They spoke of nothing else. His stories were already legends by the time I was old enough to understand them. He was my first hero. Now he's here searching for his soul. Perhaps, in some small way I can help him. He has given me a new life. What I'm trying to say, what I'd really like, is to stay with you. All of you.' His blush was painful.

'I'm sorry,' I said. My throat hurt. 'Of course you can stay with us. I never realized you wanted to. I'm sorry. I must have seemed very unfriendly.'

'You mustn't apologize. Paul told me about Millis. I suppose you blame us. But it was Voltarrix.' When he said that name he shivered.

'Who is he?' I asked.

'Some say he's a demon. Anoramix said he was a druid from the far north. From what I gathered, he is a very powerful thief of souls. He is one of the old ones, the ones who worship iron and water.'

'What *is* a thief of souls?'

'In Celtic myth, it's a druid who can steal souls.' He made a face. 'I'm not explaining this very well. I'm not Celt you see. But if Anoramix was afraid of him, I would be frightened too. Anoramix was never afraid of anything, not even death. There's one last thing I should tell you.' He licked his lips nervously. 'Selena told me never to trust you. She said you were really Persephone, the Queen of Ice and Darkness, and that your heart was like a stone.'

'She was still upset about Anoramix,' I said uncertainly.

252

'She blamed you for his death and wanted revenge. She forbade me to tell you that Voltarrix is still seeking Paul. She said that Paul would never be safe, and that no one could protect him.'

'What does he want with Paul?'

Yovanix spoke as if weighing his words. 'If it's true Iskander lost his soul, I think I know why. If Voltarrix captured Paul and put Iskander's soul in his body, can you imagine what would happen? Paul can no longer call the moon, but he can grow up to lead an army. The Druids are starting to feel the end of their world approaching. They speak of only one thing now; stopping the Romans before it's too late. Some think it's already too late. Voltarrix is one of the old ones who believe that time can be twisted.'

'Twisted?' I echoed. My voice sounded odd.

'The druids believe that time can be changed, like a river's course. They can change it, slow it, or speed it up. With enough work, they can even make it flow backward. Time is the foundation of the druid's religion'

It was starting to make sense. *Time.* The Aztecs had foreseen the date their empire would topple, and they had tried to turn back time with their ceremonies. Nothing had worked for them. Nothing would work for the druids. The Romans would take over and usher in the modern world. Unless a boy, who never should have been born, somehow changed time.

It was conceivable – there were still two hundred years. After that, nothing would halt the inexorable march of the Roman Empire and the event that changed the world; the birth of Christ.

But suppose the druids somehow managed to unite the Norsemen, Celts, and Gauls against the Romans? What if Paul were somehow the catalyst? Paul – with Iskander's soul.

I took a deep breath. I would have to think about this. There were three people in the world who should never have been born: Paul, Chiron, and Cleopatra – and I was not supposed to be in this time or place. Anyone of us could, conceivably, change the world. A butterfly's wings indeed.

Chapter Thirty-five

The sea was rough the following day, and the day after. It wasn't until nearly a week went by, that the waves smoothed and Alexander could get up. He'd been so ill, I couldn't speak to him about what was troubling me. Besides, I wasn't sure I wanted to believe it.

Poor Alexander. His face was drawn, his eyes hollow, his smile wan, and he needed a shave, a bath, and a good meal.

The shave was possible, the good meal was tentatively nibbled on, and the bath was a bucket of seawater heated to a bearable temperature and sluiced over his head while he stood naked at the stern.

'Do you feel any better, Father?' Paul asked worriedly. He was sitting near the mast, playing chess with Nearchus.

Nearchus looked at Alexander, then quickly back at the board again. His mouth drew tight. I knew how he felt. I hadn't seen Alexander look so thin and pale since he'd been struck with the arrow in India.

'I'm feeling much better,' he said. He started to smile, then the boat slewed sideways as a large wave lifted us up and slid us into a deep trough. The horizon tilted, the mast creaked, and Alexander leaned over the rail and was sick.

'Damn!' I exclaimed, and went to find Erati for more food.

Paul and Nearchus's game wasn't bothered. Yovanix had carved a special chess set with holes in the board and pegs on the bottom of the pieces, so they wouldn't slide all over the place. When I came back with warm bread, Alexander was huddled next to them, a blanket wrapped around his shoulders, his face pinched and unhappy.

I gave him the plate of food and stood by, making sure he at least tried to eat it. Afterwards, I half led, half carried him back to his bed. We'd slung a hammock in the very middle of the boat, hoping that the swing would even out the sway. He sank into the hammock and closed his eyes. Sleeping was the only thing that helped. I poured him a draught of poppy, and he sank into a restless slumber. Paul came and sat next to me. He put his head on my shoulder and I held him close.

'Will he be all right?' he asked.

'I think so. He's tougher than he looks.'

'I worry about him,' said Paul. Seeing my surprise, he added, 'When you came to the Valley of Nysa, I thought we'd be together for ever. I was so happy.'

'The hardest thing I ever did, in my entire life, was leaving you in the valley after I'd found you again. And I only did it, because I thought I would be back for you.'

'Alone, without my father.'

'He was supposed to die,' I said quietly. 'Can you ever forgive me?'

'I forgive you.' His eyes didn't waver. 'I know why you left me there. You thought you would not be able to protect me after Father died.'

'And then Olympias sent someone to seize you and take you to Babylon. You must have been so frightened.' I hated thinking of Paul's voyage. He had been seven years old, alone, afraid, and heading toward a fabled city where his father would be acclaimed king.

He looked at me obliquely. 'I wasn't scared. You want to know something strange? Before the ceremony ... you know, the one where the blood ... you know ...?' He waved his hand nervously. 'I believed I *was* the son of the moon goddess. Since the day I was born, everyone told me that. I used to look up at the moon at night and feel safe.'

'And now?' I asked.

'Now, I have you and Father. You're both here with me, and I feel like the luckiest boy in the world. Yet, I'm scared too. Because I never believed Father was a god. And, I think, he's become even more mortal than any of us.'

'Only because he's seasick. Anyone can get that greenish shade of skin. It has to do with the inner ear,' I told him.

'Really?'

'Oh, yes. Don't worry about him, don't worry about anything.'

'I won't, honest. But can I show you something odd?' He pulled up his sleeve and pointed to his arm. 'Look, since the ceremony the scar has changed. What do you think of that?'

I peered closely at his arm. On the round part of his biceps, a crescent moon had always shone. Now the moon was different. It had nearly vanished. I pulled back, startled. 'I don't know what it means,' I said.

'It's nice not being the moon's child,' he said, smiling. 'Nearchus doesn't call me the Harbinger of Destruction any more, and he plays chess with me. I feel like a real person,' he said, satisfaction in his voice. 'Do you think I'm becoming normal?'

Chapter Thirty-six

When we arrived in sight of land, we took our places and rowed. The day was grey and chilly. We'd been travelling just ahead of spring, and here we'd outrun it. It would be another two or three weeks before it caught up with us.

I shivered as I rowed. On my right was the endless ocean, on my left, a tall granite cliff and crashing surf. We had to slip the boat into a ridiculously narrow channel, and I was terrified we'd smash into the rocks. But Phaleria and Kell knew their landmarks, and the rest of the crew knew their business, so we squeezed through the narrow passage. We entered a wide, deep fjord, and arrived at a small settlement.

Phaleria shouted to someone on the docks, and the man tossed a heavy rope onto our deck. The crew tied the boat, and Phaleria turned to us with a wide grin.

'Welcome to Orce!' she cried.

Alexander tapped my shoulder. 'Say hello to the land of your ancestors,' he said.

I wrinkled my nose. 'My ancestors? Most of them have yet to be born.'

'Well, your future ancestors then.' He took a deep breath. 'Ah, land. Finally! I thought we'd never make it. Do you want to take a walk with me?'

'I want to take a bath,' I told him.

'With me?' His eyes twinkled. He was feeling much better.

'With anyone,' I said seriously.

'Let's go then.' He grabbed my hand and practically dragged me off the boat.

Paul and Cerberus had beaten us off the boat. The dog bounded onto the beach, found what looked like a hundred-year-old dead seagull, and was happily rolling in it. Paul was wading in the surf; cold or no cold, boys can't resist wading. He held his cloak tightly around his shoulders, but his head was bare and his hair whipped around his face.

Other people were on the beach as well. Women were busy digging in the sand, and I saw willow baskets full of clams. Children played on the shingle, some picking up driftwood, others throwing seaweed at each other and shouting. On the dock, men were mending fishing nets. And everyone had the same hair as Paul and I.

I looked back to the beach where Paul was now throwing a stick to Cerberus. Another boy had joined the game, and the two towheads could have been brothers.

No one gave me a second glance here. It was the first time I'd felt as if I weren't sticking out like tinsel at Easter. Everyone here had blue eyes. Everyone had high, broad cheekbones. Alexander looked at me, his head tilted to the side, and said, 'And I always thought you were unique. How disappointing.'

I shoved him off the dock.

Well, he did need a bath, and the water wasn't that deep. He grinned up at me, his teeth flashing white in his face. 'You do have feelings after all,' he crowed.

The people weren't yet Vikings. They weren't going to terrorize anything, except maybe the shoals of cod in the freezing waters off the coast. Their main industry was fishing, of course. They lived in deep fjords, braving the winter, fishing all year long, and farming during the short spring and summer. The coast was still sparsely settled.

The Gulf Stream made its way up to the Arctic Circle here, and the climate wasn't as bad as you'd think. But we were roughly four hundred kilometres from the Arctic Circle, and the wind, when it blew from the north, was like a block of ice. Where the cold air met the warmer water, there were huge, thick banks of fog. The sudden fog was deadly – a boat could get lost ten feet from shore.

We'd been lucky with the weather, and we were the first to arrive in the village that spring. It was beautiful. Rarely have I seen such majesty in nature. Alexander would often walk to the bow of the boat and just stand, his hands clasped behind his back, his face lifted toward the mountains.

The villages were set deep in the fjords. Behind them were towering pine forests, and small pockets of meadow used for grazing and hay. Tides rose and fell gently. The huge, Atlantic waves were tamed inside the fjords, and often the water was as flat as glass. The colour of the water varied according to the sky. All around were mountains, above us, and reflected in the mirror of the fjords.

The people were the strong, silent type. During the day, few words were exchanged. All this ended at night. When the work was done, and the villagers gathered in the great hall for the communal dinner, it was as if a switch had been thrown. Beer flowed from huge wooden casks. A whole sheep turned on a spit. There was codfish, of course. And stories.

I didn't understand a word of what they said. Phaleria did, and translated for us. As the evening wore on, people stood up, one after another, and told stories. There were tales about the gods, with king Odin, Thor the thunder god, or Loki, troublemaker. They told fishing tales, like the entertaining story about Olaf caught in the codfish net, or the tragic tale of Svensson and his disappearance in a fog bank. Since the men sailed far afield, there were stories about different tribes in the region, gossip from neighbouring villages, or news from faraway friends and relatives. They talked about a new invention someone saw or heard about, a new recipe, strange animals they'd seen, or even a strange weather pattern.

It wasn't only men. Women commanded as much attention as men did. One thing struck me after a while. The only people who stood up to talk were adults. Phaleria, when I asked her about this, told me that only the people over a certain age could speak. The young were supposed to listen and learn. It was, she informed me, a sort of informal education. The best stories were honed and perfected, the useful ones repeated for generations, and the whole village profited.

There were no writings here. It was a purely aural society. Everyone listened carefully when someone spoke.

No one monopolized the conversation. Phaleria was able to translate almost everything, because after someone spoke there was a lull while people discussed what they'd just heard. When dinner was over, everyone helped clean up, then bade each other goodnight, and went to bed.

Chapter Thirty-seven

We stayed at an inn. It wouldn't get any stars in modern times. It was a longhouse, with a common hearth in the middle, beds along the sides of the walls, and no windows or chimney. At the north end was stabling for animals. Luckily it was spring and the livestock had been moved outside – but the smell lingered. The hearth smouldered all night, giving off heat and smoke. A small hole in the thatched roof was supposed to let the smoke out, but the smoke didn't seem to want to venture outside.

Each bed was built as an alcove. We pulled heavy wool curtains closed around us and slept while the smoke swirled lazily. In the morning, I felt like a smoked sausage. The wooden floor was covered with brightly coloured rugs. The hearth was made of flat rocks placed in a rectangle. These stones made a good bench. When I woke, I saw Titte and Kell sitting there, drinking chicory and discussing the day's plans.

Phaleria emerged from her bed, parting the curtains and poking her head out. 'Is anyone in the bathroom?' she called.

'No, it's free,' said Kell.

Phaleria nodded in satisfaction and left the longhouse by the front door. The bathroom was right outside, and was the most comfortable I'd seen in all my travels. I suppose that cold weather would tend to make people more careful about how they built their toilets. This was a spacious affair, with smooth wooden benches, many large buckets always full of clean water, and a seemingly endless supply of clean cloths.

We settled down to stay for a month of trading. The first day was spent getting to know the village, finding the baths – sauna huts, a small pond, ducks in the water, and steaming people shooting naked out of the door and diving into the pond – and getting settled.

Paul had found a friend, and was busy learning the language by pointing to everything and repeating the words like a parrot. I was sure he'd be speaking fluently before we left.

It was the fifth day after our arrival, and I still hadn't spoken to Alexander about what Yovanix had told me. We never seemed to be alone. Plus, I wasn't sure what to say. 'By the way, the man who stole your soul wants to use Paul to lead an army and conquer Rome?' It sounded ridiculous, even to me. Alexander seemed to be in a good mood. Why ruin it? Voltarrix couldn't harm us here. He wasn't anywhere near us.

I managed to forget about him and spent my time relaxing in the sauna, playing chess with Paul, or cleaning and mending our clothes. We were starting to look ragged from so much travel. Axiom was a big help; he had always been Alexander's valet and knew how to sew up a ripped cloak or take out stains in linen. I was vain. I missed Brazza; he could spend hours brushing and dressing my hair, doing my make-up, and giving me manicures.

Without him around, my hair lived in braids, my hands were chapped, and I'd lost my make-up somewhere between Massalia and Lutetia.

Phaleria sold Egyptian kohl, carmine from Corsica, powder from Rome, blue and purple eye shadow from Persia, and lipstick and perfume made by the Parisii. I managed to replace most of my cosmetics, and Phaleria gave me a recipe for a skin cream. I only needed lanolin from a sheep, lavender oil, thyme, a cup of ass's milk, a pinch of talc, honey, and rose water. Easy. I stared at the recipe and wondered what lanolin looked like, and what part of a sheep it was from.

The weather had brightened considerably, and the fishing boats came back bursting with cod and mackerel. The village was in high spirits; three new trading boats had been sighted heading this way, and everyone hastily polished up their wares and set up stands along the beach. Soon the whole village was spread out and ready to trade. Phaleria, who'd arrived first, had been busy, but now I saw why she hadn't taken all her wares out of the boat. The villagers weren't the only ones in the region. From inland, came wagons pulled by reindeer, which made Paul cry out with delight. Even Alexander was surprised by the tame deer.

'What amazing creatures,' Alexander kept saying. 'They have webbed feet like ducks, fur like rabbits, a beard like a goat, huge antlers, and the face of a cow!' He hurried to take out his journal and sketch a picture of the beasts for Plexis. 'He'll never believe this,' he said, shaking his head. 'He'll think I'm making it up.'

'What about the narwhal?' I asked him. He kept a journal, like any well-educated man of his time, and was no mean artist. We'd caught sight of a narwhal one day, and he'd used up nearly five pages describing and drawing it.

'He'll think I made that up too,' he said. He frowned at his picture and added more height to the antlers. 'I can't wait to see him and tell him everything we've seen. But you have to be there too, otherwise he won't believe a word.'

I looked at his picture and told him to add eight more reindeer behind the one he'd drawn. 'And a bigger sleigh.' He complied, mystified, and then I drew in a stout gentleman with a fluffy beard and a sack full of toys sticking out of the back of the sled. I giggled, thinking of Plexis's face when he saw that.

'What in Zeus's name is that?' Alexander sputtered, looking at his drawing.

'Santa Claus,' I said. 'In my time we tell children stories about this fellow. He flies through the air with his sled and brings toys to good girls and boys. If you had red ink I'd make his suit look better,' I added. 'The deer all have names. There's Dasher and Dancer and Donner and Vixen, Comet and Cupid and Prancer and Blitzen. The deer in the front has a red nose that glows. His name's Rudolph. I can sing you a song about him if you like.' I was nostalgic all of a sudden.

Alexander stared at me. He drew his brows together in a scowl. 'You don't believe anything I tell you about dryads or nymphs, you mock our gods, you forget the names of the nine muses, but you know the names of nine tame deer, and now you're trying to tell me they can fly?'

'It's only a story for children,' I said. 'My nanny used to tell it to me. I used to look forward to Christmas. It was the only time my family paid attention to me. We were so rich, I had more gifts than all the children in the village put together. I thought it was wonderful until I grew old enough to be embarrassed about it.'

Alexander opened his mouth to say something then shut it. He reached over and gently brushed a tear off my cheek. 'Why are you crying?'

'Something's missing. It was when you started talking about Plexis. I miss him terribly.'

He smiled at me. 'I yearn for Plexis too.' He caught my look and grinned. 'I can picture him here, huddled in furs close to the fire, his nose blue with cold and his feet frozen. He would sneeze and say we were barbarians, impervious to cold.'

'And then he'd smile and his whole face would light up.' I said dreamily.

'He'd like your story about the flying deer and the gifts.'

'You know, I'm not too sure about the reindeer names,' I said apologetically.

'That's all right. I sometimes get the muses mixed up.' Alexander put his arm around my shoulder and put his head against mine.

I smiled. That was a huge lie. But it made me feel better.

A cold wind whipped our hair, and there were white caps in the fjord. Three trading boats were coming in under sail. Two were boats built in Roman style, and one was a Phoenician trader. Then the sails were taken down, and the boats rowed the rest of the way. They each went to a different dock. People started rushing toward the harbour. A stir of energy swept through the village. Alexander and I were caught up in the excitement. Alexander tucked his journal into his belt, and we jogged toward the boats.

The Phoenician trading boat captured my attention. It came from so far away. Perhaps there was even news from Greece. On board, the crew was busy tucking away the sails and ropes while the captain spoke to an official, showing him the tablet upon which all his goods were tallied. Already, I could see amphorae of wine, olive oil, and palm oil being rolled onto the deck. Wax seals and symbols stamped into the clay showed what each jar contained. I was fascinated. Olive oil was probably very welcome in a place where the only oil came from codfish. Bushel baskets of dried dates were next, and then there were tightly rolled packages of quality papyrus. The boat had been trading in Egypt. Alexander noticed before I did. He stepped lightly on board and tapped the captain on the shoulder.

'Have you news from Alexandria, near Egypt,' he asked, 'or from Greece?'

The captain nodded. 'I do, sir. I would be glad to fill you in on everything, but first I need to see to my crew and my goods. Perhaps you could help me. I have a passenger who is grievously ill. If you could get a healer to come look at him, I'd be much obliged. I haven't got time to do so myself.'

Alexander nodded and left the boat. I was curious though, and a little worried. Contagious diseases often travelled by boat. I thought of the Black Plague, and shivered.

'What exactly does your passenger suffer from?' I asked.

The man frowned. 'A fever, mostly. And delirium.'

'Have any more of your crew been ill?' I asked.

The man shook his head. 'No, this man was wounded even before he came on board. It was a sword fight from the looks of it. I wouldn't have taken him, but he begged me. He said he had to get to the 'Arctica' as fast as possible. He said he had to find someone.'

I was intrigued. 'Find whom?'

'He says he's seeking Iskander, the great conqueror,' said the boat captain with a twisted grin. 'Now you see why I say he's delirious. Everyone knows Iskander died in Babylon. He …'

I didn't hear the rest of his words. I pushed by him and bolted for the lower deck.

There was one room set aside for sleeping. Crew slept on the floor, on pallets, or in hammocks hanging at various levels from the floor. The man I was looking for was lying in a hammock. His face was ashen. His breathing was shallow and his eyes were closed. A bandage was wrapped around his shoulder, holding his arm against his chest. When I spoke his name, his eyelashes fluttered. He opened his eyes and looked at me.

'By Zeus,' he said faintly. 'I've found you.' Then his eyes rolled back in his head, and he passed out.

I stared as spots of blood appeared on his chest. Then I realized that my nose was bleeding. I put numb hands up to stop it. I felt as if I'd been dipped into ice. In another minute I would shatter. 'Plexis,' I whispered. 'What happened to you?' Then my self-control slipped, and I screamed.

Chapter Thirty-eight

Alexander must not have been too far away, because he heard my cry. The captain stared, open-mouthed, as Alexander leapt back onto the boat and crashed down the hatch, lunging past sailors carrying precious amphorae of oil.

'What is it?' he cried.

'It's Plexis!' I pointed.

Alexander gave one look at his friend and blenched. 'I'll get Nearchus,' he said, and left as quickly as he came.

I bent over Plexis. He looked dreadful. His face was gaunt and unshaven. Each breath he took seemed to pain him. A bandage covered his arm. It was soaked with blood and pus and smelled like rotten meat. I could barely stand close to him; the stench was awful. I held my breath. If he had gangrene, he was doomed. From what I could tell, his arm had been badly broken, cut, and hastily set and bandaged. I wondered when, and how, and especially, why. Why had he come? Why had he abandoned Chiron and Cleopatra? What had happened?

'Plexis, Plexis!' I called, my voice urgent.

Alexander and Nearchus came in a matter of minutes. They carried Plexis carefully from the boat and headed for the inn, where we had our belongings.

'I'll boil water,' I said inanely. In times like this, all I could think about was germs.

'Why? Do you think he needs soup?' asked Nearchus.

'He needs bathing, shaving, and rest,' said Alexander, assessing the situation. He'd already lifted the bandage and peered under it carefully. 'I wish Usse were here.'

'Me too,' I moaned, opening the bag of medical supplies and scanning Usse's voluminous notes for hints on what to do with badly set bones and festering sword wounds.

Alexander and Nearchus set to work cleaning Plexis. Halfway through the operation, Demos came to help. I carefully measured ingredients from Usse's pharmacy, hoping that whatever I was mixing would work. While I ground sulphur in a little mortar; I saw Demos studying Plexis' arm.

'Is he unconscious?' he asked.

Alexander looked up at him and nodded. 'He is, why?'

Demos frowned. 'This is why.' He took the arm firmly in his huge hands and gave a straight, hard pull. There was a cracking sound, and Plexis woke up screaming.

Alexander swore, Nearchus too, only more fluently.

I froze and looked up from my mortar, but Demos just whistled as he examined the new angle that he'd made with Plexis's arm.

'Now that will heal straight,' he said with satisfaction. 'Let's clean out the wound.'

A nasty gash across the forearm had been cauterized and left to heal. It was infected, though, and I winced as Demos set about scraping and cleaning. An abscess broke and pus gushed out. Alexander turned green, but he held the arm tightly. Nearchus fainted. I didn't see him, but I heard him hit the ground. Demos didn't even blink. He asked for a scalpel. 'There's more,' he announced. He asked for tweezers and pulled out a five-inch sliver of bone. 'He didn't need that in there,' he said, his voice jovial.

He whistled while he worked. Plexis woke up, screamed, then fainted again.

When I finished the balm, Demos smoothed it over the wound before binding it carefully with strips of clean linen. 'Let's see if we can save this arm,' he said heartily.

My lips moved in silent prayer. If the arm *were* saved, Plexis would have a horrendous scar for the rest of his life. I sighed and stood up, wiping shaking hands on my tunic.

'Thank you, Demos,' I said.

'No problem. I always wanted to practise medicine.'

'So did I,' said Alexander. 'But not on my friends.' He rubbed his hands across his face.

Nearchus had recovered from his faint. 'I'll stay here until he wakes up,' he said to Alexander. 'You go back to the boat captain and find out if he knows anything else.'

Paul came in the room in a rush. He leaned over Plexis. 'He looks bad. Where are Chiron and Cleopatra? Did he say anything?'

'He's been mostly unconscious,' I answered.

I began to pace. He must have left right after us. He'd been wounded roughly two weeks ago, at the most, so he had been following us closely. But what had made him leave?

While I wondered about this, Alexander came back. He pulled me to him, hugging me hard. 'The boat captain says

274

he took Plexis on board when he stopped for provisions on the coast. He was already wounded, alone, and delirious,' he said.

'What's the news from Alexandria?' I asked.

'Nothing important, but there *was* news from Carthage. Strange things are happening. The priests are predicting the end of the world.'

I trembled in his arms. 'I have to tell you something,' I said. 'Yovanix said that the druid who attacked us and killed the Romans was a thief of souls. He hasn't given up searching for Paul.' Alexander stiffened. 'He also said that the Celts believe that time can be twisted somehow. Isn't that ridiculous?' I finished with a sob.

'I don't …' He broke off.

I pulled back and looked at him.

'What?'

'I don't want him to die.' He spoke simply but his voice cracked on the last word.

'He won't,' I said.

'He's dying.'

'No.' I shook my head. 'He's not.' I pushed his hands away and walked over to where Plexis lay. His body had always been so smooth, so cool. I touched his forehead with the tips of my fingers. It was hot. Tears slid down my cheeks. 'What can we do?' I asked Axiom, who was sitting on the floor by Nearchus.

I saw he'd been praying. 'I don't know.'

Alexander sat on the bed and took Plexis in his arms, lifting him to a sitting position. His breathing eased somewhat, but he didn't open his eyes. 'He's burning up,' he said.

At that moment, Phaleria arrived. She led an old woman by the hand. 'This is the healer,' she said. 'Demos said you needed one.'

The woman was blind. Her eyes were milky-white, and her silver hair was tied back with a leather thong. She wore a brown linen robe with beautifully worked embroidery on the bodice and skirt. She didn't look like a healer. She looked like an elderly wood sprite. She even had a strand of red hawthorn berries around her neck.

'Alex, she can't see!' I whispered.

'Hush.' He moved off the bed making room for the healer. She knelt at the bedside and ran her hands lightly over Plexis's body. She crooned eerily.

'She's laying on the hands,' Alexander told me.

'What is she doing?' I asked. 'Where's the medicine? Where are her herbs?'

'You have no weird women in your land?' Axiom gave me a startled glance.

'No.' I shook my head. The woman shushed me and waved us away. We went to the other side of the room and watched. Her hands barely touched him. After a while she peeled the covers off Plexis and ran her hands over his whole body. In the dim light, I couldn't be sure, but it looked as if she were stirring the air around him.

'Everyone has an aura,' Axiom explained. 'Some people have a strong aura, and some have a very subtle one. Exceptional auras can practically be felt. Certain people see them as colours and can feel them. A healer can change it.'

'Sort of like an electric field around the body,' I guessed.

276

Since I'd already explained electricity to Axiom, he knew what I meant. 'Yes, in a way.'

'Will he get better?'

'I don't know.' He went back to his prayers.

Alexander's hands were clenched so hard they were white. I took one and slowly unfolded it. His nails had made red puncture marks in the skin. 'Why did I leave him?' he asked. His eyes filled with tears.

'He's not going to die,' I said. 'Let's be optimistic.'

'It's hard for someone without a soul to be optimistic.' He didn't say it in jest. His whole face twisted and he sat down heavily on the floor.

I sat next to him and held him tightly. I was frightened. The melancholy madness that haunted him was just under the surface. I could see it in his eyes; if Plexis died, it would submerge him. I squeezed my eyes shut and tried to pray.

The old woman stayed for nearly an hour. The silence in the room was as heavy as the pall of smoke. When the healer finished, Phaleria went to her side.

'What does she think?' I asked, waylaying them.

Phaleria shook her head. 'She won't make predictions. We'll see soon enough if it's helped.'

'We will?' I echoed dumbly.

'If he dies, it didn't work,' said Demos. He stepped back making room for Phaleria and the old woman to pass. 'But if he lives, his arm will be straight.'

I looked at Plexis. He moaned and turned his head toward me.

'Ashley?' he whispered.

'I'm right here,' I answered.

'He's coming after Paul. I had to stop him. I tried to stop him. Iskander …' His voice trailed away.

'Shhh. It's all right. We're fine, we're right here.'

'My arm hurts,' he whimpered. He didn't open his eyes.

'It's going to be all right. How are Chiron and Cleopatra? Where are they?' I couldn't keep the fear out of my voice.

'They are with … Usse …they are all right.' He drew a deep breath and coughed.

'Don't talk any more. Just rest.'

Plexis's voice was little more than a whisper. 'Must tell you,' he said. Between each word was a little gasp. 'A druid came to the house. Looking for Paul. He nearly killed Usse.'

'Usse? Where is he now? Where are the children?' Alexander asked.

'With Ptolemy. He swore he'd protect them. Brazza too. I took them to Memphis.' His voice was getting weaker.

'Plexis, if you die, I'll never forgive you,' I said, bursting into tears. 'Will you just be quiet and get better?'

'No.'

'No what?'

'I won't be quiet.' He nearly grinned.

Axiom finished mixing a potion and gave it to him, holding his head tenderly. 'Drink it all,' he said.

Plexis swallowed it, then said, 'The master druid has paid for the capture of Paul. So has the Celt king, Bran. The druids have predicted the end of the world. You must believe me. They know where you are.' His pupils were dilating. A flush reddened his cheeks. 'I only killed three of them. But there were too many ...' His voice trailed off. The poppy juice put him to sleep. His breathing was deep and sonorous.

Plexis slept for two days. Twice, the weird woman came and wove her strange magic. We changed his bandage three times. Axiom managed to find some mouldy bread and we used that on his wound. His fever flared and then subsided. His heart beat rapidly; his breathing was shallow and pained. He didn't stir when we moved him to clean him or change his bandages. His skin hugged his bones, and I thought he looked more like a cadaver than a living man. At night, we lay awake and listened to his breathing. Every time there was a falter or a sigh, I felt Alexander stiffen beside me.

Three days later, Plexis opened his eyes. They were bright with fever, but they were clear. The clouds of pain had gone. His arm was still infected, but it seemed to be getting better, not worse. His breathing was even now. He took a deep breath and didn't cough.

'Salutations,' he said.

'Plexis!' Alexander leaned over his friend and clasped his good hand. 'How are you feeling.'

Plexis frowned. 'I'm not sure. Thirsty, I think.'

Axiom gave him a cup of broth, and he managed to drink most of it. Afterwards, we let him rest. Just the act of drinking had exhausted him.

I went to the baths with Paul. The inn was becoming crowded. Besides us, there were four traders from Rome, three Phoenicians from the boat Plexis had been on, and two Celtic traders. Alexander was thinking of moving back to the boat with the rest of Phaleria's crew, but I was wondering if we shouldn't leave Orce. It was an important trading town, and if someone were looking for Paul, it would just be a matter of time before they thought to look here.

Demos and Yovanix went to bathe with us. Alexander had appointed Demos Paul's guardian, and Demos had asked Yovanix to be his lieutenant. Yovanix had been ecstatic, and now spent every free moment learning how to wield a sword, while Paul looked on jealously. Alexander still wouldn't trust him with a sword, so Paul was learning to spar with staffs. I thought they looked dangerous enough, and hardly a day went by without Paul getting a bruised wrist or finger.

Nearchus trailed after us. Since Plexis had found us, he had been strangely quiet. He was worried. Every group needs someone to defuse emotional situations, and Plexis could talk Alex out of his melancholy or make Nearchus stop frowning. He was not a tactician, or even a particularly brilliant fighter. His talent was his ability to put anyone at his ease. One thing he did better than anyone else, was training horses. Even animals sensed his gentleness. Cerberus had been lying near the foot of his bed since he'd arrived, even forsaking Paul. Plexis made everyone feel special, and Nearchus, who was a quiet, uptight sort, adored him.

The sauna was divided into two parts – one for women and one for men. Paul, Demos, Nearchus, and Yovanix went to their sauna, and I walked over to the women's hut. There were three other women there. I took off my clothes and left them in a wooden cubbyhole near the entrance. Then I went to the first room, where I slathered soft, black 'soap' made of ashes, tallow and oil over my body. Hot steam opened my pores and sweat ran down my back and chest. I only stayed half an hour before jogging outside and plunging into the pond.

The women's side of the pond was hidden from the men's side by a small grove of trees. If I swam to the middle, I could see the men as they cooled off in the dark water. Women swimming too far out in the pond were considered loose, and one's reputation in this village apparently hinged on how far you swam.

I didn't swim very far. For one thing the water was freezing. It came straight off the mountains. The pond was very deep, and the water so dark it looked black. When I couldn't see the bottom it made me nervous. There was probably a monster of the Loch Ness variety hiding under there.

I swam just enough to cool off. Back in the hut, I combed my hair and braided it. I applied the cream Phaleria had given me for my dry skin. It was greasy and smelled faintly like sheep. I dabbed some jasmine perfume on to cover the sheep smell. Finally, I dressed and dashed back to the inn.

When I arrived, I saw Alexander sitting outside with his head in his arms, sobbing. I dropped my towel and my toilet case, and rushed to his side.

'What is it? Oh, Alex, is it Plexis? Is he ...' I couldn't bring myself to say it; I choked and felt tears leaking from my eyes. 'Oh no!' I wailed, and started to cry.

'No, no. It's not that, he's better. Much better. I'm sorry, I didn't mean to frighten you.'

'You mean you were crying because he's better?' I sniffed.

'Yes, I suppose so.' He smiled shakily.

'Don't ever do that again,' I said. 'You scared me.' I put my hand over my heart. 'He's better?'

Plexis was sipping a cup of broth. His fever had finally left him.

'I'm so glad you're better,' I said, sitting next to him and trying not to jostle his arm.

He put his one good arm around me, and I wet his chest with my tears. 'I don't know why everyone's crying all over me,' he said cheerfully. 'I don't need a bath. Axiom's been washing every inch of me for three days now.'

'You scared us,' I said, leaning back to get a good look at him. I smiled shakily and tucked a stray curl behind his ear. 'I missed you. I'm so glad to see you, even though I know it's bad news. Can you tell me about it now?'

He flipped his wrist. 'When Iskander and Nearchus are both here; everyone should hear this. You look good. The land of your ancestors suits you. You don't look so out of place here.'

'No, it's short, dark-haired guys that get stared at here,' I said teasingly.

'Well that counts me out, I'm a *tall*, dark-haired guy.' He smiled, his teeth flashing in his thin face, and then he was serious again. 'I can't believe I caught up with you. I left more than a month after you did. I rode four horses to

282

death in Gaul.' He shuddered. I knew how much he loved horses. He must have been frantic.

'I heard of the sacrifice in Gaul with Paul and the druids, and I knew that I had to hurry. I was afraid I'd get to you too late.' He was silent for a moment, looking at me. Then his mouth curved in a smile again. I felt the familiar rush of heat in my belly, and my cheeks grew hot. Plexis gave a small laugh. 'I'm not *that* well yet,' he said softly.

'Soon,' I said.

'Soon,' he agreed, a faint flush on his face.

'How are Chiron and Cleopatra?'

'Chiron is heartbroken. He didn't want to be left behind.'

'Like Paul.' I grinned. 'When did you realize he was missing?'

'The next day. I wanted to kill Chiron. It was the first time I ever lost my temper with the child. Brazza took the boy and hid him in his room. The whole house was in an uproar. I found Paul's note. It was a disaster, by the way. That boy has no talent for writing. His tutor will have his hands full when he gets back.' His voice was getting strained again. I placed my hand over his mouth.

'Hush, you should rest now.'

'Lie here beside me. I want to sleep with your arms around me.'

'I don't want to hurt your arm.'

'It hurts anyway. Please?'

I carefully lay down next to him and held him while he slept. The people coming in and out of the room made as little noise as possible. They had been very considerate all during his illness, although most of them had a pitying look about them. They were sure he was dying. Phaleria came in and raised her eyebrows. I realized she was shocked. I wondered what her face would look like when she saw him with Alexander. Or with Alexander and me.

I slipped out of the bed without waking Plexis and went outside. Alexander was nowhere to be seen. Nearchus was sitting on a bench along the wall.

'Iskander went to the baths,' he said, to answer my question.

'Where's Paul?' I took my hair out of its braid and fluffed it. The sun would dry it soon.

'He's with Yovanix and Demos. They went to the docks.'

I nodded. The docks were where all the action was. Boats coming and going. People shopping, trading, talking, and gossiping. In the evenings, there was still the traditional town dinner, although now that warmer weather was coming, dinner would move outside.

As we sat there in the sun, warming our faces and shoulders, Alexander came back with Paul trotting at his heels. I smiled as they came nearer. My heart still swelled when I saw them. Alexander sat on one side of me, Paul on the other. They leaned back against the warm wood, and Alexander closed his eyes. His mouth was curled in a smile.

'What's up?' I asked.

He opened one eye and looked at me. He didn't look up in the sky any more when I asked that, as he used to. 'We're all together again,' he said, and in his voice there was a note of quiet satisfaction.

284

Nearchus heard it too. He grinned widely. 'We are, aren't we?' he said.

'Now where to?' I wondered aloud.

Alexander opened his eyes. 'We go north to find my soul,' he said.

'North.' Nearchus looked toward the mountains. 'I'd like to see the aurora borealis.'

'I'd like to see the great white owl, the white bear, and an iceberg!' Paul chimed in.

'I'd like to see a white night,' I said.

'Do you think we can, Father?' asked Paul.

'Yes. I can almost feel my soul now. It's somewhere over those mountains, north, and north some more. In the evenings, when the stars show, I see the great bear. He's showing the way to my soul.'

'The stars come out later and later, and soon you'll see them no more,' said Nearchus. He was impressed by the length of the days.

'The land of the never setting sun. When the summer solstice arrives, we'll be in reach of my soul. I know it. And then, my friend, do you know where we'll go?'

We all stared at him.

'Where?' Nearchus asked.

'Home,' he said, smiling brilliantly at all of us. 'Home. To Egypt to fetch Chiron, Cleopatra, Usse, Chirpa, and Brazza. And then we get on one of Nearchus's infernal boats, and we'll go to Ethiopia and share a banquet with the gods.'

'That,' said Paul, stars shining in his eyes, 'sounds like the best idea you've ever had.'

'I know,' said Alexander, and he leaned over and kissed me on the lips.

I felt the world tilt, spin, and settle. In my nostrils was the scent of warm pine planks, on my lips was the taste of salt and honey, and in my arms was the man I loved. The relief of knowing Plexis was getting better, of knowing my children were safe, and seeing Alexander smile, nearly overwhelmed me. Tears slid down my cheeks, and I hurried to hide them with my hair.

'A sweep of silver,' said Alexander dreamily, running his fingers through my hair.

'With only a few little nits,' I said.

'That's all right. They're probably related to the ones I have.'

'You have them too?' I pulled away with a mock scream.

'We all do. It's part of life. We're all together. You, me, the sea, the sun, the mountains, and a few lice.' He kissed me again and I felt my bones melt. 'Shall we go inside?' His breath tickled my ear as he whispered.

I nodded. In another minute I would have agreed to do it under the bench. We left Paul and Nearchus blinking sleepily in the sun and disappeared into the darkness of our alcove. Our clothes seemed to levitate off our bodies, and we came together with a rush that left me breathless. Alexander was sleek and smooth. Under his skin, his muscles were taut. I ran my hands over his belly. I knew of the places that made him suck in his breath with a gasp. I could never get my fill of his body. I wanted to make it last longer, so I started to wrestle, but he was so much better. He pinned me with his elbows and knees. His smile was wolfish.

'Did you want to do it like that?' he asked, parting my legs with his knees.

I pretended to relax and then just as he was about to lower himself onto me, I scissored my legs and threw him to his side.

He laughed softly and let me win a round, just to show me he could. Then he flipped me over and proceeded to do what he liked.

I liked it too.

When my moans had faded to sighs, and his breath had returned to normal, he rolled off me and propped his chin on his hands. 'I think we should leave as soon as Plexis is ready to travel,' he said.

'Fine with me.'

'I didn't want to worry you, but I think I should tell you. Voltarrix is heading this way. He'll be here in a few days.'

'I'm worried,' I said.

'Me too.' He lifted the curtains aside and looked out into the gloom where Plexis lay sleeping. In the dark, I could see Axiom moving quietly around the sick man's bed. The front door opened letting in a flood of spring sunlight. Demos's large form blocked the light as he came through the door.

'Something's wrong,' Alexander said, pulling his clothes on.

Demos hurried over. 'A strange boat has arrived with druids on board. Warriors from the looks of them. Not traders, despite what they may say.'

Alexander swore, then kissed me hard. 'We'll be leaving sooner than I thought. Quick, get our things ready.'

Chapter Thirty-nine

I put our clothes, Alexander's shaving kit, our toothbrushes, flint and pyrite, some onions and garlic, and a sewing kit into a leather backpack. Also in the alcove were Alexander's sword, and his large, round shield that he took everywhere. Usse's medical bag was underneath Plexis's cot. I finished packing, pulled on my footgear, and went outside. The sunlight blinded me for a moment. Nearchus and Yovanix were still on the bench with Paul between them.

'Demos told me. Don't worry,' said Nearchus, as I passed. 'We'll keep Paul safe.'

I was looking for Alexander, and I found him at the docks. He and Demos were standing on a windy jetty with their cloaks whipping around their legs. They were talking to Phaleria. Several men were standing nearby them. They were dressed in the grey robes of the Celtic druids. *Druids!* They had found us. Alexander was right. We had to leave.

My heart lurched when I saw that the new boat that had arrived. It was a long, slender boat with a single square sail and a long row of oars on either side. The bow lifted gracefully off the water and ended in a grinning dragon's head. I stared. *A Viking-style boat.* The waves moved it up and down making the dragon's head bob in a lifelike way.

The dragon's eyes glittered with chips of quartz. Its mouth was lined with rows of teeth. I was mesmerized.

A crowd of townspeople gathered near the boat. Apparently, they had never seen anything like it. Children darted in and out of the crowd daring each other to get close to the terrifying dragon boat.

Alexander drifted over to me and asked, 'Did you pack?'

'Yes. What's going on?'

'It seems like a whole congregation of Celtic druids has suddenly arrived to trade, but Demos is right. They don't look like traders. We have to get Paul away from here'

I suddenly felt strangely helpless and depressed. We had to get away from the druids as soon as possible. But how could we all go? Plexis was too weak to travel. 'Do we go by boat, or on land?'

Alexander looked undecided and then swore softly. 'I wanted to leave in secret, but there are too many of them. They'll be watching us.'

'If they saw Phaleria's boat leaving, they would follow,' I said.

'True, it would give us some time. Phaleria's plan was to lure the dragon boat after her while we go north on a wagon.'

He left me and walked back to Demos. I turned and looked once more at the dragon boat and clenched my hands.

We didn't have much time. Alexander and Demos went to buy a wagon. Then Axiom and I got Plexis ready to travel. We had to slip away unnoticed. Alexander said he'd taken care of that.

Around midnight, bells started ringing. Fires had broken out on the docks. Every able person ran to help. The druids rushed to move their dragon boat, which was closest to the fire.

In their panic to put out the fire and get their boats to safety, no one noticed that we slipped out of the inn, carrying our belongings and Plexis. No one noticed when we turned left instead of right, and disappeared behind the inn where a horse and cart waited. We secured Plexis on a soft pallet inside the wagon.

Phaleria would sail her boat far out into the fjord to give the druids a scare. Hopefully, at least some of the druids would think we were on the boat. When morning came, she would lead them on a merry chase along the coast.

I hoped no one would find out that Kell and Titte had lit the fires. The two brothers had risked a great deal that night. Fire on a dock was no laughing matter; some people had their whole lives tied up in their boats. If the men were caught, they would be punished, and I didn't like to imagine what that could mean.

We took a trading road out of the village. Axiom drove the horse. Alexander, Demos, Yovanix, and Nearchus jogged behind the wagon. Paul fell asleep under the bench and I snuggled next to Plexis and held him tightly, keeping him from being jostled too much. Once or twice, he held his breath when a bump moved his arm. I put my head next to his and we whispered.

'How are you doing?' I asked.

'I've been better.' He laughed softly. 'I've died twice for you. I hope you realize that.'

'I do.' My mouth brushed his in a tender kiss.

'Hmm. I think I like dying. Look at me, in the arms of the Queen of the Dead.'

'Very funny.'

'Did they follow us?'

'I don't know. They will probably split up and half of them will take this path.'

'That makes half as many to fight.'

'That's right.'

'You've followed Iskander too long, you're starting to think like an army general.' Plexis chuckled then winced as the wagon hit a root. 'I won't be of much help.'

The cart lurched and he took a quick breath.

'Are you all right?'

Plexis smiled at me. 'Yes. Fine. Here we are again, off to save the world.'

'Saving the world and finding lost souls. That shouldn't be too hard,' I said.

I sat up and looked around. The night was wearing thin around the edges. Stars were fading and the trees were showing more and more of their branches. In the distance wolves howled. The sky was tinged with rose and green, and the night shivered as dawn touched it with cool fingers.

The words of the oracle came back to me then. Words that had been spoken twelve years ago in a dark smoke filled room near Persepolis. *'Keep your son with you, he will find the lost soul.'* I hadn't known what it meant at the time, but now I did.

'And after this adventure's done we can go home,' I said.

'To have a banquet with the gods,' said Plexis dreamily.

'Why, that's right,' I said, brushing his chestnut hair off his forehead.

'You can count me in,' said Plexis. 'You can count on me for the adventure.'

'I know,' I said happily, and I smiled. The stars were reflected in his bright hazel eyes as he stared back at me – the stars, the faint light of dawn, and all the joy I felt to have him near me again.

In the darkness, I smiled. We were heading toward the land of the Eaters of the Dead, but I was not afraid. The prophecy would be fulfilled. Alexander *would* find his soul.

I whispered his name in the night, and the pine trees rustled it back to me like an echo. *Alexander*.

Proudly published by Accent Press

www.accentpress.co.uk